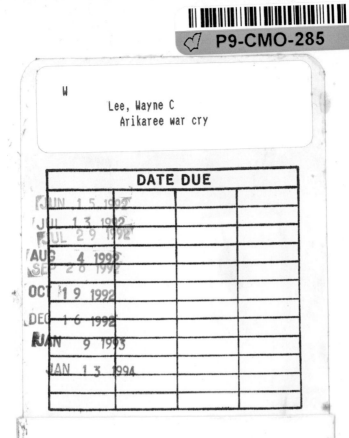

Arikaree
War Cry

WAYNE C. LEE

Arikaree War Cry

A DOUBLE D WESTERN

DOUBLEDAY

New York   London   Toronto   Sydney   Auckland

A Double D Western
PUBLISHED BY DOUBLEDAY
a division of Bantam Doubleday Dell Publishing Group, Inc.
666 Fifth Avenue, New York, New York 10103

DOUBLE D WESTERN, DOUBLEDAY,
and the portrayal of the letters DD
are trademarks of Doubleday, a division of
Bantam Doubleday Dell Publishing Group, Inc.

Library of Congress Cataloging-in-Publication Data

Lee, Wayne C.
Arikaree war cry / Wayne C. Lee. — 1st ed.
   p.   cm.
1. Cheyenne Indians—Wars—1868–1869—Fiction. I. Title.
PS3523.E34457A89   1992
813'.54—dc20   91-30531
CIP

ISBN 0-385-41573-7
Printed in the United States of America
May 1992
First Edition

10 9 8 7 6 5 4 3 2 1

W

One

DAIN TALMAGE was not a man who believed in premonitions. But as he drove his wagon out of Minneapolis, Kansas, he was uneasy and he couldn't put his finger on the reason.

Glancing at the sun low on the horizon, Dain decided to camp for the night. It was fifteen miles to his homestead over on the Saline River in Lincoln County. That was too far to drive after dark. He had watered his team at the Solomon River just as he left Minneapolis so they wouldn't need water.

He unhitched and unharnessed the horses and staked them out where they could get grass. He spread a blanket on the grass under the lumber-filled wagon. He wouldn't need any cover on this hot August night. The prairie was level under the wagon but there was a gully to the north where rainwater drained off toward the Solomon after a downpour.

Eating some dry bread and meat he had brought along, he stretched out on his blanket, thinking of the shed he would build for his cows for the coming winter. It was 1868 and this would be his first winter on the Kansas plains, but his sister, Susan, and her husband, Bert Diehl, had been here for a year and a half. They had told him what to expect. Their homestead was just up the river from Dain's.

As darkness settled over the prairie, a soft breeze whispered through the grass, cooling the hot air of the day. Dain couldn't dismiss that gnawing at the edge of his consciousness. He wished he were making better progress with Valina Kern but he knew the big reason for the slowness of their relationship was his distrust of everyone he didn't know well, which included Valina. His sister said his suspicious nature was a curse to himself and to anyone who wanted to be his friend. But he considered it a safeguard against betrayal. He trusted no one until that person had proved himself trustworthy. He went to sleep, thinking that he hadn't found many who had passed that test.

He was jolted out of his sleep by a startled snort from one of his horses. Trying to see through the darkness, he searched the area without moving. He wished he hadn't left his gun in the wagon. He hadn't expected to need it this close to town.

After a moment, he caught the movement of a shadow out near the horses. His first thought was horse thieves. But then he saw that the shadow was moving toward the wagon.

There wasn't enough light to identify the man moving toward him but he did catch a glint of starlight on a gun or a knife. His mind raced. If he climbed into the wagon to get the gun, he could be dead before he reached it.

Rolling quickly from under the wagon, he dashed toward the ravine he'd seen to the north. Until he moved, the attacker apparently had not known where he was. He'd been moving cautiously toward the wagon. Now he rushed forward.

Dain hit the ravine and rolled into it. Hiding was his only defense now. He peered cautiously over the top of the ravine. The man had come around the wagon but stopped there. Obviously he hadn't seen Dain roll into the ravine. In the deep shadows, the ravine would not be visible to anyone more than ten feet from it. Dain must have simply vanished into thin air so far as the man was concerned.

Dain expected him to begin searching and he tried to devise a scheme to get the upper hand if the man found him. But the intruder slowly backed to the wagon. There he climbed inside and began shifting lumber, apparently looking for something on the floor. Dain wondered what it could possibly be. When he found what he was looking for, or even if he didn't find it, maybe he'd go away. Dain decided that was probably his only chance to stay alive.

The man finally stopped moving lumber and climbed out of the wagon. Dain had the feeling that he had found what he was looking for. He began pacing slowly back and forth north of the wagon. Dain knew he was looking for him.

After a couple of minutes, he stopped. He hadn't come close enough to the ravine to see it in the dim light. Finally, he disappeared out beyond the horses, the way he had come.

Dain waited a half hour in the ravine. The stranger might be lying in wait to see if Dain would return to the wagon.

Finally, Dain got up and moved cautiously toward the wagon. When he was within a few feet of it, he came out of his crouch and ran forward. Climbing into the wagon, he looked for his gun. It was there, apparently undisturbed. That made the intruder's mission even more baffling. He'd surely meant to kill Dain yet he hadn't taken his gun when he had the chance.

Checking the gun to see that it was unharmed and loaded, he climbed back outside and onto his blanket. If the intruder came back, Dain would be ready for him this time.

Nothing happened to disturb Dain during the remainder of the night. As soon as it was light, he examined the wagon. The lumber had been shifted around some but nothing seemed to be missing. Then he remembered the leather band he had found in the wagon when he loaded the lumber. He had no idea how or when it had gotten there. It was a very crude piece of leather with some shells and beads on it and there had been what looked like pieces of dried hide fastened to it. Leather thongs were on each end so it could be tied around the wrist or forearm. Dain had guessed some youngster might have lost it in the wagon before he loaded the lumber.

The bracelet seemed to be the only thing missing. Could it be possible that the intruder had been after that? He got under way, still puzzling over the situation. He'd ask his brother-in-law, Bert Diehl, about it and see if he had any reasonable explanation. He also might ask his one real friend, Ron Fulton. Ron knew the people here better than Dain did.

Before he reached Alpha, the little town that served the homesteaders along the Saline River, a big collie dog came rushing toward him. Dain had left his dog, Havana, at home when he went to Minneapolis, afraid he'd get into a fight with the town dogs. Dain welcomed Havana, wondering how far the dog had gone searching for him since he'd left home yesterday noon.

The dog trotted beside or behind the wagon as they moved along. Dain was heading straight for his homestead, bypassing town, when he remembered that he had forgotten to get sugar in Minneapolis. He could get that at Scurry's store in Alpha, although he didn't like to do business with Addison Scurry. His prices were too high and Dain didn't trust the beady-eyed storekeeper. But if a man lived in this end of Lincoln County, he traded with Scurry or drove a long way to another town.

Havana was trotting in the shade of the wagon as Dain turned into the only real street in Alpha. He had gotten the dog from a man who hailed from Havana, Illinois, on the Illinois River. Although the dog was two years old now, he acted more like an overgrown pup.

As Dain pulled the team up to the hitchrack in front of Scurry's General Store, Havana dodged out from under the wagon to bark at a rider coming along the side of the building.

Jerking up his head, Dain saw that Havana was challenging a cream-colored horse carrying Valina Kern. He wanted to make a good impression on Valina and this certainly was not the way to do it.

Havana dashed straight at the horse and the sight of the big collie was more than the horse could take. He reared and Valina was caught completely by surprise. Losing her balance and then her dignity, she slid over the rump of her horse and plopped into the dust.

Dain leaped out of the wagon and aimed a kick in the direction of the dog. Havana suddenly realized he had done something wrong and ducked back under the wagon. Dropping down, he laid his head on his paws and peered apologetically up through the spokes of the wheel at his master.

Dain wheeled back to Valina, still sitting in the dust of the street. This was the worst possible place—almost in front of Scurry's store. Addison Scurry was making no effort to hide his courtship of Valina. Dain's pursuit of Valina was mostly in his own mind.

Valina had to be horribly embarrassed. There was no way that he was going to smooth this over. Still, he had to try.

"I'm sorry," he said, reaching out a hand to help Valina to her feet.

She ignored his hand and scrambled up by herself. "Do you sic your dog onto every rider you see?" she snapped.

"I didn't—" he began, then stopped. Even if he had a perfect explanation, she wouldn't listen now.

Dain remembered when his sister, Susan, had introduced him to Valina. Susan was as different from Dain as a sister could be. To her, everybody was a friend until proven otherwise. Dain approached strangers with caution, if not outright suspicion. Until they proved they were worthy of his confidence, he didn't trust them, not even a beautiful young lady like Valina Kern.

Dain hadn't seen as much of Valina as he'd like. She and her aunt, Martha Zylstra, had opened a millinery shop about two months ago and Dain found no excuse to patronize a lady's hat shop.

Valina's horse had stopped as soon as the dog went back under the wagon. Grabbing the reins, Valina stamped past Dain and turned up the street toward the millinery shop.

Dain watched her go, remembering the matchmaker's gleam in his sister's eyes when she had introduced them. If she could see the gleam in Valina's eyes now, she'd know she had made a bad mistake. About the only thing Valina would match with Dain now was a hangman's noose.

Dain was disgusted with the whole affair. To add to his disgust, he saw Addison Scurry run out of his store to intercept Valina.

"I saw what happened," he said in his smoothest voice. "That was a disgrace. Dain should be barred from bringing his dog to town. Are you sure you're all right?"

"I'm sure," Valina said, her voice several degrees softer than when she'd been talking to Dain, "but thank you for your concern."

Valina went on up the street. For a moment, Dain thought that Scurry was going to follow her. When he turned back into the store, Dain tied his team and stepped up on the porch.

Scurry stopped and turned just inside the store. "What do you want?" he demanded, his voice as frigid as river ice in January.

"I need some sugar," Dain snapped, following Scurry into the dim interior of the store. He knew the storekeeper's jealous nature and he didn't doubt that he was aware of Dain's interest in Valina. He wondered how far Scurry would go. It flashed across his mind that maybe Scurry was the one who had tried to get rid of Dain last night in that attack on his camp.

"Valina should have used her quirt on you," Scurry growled, making no move to get Dain's sugar.

"Maybe you'd like to do that for her," Dain shot back.

"I would if she'd ask."

"You don't have to wait for her permission," Dain said angrily. He waited expectantly but Scurry didn't rise to the bait. "How about that sugar?" Dain snapped. "Five pounds."

Scurry swore, wheeled around and went for the sugar. Dain was surprised. He usually had his hired man wait on customers.

"Where's your flunky, Jed?" he asked.

"Didn't need him today," Scurry growled. "He got a chance to make half a dollar by helping Bert Diehl build some fence."

A chill ran through Dain. If there was anyone he trusted less than Scurry, it was Jed Wolfcry. Wolfcry was half Indian—sullen, taciturn and as out of place here in Alpha as a wart on a beauty queen. Jed Wolfcry was short and stocky with piercing black eyes; his hair was so black it shone almost blue at times. In spite of his swarthy skin, he declared that he was white and vehemently resented being called an Indian.

"What kind of Indian is Jed?" Dain asked, knowing the question would irritate Scurry. "Sioux or Pawnee?"

Scurry scowled, fists clenched. "Half Cheyenne," he snapped. "What difference does it make? He hates all Indians worse than you do." He slammed the sugar on the counter. "Here's your sugar."

Dain dropped a quarter on the counter and stared at Scurry. His muddy brown eyes always looked angry. Dain wondered if he used axle grease on the long dirty hair that was kept combed straight back. The front of his face had a low hairline and weak chin with a long narrow nose arching like a bridge between his eyes and mouth. It was a face Dain would never trust.

Dain took his sugar out to the wagon and started to untie his team, then on impulse, turned up the street toward the hat shop. There was no way he could undo the damage Havana had done but he had to try.

Valina wasn't in the hat shop, but her Aunt Martha was. Dain had seen her only a time or two and he definitely hadn't made up his mind about her. She wasn't tall and her two hundred pounds made her look shorter and squatter than she really was. Gray flecked her brown hair and there was a twinkle that he couldn't ignore in her green eyes.

"Is Valina here?" Dain asked.

"You don't want to see her now," Martha said softly. She glanced out into the street where Havana was waiting for Dain. "That dog doesn't look like the man-eating monster Valina described."

"He's harmless," Dain said. "But he scared her horse."

"Practically ate him up, to hear her tell it." Her eyes twinkled brighter. "She wasn't hurt, if that's what is worrying you. I can just picture her plopped down in the dirt, as mad as a bee-stung bear." She laughed.

Dain found himself grinning although he wasn't sure why. He

hadn't seen anything funny about the incident. "I just wanted to explain."

"There's nothing to explain," Martha said. "And this is no time to apologize. She's mad enough now to fry every word you say. Wait until her ruffled feathers get smoothed down a bit."

He could see that Martha considered the whole incident amusing. But he also saw the wisdom of Martha's advice. Likely Addison Scurry would be the one to smooth Valina's ruffled feathers. He turned back to the door.

"Drop in any time you need a lady's hat," Martha called after him.

Dain grunted and went outside. He wanted to be angry at Martha; she'd given him reason for it. But somehow he found that hard to do. He was disgusted with the whole day so far.

Untying his horses, he sent them at a stiff trot out of town. He was halfway home when he noticed the paper under his feet. Leaning over, he picked it up. The writing on the paper was scrawled in a very poor hand.

"You stole a medicine band. For that you will die."

A chill ran over Dain. Could this refer to that bracelet he'd found in the wagon?

Two

H E READ THE NOTE AGAIN as he let his team follow the road toward home. That man who had searched his wagon the night before had been there long enough to write it. He must have been the one. He had probably put it between two boards and expected Dain to find it when he unloaded his lumber after he got home. The jolting of the wagon on the road from Minneapolis had jarred it loose and it had fallen at Dain's feet.

He had no idea what a medicine band was but it sounded Indian. In fact, the band itself, as he recalled it, looked like something an Indian would have made. But why kill the man who stole it? Going one step further, he wondered how it got into his wagon.

Dain tried to think of all the people he didn't trust. He admitted that took in most of the people he knew other than Susan, her husband, Bert, and Ron and Eve Fulton. Beyond those four, however, he couldn't say that he fully trusted anybody else.

Distrust hadn't come naturally to Dain. He had learned it. He had trusted his father when he was little. Then his father had gone off to fight in the Mexican War, leaving Dain's mother to make the living for herself and Dain and Susan.

Dain had bridged that breach in trust when his father returned after the war. But soon he was gone to California, consumed by gold fever. Dain had been seven then and he'd been ten when his father returned. Life had been hard for Dain's mother and her two children but they had dreamed of being rich when Henry got home. Instead, he was dead broke and half starved when he stumbled back in 1852.

Dain's faith in his father never recovered from that. As he grew older, his distrust of everything and everyone around him deepened.

Only his faith and love for his mother and sister remained unshaken. Then Henry, already past forty, was among the first to volunteer to fight in the War Between the States. Again he left the family without a breadwinner except for Dain, who was nineteen. Dain himself was soon in the army.

His trust in everything, already badly shaken, was completely shattered by the war. His father had been killed at Fredericksburg. His mother had died quietly before the war was over. And Susan was married to Bert Diehl.

At first, Dain had resented Bert for taking his sister away. But he soon learned that he had a staunch friend in Bert. It had been Susan and Bert who had encouraged Dain to come to the Saline Valley a year after they had settled here. He'd been on the Saline now for three months.

His eyes fell on the note he had dropped back at his feet. There was a lot about that bracelet he didn't understand. His brother-in-law seemed to know a lot about Indians. Maybe he could explain the significance of that leather bracelet. He didn't need Bert to tell him that his life was on the line, but maybe he could tell him why.

His first reaction was to blame Addison Scurry. He disliked Scurry intensely and he knew the feeling was mutual. But it wasn't likely that Scurry would go all the way to Minneapolis just to strike at Dain. Reluctantly, Dain dropped Scurry off his list of suspects.

There was something else pushing Dain right now. Scurry had said that Jed Wolfcry was working for Bert today, building fence. Dain didn't trust Wolfcry as far as he could spit against the wind. He hadn't thought that Bert did, either.

At home, Dain didn't even unload his lumber. He put his horses in the barn, unharnessed and fed them, then got his saddle horse and rode upstream to his brother-in-law's place. He expected to find Bert and Susan and his three-month-old nephew, Hiram. But he didn't see anyone as he rode up.

The spring wagon was gone. Bert must have taken it somewhere. Dain looked out at the fence where Jed Wolfcry was supposed to be working. But the only thing he saw out there was a saddled horse standing hitched to a post.

The door was open so Dain dismounted and went inside. He seldom knocked at his sister's place. Hearing a sound in the bedroom of the two-room soddy, he headed that way, expecting to find his sister and her baby.

But it wasn't Susan he saw when he stepped through the doorway. Jed Wolfcry was at the foot of the bed, staring behind the bureau pulled back from the wall.

Dain had helped Bert build an extra wall earlier in the summer. From the outside, it looked like the original exterior wall, but the inner wall had not been removed. Inside, it wasn't likely to be noticed that the room was too small. Dain and Bert had pushed the bureau in front of the small opening they had cut into the original wall. That concealed the four-foot-wide space between the walls.

Dain and Bert had built that because there had been so many rumors of Indian raids. This was a hiding place for Susan and the baby in case of an attack. Susan could pull the lightweight bureau up against the inner wall once she was in the tiny space and no raider was likely to find them. Wolfcry evidently had been snooping through the house and discovered the hiding place.

Fury swept over Dain. Jed Wolfcry had no right to be in this house.

Dain leaped into the room. "What are you doing in here?" he yelled.

Wolfcry wheeled, obviously surprised at being interrupted. He backed off. "I—I came to the house for a drink."

"Did you expect to find water back here?" Dain demanded, lunging at the half-breed.

Wolfcry leaped aside, trying to dodge around Dain and out the door. Dain swung a fist, catching him a glancing blow on the side of the head. Wheeling, Wolfcry clawed at the knife at his belt. Dain hit him again, sending him staggering through the doorway.

The half-breed regained his balance and made it through the outside door. He had his knife in his hand as he spun around, but Dain had his hand on his gun. Wolfcry, the determination on his face slowly fading, back-pedaled.

"I'll live to cut your heart out!" he hissed, then wheeled and ran to his horse.

Dain watched him mount the horse and kick him into a hard gallop toward town. His fury slowly subsided. Their hopes of keeping Susan's hiding place secret were gone.

Dain started to leave, then stopped when he saw the spring wagon coming from up the river. Bert Diehl had built his house on a bend in the river. To the north was Ron Fulton's homestead and to the southeast was Dain's. Dain met Bert and Susan near the barn.

"Did you get your lumber?" Bert asked.

Dain nodded and helped Susan out of the buggy with her baby. When she had gone to the house, he turned to his brother-in-law. "I just ran Jed Wolfcry out of your house," he said in a low voice so Susan wouldn't hear.

"What was he doing in there?" Bert asked, anger lifting his voice.

"He found that secret place behind the bed. He'd pulled the bureau out and was staring through the hole when I caught him."

"He was supposed to be building a fence!" Bert exclaimed.

"He said he came to the house to get a drink," Dain explained. "I don't trust that half-breed any farther than I can throw a bull by the tail."

"Two of us," Bert agreed. "But I had to have help today and Jed was all I could get."

"You shouldn't have left him alone on the place."

"I reckon not. But Susan is afraid of Jed so I took her up to visit with Eve Fulton this morning, then went up this afternoon to get her while Jed finished up today's work on the fence."

"Jed doesn't talk to many people," Dain said, trying to quiet his own fears. "It's not our neighbors we're afraid of, anyway. Raiding Indians aren't liable to find that secret room."

"Jed swears he hates Indians," Bert said, worry still fringing his voice. "He's not apt to tell them what he knows."

Dain thought of the bracelet he'd found in his wagon yesterday. "Do you know what a medicine band is?"

Bert frowned. "Is that an Indian bracelet?"

"Maybe," Dain said. "I found it in my wagon yesterday when I was loading my lumber in Minneapolis. It was a rough strap of leather with thongs on each end of the strap. There were a few shells and beads and some old pieces of hide fastened to it. It looked like it could have been tied around a man's wrist or arm."

"A good luck charm," Bert decided. "I've been told that Indians put a lot of store in their good luck pieces; won't go into battle without them. They're sure they'd be killed. How did you happen to get one?"

"I haven't the foggiest notion," Dain said. "Somebody must have thrown it into my wagon but I don't know where or when or who did it."

"Have you got it now?"

Dain shook his head. "Somebody took it from my wagon; sneaked up on me last night while I was camped just outside Minneapolis. One of the horses snorted and woke me up. My gun was in the wagon so all I could do was roll out from under the wagon and hide in a ravine a little ways off."

"Was the man after you or the medicine piece?"

"Both, I figured. He ransacked the wagon then searched awhile for me. But I laid low and he didn't find me in the dark."

"What all did he take from the wagon?"

"Nothing but the medicine band, so far as I know," Dain said. "Then this morning when I was leaving Alpha, I found this note." He handed the paper to Bert.

Bert read it and frowned. "I don't like the looks of this."

"At least, we know it's not an Indian. Never saw an Indian who could write that well."

"Not saying there aren't any," Bert added. "Who do you suspect?"

"I first thought of Addison Scurry," Dain said. "He would love to get me, I'm sure. But Scurry would hardly have been near Minneapolis at midnight. If I hadn't found the bracelet while I was in Minneapolis, I'd suspect Jed Wolfcry. He claims to think and act like a white man. But there's a lot of Indian there."

Bert nodded. "He also knows how to read and write the white man's language, after a fashion."

Suspicion grew in Dain. "He does, doesn't he? What time did he come to work this morning?"

"He was here ready for work by the time I got back from taking Susan to the Fultons'," Bert said. "Hardly seems likely he could have been trying to kill you over at Minneapolis in the middle of the night."

"He'd have had to move pretty fast," Dain agreed.

It was hard for Dain to eliminate Jed Wolfcry. There was little doubt that the half-breed wanted to kill him. But if that had been Jed at Dain's camp close to Minneapolis, he'd have had to make that fifteen-mile ride back to Alpha by morning and then come on out to work for Bert by starting time. Still, Dain wouldn't completely rule out the possibility that Jed had been the one.

"I never saw Jed wear anything that even resembled an Indian good luck piece," Bert said. "In fact, I never saw him wear anything that even suggested he was part Indian."

Susan came out of the house, upset that her bureau had been

moved. Dain said he'd been in the bedroom after he got here and she dropped the subject. To mention that Jed Wolfcry had located that hiding place would only make her worry.

"Did you stop to see Valina as you came through Alpha?" Susan asked, that matchmaking gleam in her eyes again.

Dain told her what had happened. "When that horse reared," he finished, "she plunked into the street like a rock dropped from a fifty-foot cliff."

Susan laughed. "That must have been a sight."

"She was mad as a hen in a horse tank," Dain said.

"Did you expect her to get up and hug you? After all, it was your dog."

As usual, Dain went on the defensive when criticized. "It was her horse," he snapped. "She should know how to ride it."

"You're not going to make many friends with that attitude," Susan shot back. "You did apologize, didn't you?"

"She was in no mood to accept apologies."

"She'll get over it," Susan said. "You'll both laugh about it someday."

"I doubt that," Dain said and turned to his horse. He was glad that Jed Wolfcry was gone. He hoped Bert didn't hire him again, no matter how much he needed help.

He thought of going up to see Ron Fulton to ask him to help build the shed for his cows. He was a good carpenter. But it was nearly chore time now. He'd see him tomorrow.

As he rode home, he thought of Jed Wolfcry again. Why had he been snooping around Bert's house? And could it be possible that he was the one who had attacked his wagon and left the note?

Arriving at his own sod barn, he put his horse away and saw to it that all the horses had plenty of grain in their boxes and could get out into the little pasture he had fenced in.

Then he went to the wagon which he had left next to the site where he was going to build his shed. Laying some posts on the ground, he began pulling out the dimension lumber, the two inch by four inch, two inch by six inch, and two inch by ten inch pieces that would be the plates, studding and rafters. He laid them side by side on the posts, then unloaded the one inch by twelve inch boards on top. The lumber would be held off the damp ground by the posts.

As he unloaded, he realized that the leather band he had found could have been tossed into the wagon at any time. When he shoved those boards into the wagon at the lumber yard in Minneapolis, he'd have pushed the band to the front of the wagon. He wouldn't have seen it until he started driving home. But the note had to have been stuffed in between the boards after he left Minneapolis. That had surely been done after the night raider had found the bracelet.

He headed for the house to get his milk bucket. He had three cows and one of them was giving milk now. Thinking how miserable it would be milking his cows outside in zero weather, he realized it was important to get his shed built before winter. His tiny sod barn simply wasn't big enough for both his horses and cows.

Going into the house, he got the milk pail, then stepped outside to go to the corral. That was the instant when something hit him from the side like the kick of a mule.

Dain barely got a glimpse of Wolfcry as he was hit. He knew that the half-breed intended to make good on his threat to cut out his heart.

Three

DAIN WAS KNOCKED BACKWARD by the force of Wolf-cry's charge. But their collision sent them in different direc-tions. Wolfcry was much shorter than Dain, built like a tree stump, with big muscular arms and legs and a bull neck. Dain guessed he was depending on surprise and superior strength to win this battle for him.

Dain dropped the milk pail as he staggered backward, trying to catch his balance. But it was useless; he went down with a thud.

With a wild cry of exultation, the half-breed leaped after him but he was so intent on reaching Dain before he could get to his feet that he failed to notice the bucket. His foot hit the pail and it rolled, sending him sprawling.

Wolfcry seemed to explode off the ground as Dain scrambled to his feet. Jerking a knife from his belt he charged toward Dain. Dain dodged frantically and scooped up the bucket, throwing it with all the force he had.

Wolfcry ducked, throwing up an arm. The bucket slammed into his arm and knocked the knife spinning across the yard. Wolfcry lunged to recover his knife and Dain leaped after him, slamming into his back just as he was stooping to pick up the knife. They crashed to the ground, Dain on top, with the knife pinned beneath Wolfcry, out of reach of either of them.

Wolfcry tried to turn over but Dain grabbed a handful of hair and jerked his head up, bending his neck backward.

"Why are you trying to kill me?" he demanded.

"You deserve to die," Wolfcry spat out through clenched teeth. "I'll kill you."

Dain slammed his face into the dirt, then jerked his head back again. "Why?" He decided the half-breed wasn't going to answer so he jerked his head farther back.

"You've got to die!" Wolfcry croaked, his breath almost shut off.

Dain got off his back and Wolfcry lunged for his knife. Dain still had his grip on his hair and he jerked with all his strength. Wolfcry literally flew off the ground and landed on his knees. Dain jerked him to his feet, then held him there on his toes, his weight suspended by Dain's grip on his hair.

Dain knew he held his destiny in his hands. Wolfcry was as vicious as any wild animal. If he didn't kill him now, he'd have to deal with him later. But no matter how furious Dain was, he couldn't bring himself to kill him now. That would be murder.

He gave Wolfcry a shove that almost sent him sprawling. "Get out of here and keep going!" he shouted. "If I ever see you again anywhere in this valley, I'll kill you on sight."

Wolfcry stumbled for several feet, then caught himself and, like a shadow, melted into the deepening shades of the twilight. The moment he was gone, Dain felt a pang of regret at his weakness. Killing Wolfcry would have been self-defense even if he had done it while he was helpless.

Reaching down, he picked up Wolfcry's knife. It was a good one, well balanced. He had a sheath in his trunk just about the right size for it. He'd carry this knife; it might come in handy sometime.

He didn't expect Wolfcry to show up again tonight but he kept alert just in case he was underestimating the fury in the half-breed.

The next morning, he saddled his horse and rode up to Ron Fulton's place. Dain prided himself in not making friends easily, but it had been different with Ron. He had taken a definite liking to him immediately and he had never questioned his honesty or loyalty to their friendship.

Ron had no work pressing him that day and he agreed to come down and help Dain start building the shed. As they rode back to Dain's place, Dain told him about the leather bracelet he had found. Ron had stayed in the army for a while after the war and had been on a campaign against the Indians. That was when he had fallen in love with the Kansas prairie and as soon as he left the army and got married, he had come here and homesteaded. During his army service, he had learned a lot about the Indians while chasing them over the plains.

"Know anything about a medicine band?" Dain asked.

"I know many Indians wear good luck bracelets. What you found must have been something like that."

"Would having that make the owner want to kill me?" Dain asked.

"If he thought you had stolen it from him, yes. That's like stealing his life. But you're talking like you thought there were Indians here. I haven't seen any."

"Jed Wolfcry is more Indian than we think," Dain said.

Ron nodded. "Maybe so. He had a white father and an Indian mother, I hear. He must have inherited the worst of both races. But he dresses white and lives with the whites." Ron rubbed his chin thoughtfully. "He might have brought some of the Indian superstition with him when he came to the whites."

"He tried to kill me again last night," Dain said. "Of course, I knocked him around some when I found him in Bert's house. That may have been why he came after me last night."

"If he tried it once, he might try it again," Ron said. "I'd keep an eye out for him."

They got a good start on Dain's shed. His horse barn was sod and so was his house, but lumber seemed the fastest way to build a shed for the cows. Before the end of the second day, they were ready to make the doors for the shed and Dain realized he had forgotten to buy any hinges. He could make leather hinges but doors always sagged on leather. He wanted iron ones for his shed.

Dain and Ron saddled up and rode to Alpha to look for hinges. The only place that might have them was Scurry's. Addison Scurry seemed to enjoy telling Dain that he didn't.

"You won't last long enough on that homestead of yours to need iron hinges," Scurry said, a sneer curling his lips.

Anger surged through Dain. He pressed against the counter. "Nobody's going to push me off my homestead. You figure on trying?"

Scurry tipped his head back until he was staring down the sides of his curved nose at Dain. "I wouldn't stoop to touching your dinky bit of land. All I'm saying is, it takes a real man to make a homestead go."

Dain lunged against the counter but Scurry backed off where Dain couldn't reach him. "Why don't you come out from behind that counter and say that?"

"I wouldn't dirty my hands with the likes of you."

Dain was preparing to vault over the counter to get at Scurry when Ron laid a hand on his arm. "Easy," he said softly in Dain's ear. "He's wearing a gun."

Dain got a grip on his fury. Scurry could shoot him as he went over the counter and claim self-defense—it would stand up in court. Dain realized that Scurry was just baiting him and he'd almost fallen for it. Ron's quick thinking had likely saved him.

"Anytime you feel like getting your hands dirty, let me know," Dain said after a moment.

He saw the letdown in Scurry's face. He'd been ready and he'd been confident. Dain was sure he wouldn't have been that confident if he'd been meeting Dain on equal grounds. Ron had outguessed the storekeeper and Dain had not. It was that simple. Dain realized that his trust in Ron was certainly not misplaced.

Spinning on his heel, he went outside. Ron was a couple of steps behind, keeping an eye on Scurry. Dain was too furious to consider the danger of being shot in the back.

"Leather hinges now?" Ron said, his voice still low, as they reached their horses.

Dain was trying to fight down the anger that had almost driven him over the counter into Scurry's gun. "I need more lumber," he said finally. "Let's take a couple of days off and go to Minneapolis and get the lumber and I can get my hinges there."

Ron nodded. "Can we take Eve along? She's been wanting to go to Minneapolis."

Dain nodded. "Sure." He looked up the street at the hat shop. Maybe he should make one more try at apologizing to Valina. "Be back in a few minutes," he said and headed up the street.

Ron followed but stayed outside when Dain stepped into the millinery shop. He was met by Valina. Before he could open his mouth, she cut him off.

"I'm sorry I lost my temper the other day," she said. "It wasn't your fault that your dog barked at my horse."

Dain was almost speechless. "It—it was my dog," he stammered, "but I sure didn't know he was going to do that."

"No hard feelings?" Valina asked.

"Sure not with me," Dain said, amazed at the way this was going. "Let's just forget the whole thing."

"That's the smartest thing either of you has said so far," Martha put in. "Looking for a lady's hat today?" she asked Dain.

Dain was rapidly forgetting the aggravation Scurry had caused him. "Afraid not today," he said with a grin. "I've got a shed to build. I'd better be at it."

He would have liked to stay longer and talk to Valina but he couldn't think of anything more to say. Valina had taken the wind out of his sails.

"That was short," Ron said when Dain got back outside the shop. "Did she bite your head off?"

Dain shook his head. "She apologized. To me! Can you believe it?"

"What did you say?"

"I don't remember. All I could think of was getting out of there before I put my foot in my mouth again."

"Let's get home now and get ready for Minneapolis tomorrow," Ron said.

They headed back down the street toward Scurry's store where they had left their horses at the hitchrack. Dain had completely forgotten his clash with Scurry. His thoughts were still back at the millinery shop with Valina. He had never expected to be on really good terms with her again. Now he felt he was on the very best of terms. Nothing could cloud his sky at this moment.

He flipped the reins of his horse free of the hitchrack and stepped into the stirrup. He was barely aware of the nervous sidestepping of his horse. The horse seldom acted that way but it didn't register that this was unusual.

As he threw his weight on the stirrup, he felt the saddle give a bit then hold. But the next second, there was a snap and Dain fell back to the ground with the saddle on top of him. His horse sidled away from him but didn't bolt.

Scrambling out from under the saddle, Dain's mind was in a whirl. It took a minute to drag his thoughts back to reality. His cinch had given way and, if his horse had been a wild one, he likely would have been trampled.

"What happened?" Ron demanded, running around the horse to Dain.

"Busted cinch, I guess," Dain said.

On his feet again, he pulled the saddle out of the street to look at it. He saw that it was a cut cinch, not a broken one.

"Cut almost in two," Ron said, fingering the fresh cut. "If it had held another second, you'd have gone right on over the horse and under mine. You're lucky."

Fury was exploding in Dain's brain again. This had to be the work of Scurry. There had been nobody else in the store when he and Ron had been there just a few minutes ago.

"This time I'm going to get him," Dain said, jerking his gun out of the saddle bag where he usually carried it when he didn't expect to need it. And he certainly hadn't expected to need it in Alpha.

"Don't go off half cocked," Ron warned. "I agree that it must have been Scurry—probably jealous because you went up to see Valina. Eve says Scurry is wild about her."

"I'll tame him down a little," Dain said.

"Better take it slow. He may be laying for you."

"Do you expect me to let him get away with this?"

Ron shook his head. "I'll go in first. He has no bone to pick with me. I'll find out where he's hiding, waiting for you, because I'll bet he is. You come in after I locate him."

Dain once again saw the wisdom of Ron's common sense. He adjusted the gun in his belt. He wouldn't bother with a holster but he wanted the gun where he could get it in a hurry if he had to have it.

Ron went through the door into the store and Dain came in a half minute behind him. When Dain stepped in Scurry was coming out from behind the stove in the middle of the store. It had made a good hiding place.

"What do you want?" Scurry asked Ron. Then he saw Dain behind him. Fury swept over his face as he realized he'd been flushed out of his ambush.

"I don't want anything," Ron said. "But I think Dain has a question or two to ask you."

"What's the idea of cutting my cinch?" Dain demanded, moving up in front of Ron.

"Who says I did?" Scurry snapped.

"I do," Dain said. "And I'm calling your hand. You want it with guns or fists?"

Scurry's face paled. "I'm no gunman—not against two of you."

"I'm not in it," Ron said. "Dain can take care of himself."

Scurry still kept his hands far away from his gun. "I'm no gunfighter," he said.

"Then put your gun on the counter," Dain said. "Real easy."

Scurry slowly drew his gun and laid it on the counter. Dain handed his gun to Ron. "Keep him honest," he said to his partner.

"I'm not fighting both of you," Scurry said.

"I'm strictly a spectator," Ron said. "I'm just going to see that it's a fair fight."

"I'm not going to fight," Scurry said. "You'd wreck my store."

"We can go outside," Dain said, realizing how much Scurry treasured his store. He guessed he was very possessive of anything he owned or thought he owned. Maybe he thought he owned Valina.

"I'm not going to fight," Scurry repeated. "If you start a fight, it will all be on your head."

"Don't think I'm going to let you get away with cutting the cinch on my saddle. You've got new cinches here in the store. Get one and put it on my saddle."

Color began to return to Scurry's face as he realized that he wasn't going to be forced into a fight. He turned and shuffled toward the rear of the store where a half-dozen cinches hung on a nail by their buckles.

Dain followed him, watching his every move. Taking down a cinch, he tossed it at Dain's feet.

"Pick it up!" Dain snapped. "And put it on my saddle."

Scurry scowled but he stared only a moment at Dain, then he picked up the cinch and shuffled out the door, moving like a man dream walking. Dain watched as he took both ends of the cut cinch off their rings. Then he fastened the one end of the new cinch solid and left the other end dangling where it would be fastened around the horse's belly.

"Now are you satisfied?" Scurry demanded.

"Not yet," Dain snapped. "Saddle my horse. And you'd better do a good job or I'll come back and finish what I should have done."

There were several spectators standing in the street and on the porch now. Scurry's face flushed as he moved to obey Dain's command. He had probably never been humiliated like this before.

"I'll get you for this!" Scurry hissed at Dain as he finished cinching the saddle on the horse.

Dain's anger was subsiding fast. "Look on the bright side," he said. "You saved yourself a beating. You should feel good correcting the mistake you made."

Scurry glowered at Dain as he stepped back from the horse. "Get out!" he snapped. "And don't come back to my store again."

"You can't entice good customers that way," Dain said and swung into the saddle.

Ron was already in his saddle and they wheeled down the street. Dain saw the wide grins on the faces of the men who had been watching.

"That was harder on Scurry than having the tar whipped out of him," Ron said as they left town.

"It may have a more lasting effect," Dain agreed.

After he got home, Dain did his chores and got his wagon ready for the trip. The next morning, he swung over to Fulton's place and picked up Ron and Eve and they headed for Minneapolis.

They took their time driving the fifteen miles. Dain bought the lumber he needed and got two pairs of hinges for the doors. In the meantime, Eve was enjoying the stores in town, buying the few things she really needed and wishing for the many things she couldn't have.

It was late in the afternoon when she finished so they camped just outside town and got an early start for home the next morning.

Back on the Saline, Dain drove past Fulton's place to let off Ron and Eve. As they came in sight of the homestead, Dain saw that things from the house were scattered over the yard and there were no cows or horses near the sod barn.

"Indians!" Ron exploded, leaping off the wagon and running toward the house. Eve was only a step behind him.

Dain waited only long enough to make sure there were no Indians around, then he whipped his horse into a run straight toward his own place, cutting across the prairie instead of following the river road that would have taken him past Bert Diehl's.

He found the same havoc at his place. His three cows were gone but his saddle horse was standing at the little sod barn. Apparently he had been down in that gully in the pasture when the Indians struck and they had missed him. The shed he and Ron had started had been burned.

Dain didn't even stop for a closer look. He urged his team into a run up the creek road toward his brother-in-law's place. Bert and Susan had surely been home when the raiders struck.

He jerked the team to a halt as he came into Bert Diehl's yard. He saw Bert instantly, stretched out in the yard, ten feet from the door of the house. Dain whipped the lines around the brake lever and leaped down.

Bert was dead. He'd been shot in the body and head with a rifle and scalped. There were two arrows sticking in his body.

Dain ran into the house, panic almost choking him. The house was empty. The bureau at the foot of the bed had been pulled out, revealing the secret room. Dain knew what that meant. Susan and the baby were gone, captives of the Indians.

Four

IF A THOUSAND-POUND ROCK had fallen on him, Dain wouldn't have felt more crushed. How had the Indians found that secret hiding place? Had they gotten into the house before Susan had time to pull the dresser over the opening?

Suddenly he knew as if he'd seen it written in blood on the wall. Jed Wolfcry! He knew about this hiding place. Dain had gone along with the general opinion that Wolfcry was more white than Indian but finding that leather wrist band and suspecting that it belonged to Wolfcry had altered his thinking.

He remembered how the half-breed had sworn to get even with Dain for whipping him. Showing the raiding Indians where Dain's sister was hiding could have been his way of striking back.

Dain scrubbed a hand through his blond hair and fought the sickness that swept over him. This was no time to despair or let his fury stand in the way of straight thinking. The Indians couldn't be very far away. He had to rescue Susan and he had to do it right away.

The unshod tracks of the Indian ponies seemed to go up the creek. Ron's place had probably been the one they hit after leaving here. Leaping back into the wagon, he urged his weary team into a run up to Ron Fulton's place. Ron and Eve were still wandering around in a daze, looking at broken furniture and dishes scattered over the yard.

"They hit your place?" Ron asked as Dain pulled the team to a halt.

Dain nodded. "They hit Bert's, too. Killed Bert and kidnapped Susan and the baby."

Eve gasped. "They took Susan?" she whispered.

"We've got to get her away from those savages," Dain choked.

"I'm with you," Ron said, sucking in a deep breath. He tore his eyes away from the carnage in the yard and looked at the wagon and weary team. "We can't catch up with them in that outfit."

Dain realized that Ron was thinking straighter than he was. He hadn't considered anything but getting on the Indians' trail as quickly as possible. "My horse is still at home. They took my cows but missed the saddle horse. I'll get him. Maybe Gunderson wasn't hit and he'd have a horse you could borrow."

Ron nodded. "Eve and I will walk up there. She can't stay here while I'm gone. I'll get a horse and meet you back here."

Dain wheeled the team around and urged them into a run again. They'd had a long trip from Minneapolis and had been running ever since Dain had seen what the Indians had done to Ron Fulton's place. But he couldn't let them lag now. They'd have plenty of time to rest after he got them home.

At home, Dain unhitched and unharnessed his horses and turned them out into the pasture. Saddling his riding horse, he headed back to Ron's place. Ron was waiting for him with a horse he had borrowed from Gunderson.

"I left Eve with the Gundersons," he said. "I think they're going to go to town. Nobody feels safe out here now."

"I'm not even sure they'll be safe in Alpha," Dain said.

"Maybe not, but it's better than staying out here alone. Are you going to take your dog along?"

Dain hadn't even realized that Havana was trailing him. He went everywhere Dain went unless he was sent back home.

"He won't be any bother," Dain said. "It's too far to send him back home now, anyway."

The trail of the Indians from Fulton's place was easy to follow. They had made no effort to hide it. Half a mile above Ron's place, still along the creek, they found another demolished homestead. John Hyett and his wife were both dead, sprawled in the yard. The trail ran on, following the creek.

"Looks like they stayed right on the creek," Ron said. "I doubt if they hit the town."

"They knew that most of the settlers were along the creek," Dain said. "Each family would be isolated. In town, they'd run into a lot of people."

Ron nodded. "I think you're right. There were probably just a few of them. They weren't looking for a fight. Maybe a small raiding party that is heading back now for the main band."

"They're going away from the Smoky Hill," Dain said. Suddenly he pointed to the ground. "Looks like they're cutting away from the creek and heading northeast. That doesn't make sense."

"Few things an Indian does makes sense. That's why they're so slippery."

Swinging away from the creek, they followed the trail. It was not so plain on the open prairie but still, by watching closely, they could stay on it.

Ron suddenly reined up. "They split up here. Looks like three or four of them went toward town. The rest went on northeast."

"Which bunch do we follow?" Dain asked.

"Let's follow this bunch headed toward town. They may be planning to dump off their captives somewhere."

Dain doubted that but he knew that Ron was more familiar with this land than he was so he was willing to defer the leadership to his redheaded partner. Ron was a year younger than Dain's twenty-three years and he was also an inch shorter and twenty pounds lighter. Dain had always heard that red hair meant a hot temper but in Ron's case that wasn't so. Ron always seemed to be in control of his temper. Dain's temper was much more volatile. His blond hair and blue eyes were inherited from his Scandinavian ancestors but his temper and impatience must have come from some other offshoot of his ancestry.

Dain hoped they would catch up with this splinter party of raiders but they found another homestead destroyed, the man and woman dead and scalped, the children, if there were any, gone.

"Don't think the Bonnevilles had any kids," Ron said in hushed tones as they looked over the damage.

"Looks like the raiders headed back toward the main party," Dain said.

Ron nodded. "Must have seen the smoke from the chimney and knew there was a house here. There's no fire now so this must have happened hours ago."

Dain felt as if he'd been kicked. "Then we don't have much chance of catching up with them?"

"Probably not before they join up with their camp. We'll need more men. We'd better ride into town and see if we can get enough men to tackle a small Indian camp."

Reluctantly Dain agreed. Two men couldn't tackle an Indian camp even if it was a small one. And there was no guarantee that it would be small.

They rode over the undulating hills to town. Dain hadn't seen anything to suggest that Susan and her baby were with these Indians. But they hadn't been back at the homestead. They must be with the raiders somewhere.

A surge of fury swept through Dain as he thought of Jed Wolfcry. Wolfcry had to be the one who uncovered Susan's hiding place. There was just no other way that the Indians could have found that spot. He'd find Wolfcry if it took him the rest of his life and he'd kill him just as he would a rattlesnake.

"We'd better make sure there aren't any Indians around town before we ride in," Ron said.

"Seems like there'd be some shooting if there were any," Dain said.

They topped the last rise of land and looked down on the town lying quietly in the afternoon sun.

"Looks pretty empty from here," Ron said. "We want to make sure we're recognized when we ride in. I imagine there are some nervous fingers down there right now."

Coming in from the north end of town as Dain and Ron were doing now, they came to the millinery shop first. The place appeared deserted. So did the other stores and most of the homes. But down in front of Scurry's General Store, there was a crowd. Dain decided that everybody in town was there, huddled together like frightened sheep. Most of the people were watching Dain and Ron but nobody was moving.

Addison Scurry was on the porch steps. He seemed to be the only one who wasn't paralyzed by fear. Dain looked over the men in the crowd as he rode closer. There were enough there to raid an Indian camp if he could get them to go with him. He couldn't imagine anyone refusing to go when it was explained that a white woman had been kidnapped.

"Where have you been?" one man yelled as they reached the fringe of the crowd.

"We've been trailing Indians," Ron said. "They hit every place along the Saline and even struck Bonneville's place over north, more than a mile from the creek. Killed both the Bonnevilles."

"They hit my sister's place," Dain added, trying to keep the tremble out of his voice. "They killed Bert and kidnapped Susan and the baby. We were trying to catch them and rescue Susan. But they had too much of a start. We need help to run them down and get the white women they have taken."

Dain stopped, his voice breaking as he thought of Susan in the hands of the savages. He looked over the crowd, expecting to see men step forward ready to go. But they stood there as silent and stone-faced as if they hadn't heard a word he said.

Scurry stepped back up on the porch where he was above the crowd. "Let's use some common sense here," he said, his voice loud and harsh. "The Indians have struck and run. What they've done, we can't undo. But if we dash off half cocked after them, they could move in and wipe out our town."

"That would be no worse than what they've done to the homesteads!" Dain shouted. "No telling how many women they have kidnapped. Are we going to leave them in the hands of the savages?" Dain's voice was steady now, weighted with anger.

"If we go after them, we'll all be killed," Scurry shouted. "If we stay here we can defend this town."

"You and your cowards stay here!" Dain shot back. "Those who want to rescue the women, come on!"

Some of the men began to stir and move out of the crowd toward Dain and Ron. Scurry shouted at them.

"Don't be fools! If you catch the Indians, you'll all be killed. We are still alive. Let's make sure we stay alive."

"They don't kill cowards, so you'll be safe enough," Ron shouted. He turned to the crowd. "We need men who aren't afraid to fight for our women."

Several men moved out, many with women clinging to their arms, trying to persuade them to stay.

"We won't take unnecessary chances," Dain promised. "But we have to rescue those women if we can."

A dozen men headed for their horses. Scurry screamed from the porch. "You are leaving your women at the mercy of the Indians! You've got to stay here and defend them."

Dain ignored him. There were more than enough men left here to defend the town in case the Indians returned, which seemed highly unlikely. Motioning for the men who had stepped out to follow, he headed back to the north.

As they rode past the millinery shop, Valina stepped out. She must have been hiding somewhere inside when they rode in.

"Do you really think you can catch the Indians?" she asked as Dain reined up.

"Got to try," Dain said. "My sister was kidnapped. You know how Indians treat captives."

Her face blanched and she stepped back. "Be careful," she said softly. "I hope you can find her."

As Dain nudged his horse to catch up with the others, he thought how the Indians would love to grab a prize like Valina and a chill ran through him. He didn't know how Indians rated beauty but Dain couldn't see a blemish in Valina. Even just now, with the anguish pulling at her lips, she had been the picture of perfection to Dain; blue eyes, long auburn hair done up in a bun on the back of her head, skin that had taken on a rosy tan, slim figure.

They picked up the Indians' trail about where Dain and Ron had left it. The men had seen the dead bodies of the Bonnevilles and determination was etched on every face. But the trail grew dim as they moved forward. One man was serving as tracker and leaning far over the saddle to read the signs. He finally reined up.

"They've scattered. They likely knew we'd follow them so they split up. Not more than two went in any one direction."

"Where would they go?" one man asked.

"They probably agreed to meet somewhere up ahead," the tracker said. "Or they might be heading for their main camp."

"Or maybe circling around to hit the town," another man added. "It's a cinch we're not going to catch up with them so we'd better get back to town and protect what we still have."

Dain wanted to shout that they couldn't give up. But he knew their reasoning was sound. They didn't have much chance of catching up with the Indians and they had no way of telling which Indians were holding Susan. Most of these men had families back in town; they were going back to guard them. He couldn't blame then.

Once the decision was made, the men wheeled almost as a unit and kicked their horses into a gallop toward town. Only Ron stayed with Dain.

"They make sense," Ron said. "An Indian isn't liable to be found unless he wants to be. Let's go back to town and decide what our next move should be. It will soon be dark, anyway."

"I have to find them," Dain insisted.

"I agree," Ron said, "and I'll help you all I can. But riding around in circles in the dark out here on the prairie isn't going to do it."

Dain nodded and turned his horse back toward town. His mind racing, he searched for a plan he could use to find and rescue Susan.

On their way back to town, they followed a different path than the men ahead of them had used. Suddenly Ron held up a hand.

"Riders coming," he said softly.

Dain jerked the rifle out of its boot.

Five

BLOOD POUNDED through Dain's head as he tensed, preparing himself for the encounter with whoever was coming. There were ravines cutting through the prairie where rainwater washed down toward the river after every heavy downpour. The prairie itself was not really flat, although it looked almost flat to Dain. Whoever was coming was on the other side of a low ridge.

Then suddenly they burst over the ridge and Dain's fingers tightened on his rifle. But in a moment, they relaxed. These were two of the men who had chosen to stay in town rather than go out in search of the Indians.

"Find them redskins?" one man yelled as he reined up his roan horse.

Ron answered. "Lost their trail. What are you doing out here?"

"We decided there were enough men left in town to protect it so we came out to help you."

"The Indians split up into little bunches," Dain said. "We had no idea which bunch had Susan."

"Couldn't see the trail well enough to follow any of them very well," Ron added. "The other men all headed back to town. That's where we're going, too."

The men nodded, relief showing in their faces. Apparently it had been guilty consciences that had driven them out here. "We'll just ride back with you," one said.

As they trotted their horses toward town, Dain thought of the monumental task ahead of him. But he wouldn't allow himself any doubts about his ability to find his sister and nephew and rescue them.

It was late afternoon when they got back to Alpha. Those who had hurried back from the hunt for the savages had been in town for some time. They were gathered in front of the store, making new plans.

"It's too late to do anything tonight," Herbert Gunderson said as Dain came within hearing distance. "But first thing in the morning, we have to gather up the dead bodies and give them a decent burial."

Dain thought instantly that these men could do that tomorrow without his help. He was going after the Indians. He'd find them somewhere. Then he thought that one of those bodies was Bert Diehl. It wasn't right to let some disinterested neighbor take care of Bert. But it wasn't right to leave Susan in the hands of those savages a minute longer than absolutely necessary, either.

"I know what you're thinking," Ron said at Dain's side. "You can't go after them alone. Those Indians already have a long head start. A few more hours, even a day or two, isn't going to make that much difference now. After we get past the funerals, maybe we can gather a fighting force to go after the Indians and rescue Susan."

Dain knew that made sense. But he also knew that every hour Susan was a prisoner of the Indians could mean a lifetime of torture.

The wagons rolled out of town at dawn the next morning and Dain rode with them. He knew he had no chance of rescuing Susan alone. The funerals were set for the afternoon. The bodies could not wait any longer than that in this hot weather. There would be a funeral service for all the victims at the small church in town. Half the men who had come to town to wait until they knew it was safe to return to their homesteads went to the cemetery just outside town to dig graves while the other half found teams and wagons in town and went out to gather the dead.

The only two places along the creek close to town that didn't have any bodies to pick up were Dain's place and Ron Fulton's. It was an odd quirk, he thought, that it had been Scurry's lack of hinges that had spurred Dain to go to Minneapolis for them. Now he had the hinges but no shed to put them on.

Dain rode on the wagon with Herbert Gunderson. When they stopped at Bert Diehl's place, Dain had to pinch back the tears and swallow the emotion that surged up in him. Bert and Susan might have gone to Minneapolis with him if Bert hadn't wanted to finish his fence. Now he had no need for the fence. And Susan and little

Hiram? Dain let his fury rise as he thought of his sister, a captive of the Indians. Anger was easier to live with than sorrow and regrets.

Dain and Gunderson had four bodies in the wagon when they turned back toward town. All the wagons arrived there before noon. Dain knew he'd have to wait until the funerals were over to recruit men to go with him. No one was going to leave before the funerals. Dain knew he should stay. He owed his brother-in-law that much. But he owed his sister and nephew even more.

Scurry came to the funeral service at the little church. Dain found it hard to tolerate the surly storekeeper. He looked for Jed Wolfcry although he was sure he'd be with the Indians now. He'd have been amazed if Wolfcry had been with Scurry. He'd have killed him if he'd been there. He was that certain that he had betrayed Susan's hiding place to the raiders.

The funeral service was short; the burials took a little longer as the rough boxes that had been slapped together were lowered into the graves. Dain followed the box that held Bert Diehl and placed a small cross at the head of the grave when it was filled. He had whittled the cross while he waited at noon for the funeral to begin.

He was surprised as he turned away from his task to see Valina and her Aunt Martha waiting for him.

"We're sorry about Bert," Martha said. "He was a fine young man."

"Even more sorry about your sister and nephew," Valina said. "I can't imagine how awful that must be."

Valina's face was flushed and she was biting her lower lip until he wondered if it would bleed. Tears beaded her eyes. She had no relatives who had been struck in the raid but she shared the community's sorrow.

"I'm going after Susan and the baby," Dain said. "I won't stop till I find them."

"That will be dangerous," Valina said, concern in her voice.

"Getting yourself killed isn't going to help your family," Martha put in, her plump face holding the stern look of a schoolteacher reprimanding a recalcitrant child.

"Be careful," Valina said as the three started back toward town. "Is there anything I can do?"

"As a matter of fact, there is. My dog will follow me if he can. Could you keep him for me? He'll be a good guard dog for you."

"Are you sure he won't attack us?" Martha said.

Dain wondered if his face showed his embarrassment when he thought of that day when Havana had caused Valina to get dumped in the dust of the street.

"I like dogs," Valina said quickly. "I know I can get along with Havana. I just won't let him get close to my horse."

At the end of the street, the two women moved on up toward their millinery shop. Dain turned toward Scurry's General Store. He saw Scurry inside. The other business places had closed for the funerals but Scurry hadn't. The funerals hadn't lessened Scurry's greed.

Scurry was scowling when Dain stepped inside the store, a mixture of apprehension and fury on his face.

"I see you're playing on Valina's sympathies for all you're worth," he snapped.

Dain almost went over the counter where Scurry stood. He'd love to smash in his teeth. He knew that Scurry resented Valina even talking to him but to intimate that Dain was using his sister and nephew to play on Valina's sympathies was stretching Dain's restraint to the limit. Still, he knew that if he smashed up Scurry it could very well backfire on him. Valina wouldn't want anyone fighting over her. And if Dain started such a fight, he'd be the one in bad with her, not Scurry.

"I just want to know where Wolfcry is," Dain demanded.

"I don't know," Scurry growled. "He left a couple of days ago and I haven't seen him since."

"You haven't seen him since the Indian raid, have you?"

Scurry lunged against the counter, leaning across it, his black eyes blazing. "What do you mean by that?"

"He joined the Indians, didn't he?" Dain demanded.

Scurry reminded Dain of an angry ape as he leaned far over the counter, his upper body supported on balled fists jammed against the countertop. His black greasy hair was combed straight back as always and Dain guessed he had added a generous amount of grease to it this morning.

"Where he is is none of your business!" he shouted.

Dain knew he had guessed right. Scurry apparently realized his actions were saying more than his words. He backed off suddenly, his voice lowering.

"You know he hates the Indians," he said. "You have no proof that he went anywhere near those Indians."

"I have plenty," Dain said. "Nobody but Jed knew where Susan was hiding. He told the varmints where to find her."

Scurry lunged against the counter again, then seemed to think better of it.

"You don't know what you're talking about. Anyway, I have no control over what Jed does."

"I didn't say you did," Dain snapped. "But you do know where he is now."

"I said I didn't know and I don't. You can think what you like."

"I'll do that," Dain said. "I think people would like to know what your helper here in the store is doing now."

Scurry did lunge forward then. "You dare to say a word about that and I'll tear your heart out."

Dain knew what he was thinking. The people of this town would lynch Scurry if they couldn't get their hands on Wolfcry just because the two were associated together in Alpha.

Dain was struck by the similarity of the threat that Wolfcry had made against him that night out by his soddy and the one Scurry was making now. The two had been together so much they must think a little alike even if there was no Indian blood in Scurry.

"You walk a straight path and I'll keep your secret," Dain said.

He wheeled and walked out of the store, feeling prickles along his back as he walked. Scurry had to realize that Dain knew where Jed Wolfcry was and what he had done. If he was afraid Dain might spread that knowledge among the people of Alpha, he might decide to kill Dain now. If people suspected that the man who had been working with Scurry in the store had helped the Indians, things could get ugly.

Dain had barely gotten back in the street when he saw a rider coming in from the northeast. The rider pulled up in front of the store where most of the people congregated when any news hit town.

"The Indians raided along the Solomon yesterday," he shouted. "They may come back this way. People think their main camp is to the west."

"What can we do?" one man shouted nervously.

"Head for Minneapolis until the Indians leave the country," the messenger advised.

"Minneapolis is on the Solomon River," another man said. "Why go there?"

"They didn't raid near Minneapolis," the messenger said. "And they won't. Too many people there. They like to hit the isolated homesteads."

"We'll all go to Minneapolis tomorrow," Herbert Gunderson announced. "Too late to start tonight. We'd be caught out on the prairie overnight."

The idea appealed to almost everyone. It didn't to Dain. He intended to look for Susan. He couldn't do that in Minneapolis.

"I suppose you're not going," Ron said to Dain, who was standing some distance from the storefront.

"You're right," Dain said. "I have to look for my family."

"I'll have to see that Eve gets safely to Minneapolis tomorrow," Ron said. "Then I'll go with you, if you'll wait. Maybe some of the other men will go, too."

Dain knew it was the best he could do. He had to have help but he'd have to take it when he could get it.

"We'll post a guard tonight," Gunderson said, "in case those redskins come back this way. At dawn, we head for Minneapolis. Get ready tonight to move."

A few were impatient and wanted to start out immediately. But when they considered what would happen if they ran into the Indians coming back from the Solomon, they wisely decided to wait and go with the group.

Dain decided he would have to go to Minneapolis, too. If he was going to recruit men for his mission, he would have to do it there. Alpha would be deserted.

Gunderson handed out guard duty assignments. Dain drew a post on the west side of town. He would be on duty until midnight, then another man would take his place. He wasn't sure where the others were stationed but he knew the town was ringed with men carrying rifles. He was sure the Indians would not come back this way but if they did, they'd find an armed camp. They weren't likely to test its efficiency.

His thoughts turned to Jed Wolfcry. After seeing Scurry's reactions to Dain's accusations, he was convinced beyond a doubt that Wolfcry was with the Indians now. If Dain found the Indians who were holding Susan and the baby he'd likely find Wolfcry, too.

Since he didn't expect any trouble, he relaxed his watchfulness. Still he kept an eye toward the shadows in front of him. Behind him was the town. There should be no trouble from that direction.

The first inkling he had that someone was creeping near him was a slight rustle in the grass and it was behind him. Wheeling around, he was just in time to meet a hard smash over his head with some kind of club. He felt his legs buckle under him.

He came to enough to realize he was being dragged like a sack of potatoes through the grass. He didn't know how long that went on but to his fuzzy thinking, it seemed like an eternity.

Then the dragging stopped and a man stooped over him. He lifted him and pulled him forward until his feet suddenly dangled over empty space. In the split second before he started falling, he realized he must be over an open well.

Six

VALINA TRIED to feel safe, knowing the town was guarded on every side by armed men. But she didn't. She was frightened. The possibility of Indians attacking the town was very remote. Yet she was shaken to the depths of her being and she knew that most of the other residents of the town were, too.

Martha was moving around the big room behind their millinery shop, sorting out things they would take with them on their dash to Minneapolis. Valina could see by the flash of her aunt's eyes that she was not as calm as her actions would indicate.

"Do you really think the Indians will come back this way?" Valina finally asked, irritated at Martha's outward calm.

"Makes no difference what we think. The fact is we're running to Minneapolis to get away from the threat of the savages. Do you have everything packed?"

"I can't decide what I should take," Valina said. "I can't believe the Indians will attack when we have all these armed men with us."

Martha laid one more dress in her valise. "Of course they won't. But if we tuck our tails and run and leave nobody here, the Indians could have a great time stealing and destroying everything we leave."

"You don't think we should leave?"

"I sure ain't going to stay here if everybody else leaves," Martha said emphatically. "But there's no sense in being nervous. We're safe now and we'll be safe on the road to Minneapolis. We'll sure be safe in a town that size. So finish your packing and get to bed. We've got a trip ahead of us tomorrow."

Valina knew that was good advice. But she couldn't calm down.

She felt something was wrong. She wanted to talk to Dain once more before he left on his mission. She'd heard him say that he wasn't going to Minneapolis; he was going to look for his sister and Hiram. So if she wanted to talk to him, she'd have to do it tonight. He'd probably be on his way before the people of Alpha were up in the morning.

Going into the millinery shop, she began taking the hats out of the window. She packed them carefully in boxes and pushed them against the back wall. If Indians came to town after everyone left, she didn't want anything in the window that would attract them. They'd probably burn the town, anyway, but she didn't want to invite disaster.

She was just turning away from the window with the last hat when a knock rattled the door. She couldn't imagine who would be wanting anything in the millinery shop this late. People should either be packing for the trip or in bed resting up for it.

She opened the door cautiously, then saw that it was Addison Scurry. Pulling the door back, she invited him in.

"Just checking on everyone," Scurry said easily. "I don't want to leave you behind when we go to Minneapolis tomorrow."

"Don't worry," Valina said. "We'll be ready. How about you? What are you going to do with your store?"

A pained look swept across Scurry's narrow face. "I'll have to leave it like it is," he said. "The important thing is to get you women to Minneapolis." He dropped down on a settee the shop kept for customers.

Valina wanted to keep working but she couldn't be rude. She sat beside Scurry. "Where is Jed?" she asked. "I haven't seen him lately."

"He's gone," Scurry said. "Left me with all the work to do around the store."

"Maybe the Indians got him," Valina suggested.

"That's possible. He disappeared about the time they struck."

"Isn't it terrible about Dain's nephew and sister?"

Scurry shrugged. "At least, they're probably still alive." He scowled. "Too bad Dain wasn't the one at home instead of his brother-in-law when the Indians raided the creek homesteads."

Valina caught her breath. She had momentarily forgotten about Scurry's antagonism toward Dain. She had suspected it was jealousy because she had made no secret of her interest in Dain. She hadn't spurned Scurry's attentions and she suspected he still considered himself in the race for her favors. She wished she had made her position clear before this.

"I'm glad Dain wasn't home then," she said.

Scurry frowned. "You can't depend on him to protect you."

"I don't need anyone to protect me," Valina said sharply. "I can take care of myself."

"Every woman needs a man to take care of her," Scurry said confidently. "This is Indian country. Indians are hard on women captives."

Valina saw that Scurry was trying to establish himself as her personal protector. She found that disgusting. She had made a special effort to be nice to Scurry. After all, he had the only general store in Alpha and he had treated her like a queen. But since she had met Dain, any personal interest she might have had in Scurry had faded.

"I'll personally see that you get to Minneapolis safely," Scurry added, sliding over close to Valina.

Valina couldn't believe this was happening. Right now she was worried about Dain, and she was in no mood for any trifling from Scurry. Just behind the settee was a box of hat pins that they kept for sale. She reached back and picked up one.

As she expected, Scurry did slide over against her and lifted an arm around her shoulders. Without a word of protest, Valina jabbed the hat pin into Scurry's ribs. With a screech, he leaped off the settee and landed halfway to the door, glaring at her.

"I can take care of myself, Mr. Scurry," Valina repeated softly.

Scurry scowled at her for a moment, then wheeled and stamped out the door. Valina was just putting the hat pin back in the box when Martha came rushing in from the back room.

"Who was that screaming in here? Sounded like a wounded lion."

"Addison Scurry," Valina said. "He was getting too familiar."

"He's the scum of the earth," Martha said angrily. "What did you do?"

Valina smiled. "Stuck him with a hat pin. He was insisting he'd take care of me on the way to Minneapolis. I had to convince him I could take care of myself."

Martha chuckled. "A hat pin is a convincing weapon in the hands of a woman. Now let's finish our packing."

In her room behind the living room, Valina waited until Martha had gone to bed. If she was going to see Dain, it had to be now.

Slipping quietly past Martha's room and out the front door, she headed up the street where she knew a guard would be. She was thankful it was Ron Fulton.

"Where is Dain stationed?" she asked.

"His post is on the west side of town," Ron said. He grinned. "Just don't take his attention entirely off his job."

"I just want to talk to him a minute."

She turned toward the spot where Dain would be standing guard. She didn't mind Ron's teasing but she didn't want him to see that.

She had Havana at her heels. He had been just outside the door when she came out and he followed her. She liked dogs and long ago had forgiven Havana for spooking her horse. Havana stayed as close to her now as he had stayed to Dain. She didn't understand why. It was as if he understood Dain when he said Havana would help protect her.

Valina got to the west side of town but she didn't find Dain. She wandered to the north and south until she could see the guards there but she saw no sign of Dain. Each time she passed the spot where she thought Dain ought to be, Havana sniffed the ground and whined. Once he trotted off to the west a few feet then came back. Valina wondered if Havana was trying to tell her Dain had gone off in that direction. If so, he'd soon be back.

While she waited, she thought that she hadn't told Dain about her own background. That seemed important now. She had been orphaned several years ago and had gone to live with her Aunt Martha and Uncle Jeremiah. When her uncle died a few months ago, Martha decided the best thing for her to do was get completely away from old surroundings and make a new start. Valina had come along.

She wasn't sure why Martha picked Alpha. It was a small frontier town, which Martha liked. Valina was rapidly learning the hat-making trade and she liked it. She enjoyed life here in Alpha more since she had met Dain.

Now she wished she could see Dain again. She went back to the end of the main street where Ron Fulton was standing guard. Havana was still right at her heels.

"He's not there," she told Ron.

"He wouldn't desert his post," Ron said, worry fringing his words. "Let's go look. I'll get Bruce to take my place here."

Valina waited for him to get a man to watch his post, then together they went to the west side of town. The area was still without a guard.

Ron walked over the beat that Dain would have covered. Havana was close behind him, and again he sniffed the ground. Ron concluded that Dain had been at that spot and Havana got his scent there.

"Let's check the next guard," Ron suggested.

"I noticed he was gone a while ago," the guard said. "I have no idea where he went but Scurry said that Dain told somebody he was going after his family. Maybe he left before his guard duty was up and headed out where he could pick up the Indians' trail as soon as it's light."

"Could be," Ron said slowly. "But I don't think he'd leave his post. Who told Scurry that?"

"I don't know," the man said.

"Let's find Scurry and ask him," Ron said to Valina.

Valina agreed, worry pressing down hard on her. Something terrible had happened to Dain, she was sure. Maybe an Indian had crept up and killed him or dragged him off. It would leave an opening in the circle of guards for the warriors to get into town unnoticed.

They stopped at the store but the door was locked. They didn't find Scurry at his house. They made the rounds of the guards. He wasn't there. Valina was sure he wouldn't be on guard duty. He'd been at the millinery shop after the guards had been posted.

"He's probably hiding out somewhere," Ron guessed, "so he won't have to take a turn at guard."

"I'm worried about Dain," Valina said.

"Two of us," Ron said. "You go on to bed. I'll watch for him. He may have been called away from his post for a while. He'll be back soon."

Valina went home but she knew that Ron didn't believe what he'd said about Dain showing up soon. Maybe he really had gone. He was very worried about his sister and Hiram. Every minute he'd been forced to wait to start searching for them had been torture. Still Valina couldn't believe he'd have taken a post on the guard line if he hadn't intended to stay for his four hours.

There was nothing more she could do about it tonight. She went to bed but with every passing hour, her worry increased. And slowly she became aware that Dain meant much more to her than she had cared to admit. If anything had happened to him, her life would never be the same again.

She was up before dawn. She couldn't remember that she had slept a wink. She didn't stop for breakfast but searched out Ron Fulton. She found him as worried about Dain as she was.

"I just thought of something," he said. "Dain rode his horse into town. If he left, he'd have taken the horse. We'll check on that."

Eagerly, Valina went with Ron to the livery barn. It was still dark inside and Ron had to light the lantern to be able to see the horses. He walked down the line of stalls where horses were standing. One stall was empty.

Ron pointed. "That's where Dain's horse was. He's gone now."

"Maybe he did go after his sister," Valina said hopefully. Clinging to that possibility was better than thinking of all the other things that might have happened to him.

"Let's hope so," Ron said, but Valina read the worry still in his voice.

Reluctantly, Valina joined the trek to Minneapolis. If she hoped to find out what had happened to Dain, it would surely have to be here at Alpha. She felt she was losing her last chance to find him. Not finding him was a torture she wasn't sure she could endure.

The wagon that had brought Martha and Valina to Alpha was now taking them back east to Minneapolis. They fell in behind Ron and Eve Fulton. Addison Scurry was coming, too, and he stayed close to their wagon though he didn't press his luck. Valina was sure he remembered the hat pin.

Valina was deep in thought when Martha reached over and patted her hand. "Don't worry, honey," she said. "Dain is a tough man. You'll see him again." She clucked to the team and slapped the reins to keep up with the other wagons.

"I should have stayed and looked for him in daylight," Valina said.

"You couldn't stay alone," Martha said. "If you go back, you'll have to have someone to go with you."

Valina knew she was right. She felt so helpless. If Dain was somewhere hurt, he might die before she could find him.

The caravan of wagons, buggies and riders got to Minneapolis just before noon. They found so many people there that they had to set up camp just outside town, where they'd stay until the crisis was over. It seemed that every surrounding settlement had picked Minneapolis as their refuge.

Valina helped Martha set up their little part of the camp. But her mind was on Dain. She'd go back to Alpha and look for him once more. She had her cream-colored saddle horse. She could get there before dark if she went right away. But she'd be caught at Alpha for the night.

She'd have to have help. She thought of Ron Fulton. He had helped her last night. But she couldn't ask him to leave his wife to go on what certainly appeared to be a hopeless search. What could she do?

Seven

DAIN CAME TO, shivering as if he were sitting on a frozen pond in January. A fog clouded his thinking. It was the chill of the cold water that finally cut through the haze in his brain.

He was sitting in cold water up to his chest, his back against a hard board. When he moved his head, pain shot through him. He must have banged his head against the board when he fell. Then he remembered his fall. Somebody had dropped him into a well.

Feeling down his body, he hit the mud at the bottom of the well. His legs were stretched out in the mud. Slowly he moved one then the other. There were no broken bones. His thinking was gradually clearing. He only vaguely remembered his fall. Likely his unconscious state had prevented any broken bones. If he'd been fully conscious, he'd have stiffened himself and likely broken his legs.

It took an effort to pull his feet free of the mud. He wondered what time it was. He knew it was night. Against the star-studded sky far above, he could make out the top of the well. It looked a long way above him but it couldn't be too far or his fall would have killed him.

He managed to stand up, letting the water run and drip off his clothes. The water came up past his knees. If it had been a foot deeper, he'd have drowned. He guessed that he had hit the bottom of the well about where his feet had been stuck in the mud and then he had fallen backward against the board casing. The lump on the back of his head might have come from that crash into the casing. But it had kept his head above water.

The top of his head was sore, too. He was remembering now. He'd been standing guard at the town when somebody had given him a hard lick on the head. That must have been the same man who had dropped him in the well. In Dain's rapidly clearing thoughts, only one man met those qualifications—Addison Scurry.

Scurry hated Dain, no doubt about that. Maybe it was jealousy, because he knew that Dain had eyes for Valina. Maybe it was fear that Dain would tell what he knew about Wolfcry and turn the town against him. Scurry had no tolerance for anyone who opposed him. That fact alone would have made Dain Scurry's enemy.

He tried to decide just where this well was. It was not as deep as most homesteaders' wells. Some homesteaders didn't even have a well. They just carried water from the creek. He surely hadn't been dragged far from town. The only well outside town that was reasonably close was on Tom Willis's place. It was near the creek so the well didn't have to be so deep to get water.

If Dain could rouse Willis, he'd be out of this well in a short time. Then he remembered that everyone from the surrounding area was in Alpha getting ready to move to Minneapolis at dawn. There would be nobody home at Willis's place.

The water was cold. It was hard to believe it was August. It certainly didn't feel like August down here. Against the night sky, he could see the outline of the windlass over the well but the bucket evidently was sitting on the well curb. If it had been hanging in the well, he might have been able to climb the rope. He had to find another way to get out of here.

As he stared at the top of the well, trying to think of a way to get up there, his hand came in contact with the knife he had taken from Jed Wolfcry. It was still in the sheath he wore at his waist. Immediately he had an idea.

Taking the knife, he began whittling out finger and toe holds in the wooden casing. It was slow work, but before long he had enough dug out that he could climb up out of the water. However, he couldn't hang like a lizard on the side of the well very long.

The well casing was square, meant to keep the dirt from caving in and filling the well. Reaching up to eye level, he cut two deep notches in two sides of the casing, then, reaching across the well, he tore off a piece of casing and fit it into the notches. This made a seat for him across one corner of the well. Lifting himself up to the board, he seated himself where he could drip partially dry.

He sat there until the light coming into the well told him that dawn had arrived up on the prairie. Now he began the task of cutting notches all the way to the top of the casing so he could climb out.

It was a monumental assignment, clinging to the wall with toe holds and one hand hold while he whittled out more notches with his knife. His fingers and toes ached until he thought he couldn't stand it another minute. But to let go would drop him to the bottom of the well again.

Finally he got high enough to grip the top of the casing. He was glad the wood in the casing was fairly new. If it had been rotten, he'd have never made it.

With all his remaining strength, he heaved himself up onto the curbing of the well. The sun was hot but it was the grandest feeling in the world to him. Glancing at the sun, he saw that it was near noon. It didn't really matter to him now. He was alive and, with the exception of a bad headache, was in fine shape.

He'd go into Alpha as soon as he had strength enough to walk, and see if Scurry was there. He doubted if Scurry would go to Minneapolis with the others. He was so possessive of everything he owned that he'd probably stay to protect his store.

While waiting for the strength to return to his legs, he heard a horse snort down at the barn. He hadn't expected to find a horse here—the settlers were taking very good care of the horses the Indians hadn't stolen.

Dain got to his feet with an effort. The strain of hanging on that well casing in those toe holds had drained most of the strength from his legs. He wobbled toward the barn, gaining equilibrium with every step.

At the barn, he pulled open the door. A horse was there, already saddled and bridled as if his master had just left him there for a minute. Was somebody around here?

Then he looked closer. That was his horse. He had left it in the livery stable in town. How had it gotten out here? He knew he hadn't ridden it out from town. Then the solution came to him. Scurry had brought his horse out here, all saddled and bridled, and left it. When people found Dain dead in the well, they would assume that he had ridden his horse out here and had accidentally fallen into the well. Scurry had covered his tracks.

Getting on the trail of the Indians who had kidnapped his family was still a priority with Dain but if he got a chance to settle with Scurry, he'd take it.

Leading his horse out of the barn, he took him down to the river and let him drink, then he swung into the saddle and headed for Alpha. He'd see if anybody was still there.

It was only a short distance to town from Willis's homestead. The horse, restless after standing so long shut in the barn, was eager to go and Dain let him have free rein.

As he expected, the town appeared totally deserted. It would be easy picking for the Indians to loot and burn if they came back this way. Riding past Scurry's store and his house, Dain made sure that the storekeeper wasn't still in town.

Dain thought of heading out to the spot where they had lost the Indians' trail yesterday but he knew that the job of rescuing Susan and any other women the Indians had kidnapped was more than one man could do. He had to have help. That meant he'd have to go to Minneapolis to get it. There was no possible help to the west short of Fort Harker and that was quite a distance to the southwest. That wasn't the way the Indians had gone.

Also, if he went to Minneapolis, he would probably find Scurry with the other residents of Alpha. If he found Scurry, he'd let the storekeeper pick the weapons—fists, guns or knives. Dain had every intention of winning that fight.

The afternoon was nearly half over when Dain saw two riders coming toward him. A moment of watching told him they were not Indians. Somebody must be coming back from Minneapolis for something he had forgotten.

Then, before he could recognize either rider, a dog came charging toward him. It was Havana. After calling to the dog, he urged his horse to a faster pace. Valina was supposed to have the dog so maybe she was one of the riders.

Soon he recognized Valina and Ron Fulton. He couldn't have asked for a better reception party. He wasn't so surprised that Ron had come looking for him but he hadn't expected Valina.

"Where have you been?" Ron called before they got together. "You look like you've been pulled through a knothole backwards."

"Are you all right?" Valina added quickly.

Dain detected the concern and relief in both voices and his surprise grew as he realized that Valina had risked leaving the safety of Minneapolis just to search for him.

They dismounted and let their horses rest while they exchanged stories about what had happened.

"You think it was Scurry who did it?" Ron asked.

"Positive," Dain said. "Nobody else hates me like he does."

"Did you say or do something to Scurry to make him try to kill you?" Ron asked.

"I threatened to tell people that he knows Jed Wolfcry showed the Indians where Susan was hiding," Dain said. "That seemed to rattle his hocks."

"He admitted that?"

"Practically. He left no doubt that he knew that Wolfcry was with the Indians."

Valina moved over to examine Dain's head. "When we get back to town, I'll doctor that," she said.

Dain nodded. He liked the soft touch of her hand. But he spoke to Ron. "If Scurry is in town, I want to find him."

Ron shook his head. "You need to be at your best when you tangle with him."

"I can't let him get away with what he's done," Dain said.

"You can't risk getting killed, either. You just escaped one of Scurry's attempts to kill you."

Dain would have ignored that advice if it had come from anybody but Ron. He trusted Ron.

Looking at Valina, he realized that he trusted her, too. But he was feeling more than trust. He had never met anyone like her.

They mounted their horses again and turned back toward Minneapolis. Tomorrow, Dain promised himself, he'd get help and get on the trail of the Indians.

At the wagon camp just outside Minneapolis, Valina led Dain to the wagon she and Martha had driven over from Alpha. She found some medicine there for the cut on Dain's head. The medicine burned like fire but he didn't complain.

"You'd better be more careful where you put your head," Martha said as she helped Valina with the medicine.

"It's my head," Dain snapped. "I can be careless with it if I want to."

"You've got no right to worry Valina that way," Martha shot back.

Dain stole a glance at Valina and saw the flush rise in her face. He saw Martha's point. She was letting him know just how concerned Valina was over his well-being.

With his head feeling some better, Dain wandered around the

camp but Scurry was nowhere in sight. No one had seen him since midafternoon. Dain even went into town but there were a thousand places where Scurry could hide so he gave up and went back to camp to rest his aching head.

Just before Dain was ready to roll into a blanket under Ron Fulton's wagon for the night, a rider came charging in from the southwest. He reined up and made his announcement loud enough for all to hear.

"Colonel George Forsyth is raising a company of scouts to go after the Indians who have been raiding over this country recently. The army can't spare regular soldiers for a campaign."

Dain's interest exploded. "Where do we sign on?" he shouted. "When do we leave?"

"Report to Fort Harker as soon as possible. Forsyth has authority to sign only fifty men. He will leave immediately."

Dain didn't need to hear more. Forsyth was after the Indians who had kidnapped Susan and Hiram. Dain could never get more help than this. It was his best chance. Jed Wolfcry was surely with these Indians, too. It might be his only chance to get to Wolfcry.

"Count me in!" Dain shouted to the messenger. "I'll leave for Fort Harker in the morning."

Eight

IN SPITE of a dull headache, Dain felt better than he had since Susan was kidnapped. At last, he was going to do something to try to rescue Susan. He really hadn't expected to get enough help from his neighbors. The only one he could fully depend on was Ron Fulton. He didn't totally trust anyone else and he doubted if they trusted him.

Ron had moved up to hear what the messenger had to say and he was standing just behind Dain now. "I'm going, too," he said.

His wife, Eve, usually quiet, suddenly erupted in protest. "No, Ron! That's too dangerous."

"It could be more dangerous for you and everybody else if we don't go," he said. "Those Indians will make more and bigger raids if they're not stopped."

Eve said no more but the worry didn't leave her face. Dain doubted if it would leave until they got back from their mission. Dain's only worry was that they wouldn't find the Indians who had kidnapped Susan or that he wouldn't be able to rescue her or find Jed Wolfcry.

"You'd better go tell Valina," Ron said softly to Dain. "I'm not the only one with a woman who will worry about him."

Dain started to object, then stopped. He'd never had anyone who worried about him other than his mother and sister. But today had proved to him that he did now.

He looked over the crowd that had gathered around the messenger but he didn't see either Valina or Martha. Their wagon was on the far side of the camp. Dain started across the camp. He saw a lantern sitting near the wagon, so they hadn't gone to bed yet.

As he approached the wagon cautiously, for fear of interrupting their preparations for bed, Valina came around the wagon. She saw Dain and waited for him.

"What's going on?" she asked.

"Fellow rode in from Fort Harker. A colonel is recruiting fifty men to go after the Indians." He watched the rider leave the circle and head into town. "Looks like he's going to pass the word to everybody."

"That's wonderful news," Valina said. "But why did he make that long ride just to tell us that?"

"Colonel Forsyth isn't taking regular soldiers. He's asking for volunteers."

Valina's eyes widened. "You're going, aren't you?"

Dain could hear the fear in her words. "It's the best and maybe the only chance I'll have to rescue my family. And I want to get my hands on Jed Wolfcry. He's the one responsible."

"But it will be dangerous," Valina objected. "You don't know how many Indians there are."

"Doesn't make any difference," Dain said stubbornly. "I could never get fifty men to help me go after Susan. This is an ideal chance for me. I'm not going to miss it."

Valina drew a big breath. "Haven't you lost enough?" she said almost in a whisper. "Your brother-in-law and maybe your sister and nephew."

"It's because of them that I have to go." He paused. "And it's because of you, too," he added, his voice dropping. "If we don't stop them, they'll raid again."

Impulsively, she reached out and touched his arm. "I couldn't stand it if anything happened to you."

Dain's resolve to go was struck a hard blow. He hadn't expected anything like this from Valina. He wanted to reach out and pull her to him but he knew that he must not let anything, even Valina, keep him from going with Forsyth after those Indians. He knew he stood a good chance of getting killed. But that didn't lessen his determination to go.

"I have to go, Valina," he said, his voice husky. "You know that."

"You will be careful?" she pleaded.

His resolve to curb his emotions crumbled. He held an arm out and she came to him like a magnet. He had only dreamed of holding

Valina like this and it was much nicer even than he had dreamed. His natural restraint fought against the thrill of the moment.

Dain knew he had to get away. These emotions were new to him and he couldn't handle them. His dog, Havana, was at his heels. "Take care of Havana," he said. He backed away to pet the dog and push him toward Valina.

"I'll keep him," Valina promised. "He'll be company for me till you get back. Please be very careful."

Dain felt the urge to take her in his arms but he fought it. "I will," he said and turned abruptly toward the far side of the camp.

Before daylight the next morning, Dain and Ron left the camp. Dain would carry the memory of that moment with Valina all the way on this expedition but he couldn't afford to let his emotions get in the way of clear thinking.

"I didn't wake Eve," Ron said. "It was hard enough to get her to accept the fact that I am going. I feel I have to go. She understands but that doesn't mean she approves. It's better for both of us to leave without any more good-byes."

Dain nodded, understanding what he wouldn't have understood yesterday. "We'll be going close to Alpha," he said. "Let's ride in and see if everything is all right."

Ron agreed and they touched their horses into a ground-eating trot. At the end of the street in Alpha, they reined up. A team and wagon was sitting in front of one of the houses along the street. The wagon was almost full of furniture and sacks stuffed full of small items.

Just then, Addison Scurry came out of the house with a gunnysack slung over his shoulder. It was full and, from the way he walked, it was heavy.

"He's stealing everything in town," Dain exclaimed.

"We'll put a stop to that," Ron said, touching his heels to his horse.

Dain kept pace and he pulled the revolver out of his waistband.

They were halfway to the wagon when Scurry noticed them. Dropping the sack like it was full of hot coals, he dashed for the wagon. Dain guessed he had a rifle leaning in the front of the wagonbox. Dain fired a shot at the wagon even though it was almost out of range of a revolver. It had the desired effect. Scurry skidded to a halt a few feet from the wagon.

"Don't move, Scurry!" Dain yelled. "The next one will be right at your head."

Scurry stood petrified, staring at the riders. Dain and Ron pulled the horses to a halt.

"Just what do you think you're doing?" Ron demanded.

"Looks pretty clear to me," Dain said. "He's stealing everything worth stealing in town." He turned on Scurry. "Were you going to burn the town, then try to make people think the Indians did it?"

"He wouldn't burn his own store," Ron said. "He might burn the rest of the town, though." He glared at Scurry. "Now let's see how long it will take you to put every item back in the house where you got it."

"I—I can't remember where all this came from," Scurry stammered.

Dain pulled the trigger again, the bullet hitting the dirt and spurting dust over Scurry's boots. "I'm just that close to killing you right now," Dain said. "You hit me on the head and dropped me in that well and now you're stealing everything in town. You deserve to die."

"No, no!" Scurry shouted. "I'll put everything back." He rushed to the wagon and grabbed a chair and ran back to the house with it.

"It will take an hour for him to return everything," Dain said to Ron, "but it will be worth it. Then we'll kill him."

Ron lifted a hand. "Easy. He may deserve killing but who wants to commit murder?"

They followed Scurry around as he returned things to the houses. He was either getting tired or more worried about what would happen to him next because he was beginning to shake before the job was done.

"Where were you going to take this stuff?" Dain demanded.

"Salina," Scurry said. "I could sell it there." He looked at Dain. "I—I didn't drop you in the well."

"Poor liar, too," Dain said.

It was plain in Scurry's face that he was lying. His long greasy hair was falling over his face. His arrogance was completely gone.

Suddenly an idea hit Dain. "Did you put that leather bracelet in my wagon when I was going to Minneapolis that day?" he asked.

Scurry nodded reluctantly. "Jed laid it down and I got it."

"Then you told him I stole it, didn't you?"

Again Scurry nodded. "I knew he'd try to kill anybody who stole his good luck bracelet."

"Then it was Jed who came and got it out of my wagon. Did he write that note or did you?" Dain pointed the gun closer to Scurry.

Scurry swallowed hard. "I put it in when you were on your way home. I thought that you would question Jed and he'd kill you then."

"Do you think you have any right to live?" Dain asked.

Ron intervened quickly. "If there is anything missing from these houses when the folks come back, we'll hold you responsible."

"It will all be back," Scurry said eagerly, turning to Ron and away from Dain. "I promise."

Dain felt no sympathy for him. He deserved the worst punishment available but Dain knew Ron was right. To kill Scurry now would be murder. There was no fight left in the storekeeper.

"Unhitch your horses," Dain ordered. "Unharness them and turn them into a pasture."

Scurry swiped a hand over his face, brushing the long hair out of his eyes. "What are you going to do to me?"

"Put you in the same place you put me," Dain said.

Scurry's eyes widened in fear. "No, no!" he whimpered.

"If it was good enough for me, it's good enough for you," Dain said, remembering how he had felt when he came to in the well. The memory left no room for compassion.

Ron nodded approval. Scurry fumbled through the chore of unhitching and unharnessing the horses. Dain helped him turn them into a pasture where there was good grass and plenty of water. They would do well until Scurry got out of the well or somebody returned from Minneapolis.

Dain thought he had been dropped from a height above the well but he and Ron each took an arm and lowered Scurry as far as they could before they dropped him. Scurry was screaming and cursing every second but they ignored his pleas. His drop would be much shorter than Dain's had been. Dain didn't want Scurry to break a leg in the fall.

"How will I get out?" Scurry screamed from the bottom of the well after he fell. Dain knew then that he hadn't been injured in the fall.

"Same way I did," he shouted back. He'd let Scurry find that way. Dain had already cut the finger and toe holds.

Before Dain had gone a mile farther toward Fort Harker, he regretted leaving Scurry alive. He'd be a menace to every decent person in Alpha. He'd been stealing everything they had when Ron and Dain had caught him. That dip in the well wasn't likely to improve his morals.

They had lost so much time with Scurry that darkness fell before they got to Fort Harker. They made camp on the prairie and were up at dawn, moving on to the fort. They arrived fairly early.

There were soldiers drilling on foot and others at the stables grooming and saddling horses. Dain was interested only in finding Colonel Forsyth. He hoped he and Ron were not too late to join his company of scouts.

A question to a passing corporal brought the answer Dain sought. "Major Forsyth is in that tent at the far end of the parade ground," the corporal said. "He's a brevet colonel, raised to that rank for this campaign. This is his last day for taking recruits here. He'll finish his allotment at Fort Hays."

Dain detected a touch of disapproval in the corporal's voice. The corporal apparently thought little of the campaign.

Dain and Ron lost no time. A man sitting at a small table in front of the tent watched them approach. He looked quite young to be a colonel, even a brevet colonel. But Dain knew that the recent war had promoted many young men to ranks well above their age. Colonel Forsyth was an average-sized man with black hair, parted slightly to the left of center. His heavy moustache matched his hair. His dark eyes sized up the two men approaching the table.

A younger man, slim and muscular, wearing a lieutenant's bar on his shoulder, stood beside Forsyth. He wore a neatly trimmed beard with the cheeks and lower lip shaved but leaving a complete circle of dark whiskers around his mouth and chin. Forsyth introduced him as Lieutenant Fred Beecher, second in command on this campaign.

The colonel asked Dain and Ron a few questions and was delighted that they had both been in the army in the recent war. He handed them papers to sign.

"The enlistment is for the duration of this expedition but no longer than ninety days," the colonel said. "The pay is a dollar a day and thirty-five cents a day for your horse if you can furnish your own mount."

Dain nodded. "I can. When do we start?"

"The lieutenant will see that you are properly equipped for the campaign," the colonel said. "We leave for Fort Hays tomorrow. We will complete our roster there."

Dain and Ron followed Lieutenant Beecher to a building where they were asked to leave their rifles and revolvers. The lieutenant handed each a seven-shot Spencer repeating rifle and a Colt revolver. Each one received one hundred and forty rounds of ammunition for the rifle and thirty rounds for the Colt revolver. Dain noticed some men, apparently recruited for Forsyth's scouts, who had Springfield breech-loading rifles. Evidently they preferred them to the new Spencer repeating rifles.

Since Ron was mounted on a horse borrowed from a neighbor, he decided to leave his horse at the fort and take an army issue. Ron took everything the lieutenant offered while Dain took a blanket, lariat, picket pin, canteen, haversack, butcher knife, tin plate and tin cup.

They spent part of the day arranging everything into as small a pack as possible, one that tied neatly behind the saddle. Dain filled his cartridge belt with ammunition for his rifle. From the amount of ammunition issued, they obviously expected them to use the rifles much more than the revolvers.

Each man would carry a seven-day supply of cooked food in his haversack. That wouldn't be loaded until morning when they moved out. Dain helped load some packs that would go on the four pack mules the expedition would take. There were big camp kettles, picks and shovels in case they made a dry camp and had to dig for water, four thousand rounds of ammunition, medical supplies and extra salt and coffee. Dain decided that Colonel Forsyth meant business.

Dain mingled with some of the expedition's recruits. They were all ages from eighteen to over fifty. The fuzzy-cheeked youngster of the bunch was Jack Stillwell, but somebody told Dain that he was more trail-wise and Indian-wise than most men twice his age.

One man who caught Dain's attention scouted regularly for the army—Sharp Grover. He was an average-sized man with sharp, piercing black eyes. Dain was told that he had just recovered from a serious wound inflicted by Indians at Turkey Leg's camp. William Comstock, another scout, had been killed in that skirmish. In talking to Dain, Grover made no bones about the danger of the mission ahead.

Nine

DAIN FOUND HIMSELF very interested in Sharp Grover. He obviously knew how Indians thought and acted. He should know what chance Dain had of finding and rescuing his sister.

As the afternoon wore away, Dain found a chance to talk to the scout. He told him that his brother-in-law had been killed and his sister and infant nephew kidnapped in the raid along the Saline. "I intend to find and rescue them, if possible. What chance do you think I have?"

Grover scratched his nose thoughtfully. "I wouldn't bet the ranch on that," he said finally.

"Aren't these raiders the ones we're after?" Dain demanded.

"Hopefully, those are the ones we'll find," Grover said. "But there's no way of telling what band of Indians kidnapped your sister. And there's no guarantee that they haven't traded her and the infant to some other band by now—if they are still alive."

Dain frowned. "What are we going out for if it isn't to punish the Indians who made those raids?" he asked angrily.

"We're going out to kill some Indians," Grover said. "If we get lucky and hit the ones who made those raids, fine. If we don't find them but do locate some others, that will be fine, too. If we kill some warriors, the others will get the message. One Indian looks just like another. And who can say what band made those raids?"

Dain wasn't satisfied with that answer. He wanted to find the band that was holding Susan captive.

"Are you telling me I don't have a chance of rescuing Susan?"

"I didn't say that at all," Grover said hastily. "I just don't want you to get your hopes up. If you want to find your sister, this is the best chance you'll have. We're going after Indians wherever we can find them. If we find the right band, we'll have an outside chance of rescuing any captives they have. But remember, our mission is to kill Indians, not find any particular band."

That attitude was at cross-purposes with Dain's mission but he supposed that was to be expected of a scout who had been on several campaigns against warring tribes. One atrocity more or less meant little to him.

From other men who had been waiting here a couple of days, he learned that there would be only three army officers on the campaign. Besides Colonel Forsyth and Lieutenant Beecher, Acting Assistant Surgeon J. H. Mooers would go along to tend to medical problems. That was some consolation to Dain.

Well over half the men already recruited were veterans of the recent war. None were in the army now. Here they were called civilian scouts. The army had no men to spare so Forsyth had been given authority to hire any men he could find. One man, William McCall, had been a general of a Pennsylvania regiment in the war. Forsyth talked to him twice that afternoon. Dain guessed they talked military strategy even if McCall was a civilian now.

Many men had personal reasons for signing up. They had come from Lincoln and Ottawa counties, where the Indians had struck hardest in their last raids. Dain was sure they hoped to find the raiders who had hit their homes.

Forsyth led his recruits, about thirty men, outside the fort to camp that night. They picketed their horses where they could get good grass.

Supper was barely over when Dain's horse began fighting with the horse next to him. Dain rushed out and found that another man had picketed his horse too close and the two had gotten into a kicking match.

Dain had barely gotten the horses separated when a huge man came lumbering out from camp to claim the other horse. Dain hadn't noticed him before.

"What's the idea?" he roared. "You staked your horse too close to mine."

"There wasn't any other horse here when I picketed mine," Dain shot back. "You staked your horse too close to mine."

Dain pulled his picket pin and moved his horse to an area where no other animal was near. The big man shuffled after Dain.

"Don't try to blame me for your mistake," he bellowed.

Dain turned to look squarely at the man. He was a huge, broad-shouldered man, at least two inches over six feet tall and well over two hundred pounds. He had a full beard that was as black as his hair and eyes. His bushy hair made him look even taller and bigger than he really was.

Dain considered himself a fairly big man, but his six feet and a hundred and seventy-five pounds seemed small compared to this big man. There was a little brown-haired, brown-eyed man with him. He would have been small in any crowd but standing beside the giant, he looked like a boy. Dain guessed him to be a foot shorter and close to a hundred pounds lighter than his companion. He could easily go unnoticed, even in a small crowd.

It was obvious that the big man was itching for a fight. Dain imagined he'd been in many fights. He would surely feel confident in any brawl.

But there would be no brawl tonight. Lieutenant Beecher came from the camp on the run. "Quiet down, Bystrom," he called. "This may not be regular army but it will go by army rules. One rule is no fighting among the men."

"He picketed his horse right next to mine so they'd get into a fight," Bystrom blustered.

"Come on, Gus," the little man said. "Let's get back and hit the sack."

The big man looked at his small companion then back at Dain, then turned and headed toward the camp. Dain wondered about that pair. They seemed to be good friends and the little man had some influence on his companion.

"Who is that, Lieutenant?" Dain asked, watching the two move away.

"The big fellow is Gus Bystrom. He seems to carry a chip on his shoulder, just hoping someone will knock it off. The little man is Bystrom's cousin, Ken Calhoun. They're always together."

"I suppose they had some relatives killed in the Indian raids."

Beecher shook his head. "Bystrom just loves to fight. Claims to be a great Indian fighter. We can use more men like that."

"He must have enjoyed the war," Dain said.

"To hear him tell it, he did," Beecher said. "Ken told me, however, that Bystrom was in charge of a prison holding captured Confederates."

Dain could imagine what it must have been like to be a prisoner in a camp run by a man like Bystrom. Likely Bystrom hadn't been in any battles himself.

"Got to watch that fellow," Ron warned after Beecher went back to camp. "I've seen him picking on some other men. He's a quarrelsome hothead."

Dain agreed but he forgot about Bystrom the next morning when Colonel Forsyth moved his scouts out at dawn on the way to Fort Hays.

In two days, they made the march along the Smoky Hill River, then up the tributary called Big Creek to the fort. There, in one day, Forsyth found twenty more men to add to his company. There were several volunteers who were turned away because Forsyth had authority to enlist only fifty men.

Dain's impatience to get on the trail of the Indians was finally dispelled by orders to move out. It was the twenty-ninth of August. The orders came just after noon and they headed north. Dain had heard that they were going to Fort Wallace but Wallace was west and a little south of Fort Hays.

Dain was glad to be heading north. He was certain that the Indians would be up there somewhere, maybe along the Republican River. The sooner they caught up with them, the quicker he'd have a chance to find the two captives. Each hour he thought of the torture Susan must be going through.

By sundown they were out of sight of any sign of civilization. It was an empty land in any direction he looked. Used to the rolling hills of Indiana, Dain found this land comparatively flat, cut only here and there by a small stream heading toward a confluence with a larger stream. It was an empty land except for Indians. He couldn't imagine it ever being settled by white people.

They came on a herd of buffalo and Bystrom swore when Forsyth wouldn't let them stop and kill some. They had a week's rations in their haversacks. They had neither the time nor the need to secure more meat. The buffalo were evidence that Indians were not likely to be in this area.

At camp, as Dain was making his way from the coffeepot to the spot where he was eating his supper, Bystrom reached out a foot and tripped him. The coffee spilled from Dain's cup and splashed on

Bystrom. The big man lunged to his feet, swinging a fist at Dain. Dain dodged and wheeled to meet Bystrom's challenge.

The fight was stopped by three men who grabbed Bystrom and pinned his arms to his side. Bystrom screamed that Dain had deliberately spilled coffee on him. One of the men holding Bystrom yelled that he saw Bystrom trip Dain.

Bystrom swore again and growled that Dain was clumsy but he turned back to his supper. Dain knew that sooner or later he was going to have to fight the big man. Bystrom had picked Dain for his target although Dain didn't know why; unless it was because he refused to back down meekly before his badgering.

"Better steer clear of him," Ron warned Dain. "He's mean."

"I won't take that kind of tormenting this whole trip," Dain said. "If he keeps it up, we'll settle it one way or another."

They reached the Saline River, far upstream from the spot where Dain and Ron had their homesteads. They paused here only long enough for their horses to drink and catch their breath, then Forsyth led them on, bearing more to the northwest now.

They came to another creek, which one of the men said was the south fork of the Solomon. It wasn't much of a creek, Dain thought. But there was a big area of grass on the south bank that was beaten down.

"Indian camp?" one man asked, turning to Sharp Grover.

Grover nodded. "Looks like they had quite a powwow here. Maybe a war dance before they hit the settlements."

"How long ago?" Dain asked.

"A month ago, maybe two," Grover said, examining the area. "This might have been where they decided to make those raids downstream on the Saline and Solomon."

"Can you tell what tribe?" Calhoun asked.

Grover shook his head. "Not unless you can find an arrow or something that will identify them. They all hold war dances. I'm guessing these Indians are the same ones that raided along the rivers."

"Think they camped here on their way back west?" one man asked.

Grover shook his head. "No sign that they did."

"Doesn't look like we're on their trail yet," Dain said to Ron, fighting his disappointment.

"If they came this way, they'll likely go back this way," Ron said. "Their families are almost sure to be where they left them."

Dain nodded. Ron was a clear thinker and what he said did make sense. He felt better as they moved on and camped a little farther up the creek. The creek was dry and they had to dig potholes in the creek bed to find water for their horses and for themselves. The stream bed of sand was wide, indicating the width of the stream during spring floods. But there was none of that water here now.

Dain found a place to eat some distance from Bystrom. He wouldn't invite trouble but he wouldn't dodge it, either. There were six cooking at the fire where Dain was sitting. Bystrom was cooking at another fire. Still, Dain was caught by surprise when his plate suddenly flew up in his face and the contents were dumped in his lap. He hadn't seen Bystrom make a wide detour to the closest fire for coffee and come back past Dain. He had kicked the bottom of his plate and upset it.

Dain came off the ground in one angry leap. But again men jumped up from their suppers to grab both men.

"He spilled his coffee on me," Bystrom roared. "I just got even."

A man named Farley was helping hold Bystrom. "You just made a jackass of yourself," he snapped.

The three officers were eating at the far side of the camp and they watched the uproar, but since there was no fight, they didn't come over.

"We'd better settle this," Dain said through clenched teeth. "I won't put up with any more."

Bystrom grinned. "Fine with me. Where and when?"

"Outside camp after dark," Dain said.

"I'll be there," Bystrom said. "You'd better be there, too."

Dain got more food and finished his supper but he wasn't really hungry any longer.

"You'd better stay away from Bystrom," Ron said softly as he finished his supper. "A brawler like that can hurt you. You didn't come out here to fight the likes of him. You came to fight Indians."

"I can't fight Indians while he's pestering me constantly," Dain said. "I've got to put him in his place."

"That would be six feet under the bottom of the creek," Ron muttered. "I'll stand by to help you if you need it."

"This isn't your fight," Dain said. "He hasn't been picking on you. I'll fight my own battles."

"Maybe the officers will stop it," Ron said.

"We'll watch until they turn in for the night," Dain said. "I've got to stop Bystrom myself."

As the campfires died down, Dain watched Forsyth, Beecher and the surgeon, Mooers. They stayed by themselves. They were the only regular army personnel in camp.

The camp quieted down and the officers rolled up in their blankets. Dain still sat on his blanket, waiting for everything to get quiet. He didn't see Bystrom and he guessed he had already slipped out of camp. He was obviously looking forward to this battle.

Dain wasn't, but he felt it was unavoidable. It was not in his makeup to back off from a challenge. Maybe that was because of his distrust of people. He had grown up with that distrust and he hadn't found many people who had proved themselves, in his eyes, to be worthy of his complete trust.

Darkness settled over the river bottom. It was time to go out and meet Gus Bystrom. He didn't look forward to it.

Ten

WHEN DAIN GOT UP to leave, Ron followed. "I have to do this alone," Dain said softly.

"I don't intend to interfere," Ron said. "But I do intend to see that it is a fair fight. I don't trust Bystrom."

Dain didn't trust him, either, and it was gratifying to know that Ron would be watching for any unfair tricks the big man might resort to.

They hadn't designated any specific place to meet but Dain was sure that Bystrom would find him wherever he was. The land sloped down from the campsite to the wide sandy bed of the creek. The grass was fairly tall near the creek bed but shorter up the slope. Most of the grass back from the stream was buffalo or grama grass. Neither got very tall. The grama grass had five-inch stems on it with the seed at the top that bent over, reminding Dain of a tiny flag. The grass itself was very short. The same was true of the buffalo grass. It had seed, too, but it was on a very short stem, not visible unless a man bent to examine it.

Dain didn't like the idea of fighting on the slope where he might fall or where the tall grass could wrap around his feet. The sandy creek bed was better. He moved upstream from the holes in the creek bed where the men had watered their horses and dipped water for themselves. Here the sand was level.

"This looks like a good place," Dain said.

He was surprised to see a couple of men come quietly down from camp. Others followed. Apparently news of the fight had spread and they had come to watch.

More arrived and several came by Dain to wish him luck. More than one man offered to help. Dain was surprised at the antagonism Bystrom had stirred up.

"I don't want anybody helping me," Dain said. "This is between me and Bystrom."

"He's tough," one man said. "You may need help. I don't know of anyone who likes the big blowhard."

"If you hadn't been so edgy," Ron said softly, "one of them might have challenged him. Now you're the one who's going to get pounded."

Gus Bystrom came through the grass then and stepped out on the sand. He was stripped to the waist, showing that all that bulk hadn't been just an oversized shirt.

"Looks as big as a skinned mule," Ron whispered.

Dain didn't say anything. He knew that if Bystrom had any skill at fighting, he'd be a match for almost anyone because of his size.

Dain peeled off his shirt to get ready. He realized with misgivings just how formidable an opponent Bystrom was going to be. He was at least two or three inches taller than Dain, which would give him an advantage in reach. And he must weigh forty or fifty pounds more than Dain.

There was excitement and anticipation in Bystrom's black eyes. He ran a beefy hand through his unruly hair.

Dain was still getting himself mentally prepared for the fight when Bystrom charged like an angry bull. Dain barely had time to jump out of his way. Bystrom's arm swept wide and hit Dain on the shoulder, knocking him sideways. Dain hit the sand but came to his feet like a coiled spring. It raced through his mind that he dare not let Bystrom get him down. He'd kill him before anybody could drag him off.

Bystrom skidded in the sand and turned around. Then he came back at Dain in another charge. Dain was prepared for it this time and agilely leaped aside, letting Bystrom expend his energy in getting his huge bulk stopped.

As he wheeled around, Dain struck a blow that Bystrom caught on his shoulder. Dain saw the one advantage he had. He was much faster than Bystrom. Bystrom was like a big Percheron horse. It took him twice as long to turn around as it did Dain. But all Bystrom needed was one mistake on Dain's part and Dain would be ground into the sand of the river bed like a burned-out cigar.

Bystrom bellowed like a frustrated bull. "Stand still and fight, you coward!" he screamed.

"Come on, big boy," Dain taunted. "You're the one who wanted this fight."

Howling in rage, Bystrom charged again. Dain dodged to one side but barely escaped those flaying arms. Bystrom was already getting tired from charging up and down in the loose sand of the creek bed.

Dain decided all he had to do was keep Bystrom running until he played out. But Bystrom saw that, too. When he came back toward Dain, he moved slowly. He looked awkward but he was conserving his energy. Apparently he had won his brawls by simply grabbing his opponent and mauling him into submission. So far, he hadn't been able to catch Dain.

Giving ground slowly in front of Bystrom's advance, Dain concentrated on keeping out of Bystrom's grasp. When Bystrom got close, Dain feinted to the right and got Bystrom to lunge at him. Ducking under his powerful swing, Dain got in two good licks at Bystrom's head. Neither seemed to bother the big man. He simply turned and began a slow march toward Dain again.

Dain heard the men cheering him on. He barely had time to glance their way. In that glance, he saw the three officers standing behind the men. If the fight was stopped, Bystrom would go on being just as aggravating as ever.

Nobody called for the fight to stop and Dain turned his full attention to Bystrom. Bystrom wanted a toe-to-toe slugging match. That would throw all the advantage his way.

Dain waited till Bystrom got close, then ducked low and drove two hard fists to Bystrom's stomach. The big man backed off with a curse. Dain had found a soft spot in Bystrom's armor. A blow to the head hadn't seemed to faze him but a blow to that soft belly was something he didn't relish.

As Bystrom came at Dain again, Dain watched for an opportunity and ducked low to land another hard blow to his stomach. Bystrom was expecting it this time and swung a huge fist at Dain, catching him on the shoulder.

Dain reeled backward in spite of his efforts to catch himself. He finally caught his balance but Bystrom was almost on him. Bystrom swung a big fist in a huge circle, aimed at Dain's head. Dain ducked and the fist went over his head but the effort cost Dain his balance again.

Staggering backward, he found the sand an enemy instead of an ally. His foot slipped in the sand. He felt himself falling and he flipped his eyes at Bystrom. The big man was staggering a bit himself as he tried to recover his balance from his mighty swing at Dain that hadn't connected.

Putting out a hand, Dain tried to catch himself and get back to his feet. But again the sand under his feet slid and he went down hard in the sand. Bystrom finally got his balance. Seeing Dain sprawled in the sand, he wheeled toward him. Before Dain could get control of himself, Bystrom charged and threw himself at Dain. With the force of his charge and his weight, he would crush the life out of Dain if he hit him.

Rolling frantically, Dain threw himself to one side. Bystrom saw that he was moving and tried to change the direction of his fall. Dain avoided most of Bystrom's weight as he crashed to the sand but an outstretched arm hit Dain like a club. Bystrom slammed into the sand with the force of a falling tree.

Dain crawled to his feet, almost numb from the blow of Bystrom's arm. Bystrom got up slowly, sand in his hair, gasping for breath. The crash onto the sand had apparently knocked most of the wind out of him.

Still, he gritted his teeth and made another charge at Dain. Dain saw the big man's wobbly legs. Drained as he was, Dain went forward to meet Bystrom, dodging his wild swing. He drove a fist with all his remaining strength into Bystrom's already bruised stomach.

Bystrom doubled over with an explosion of air from lungs not yet recovered from that jolt on the sandy creek bed. Bystrom's guard was down now. Dain stood his ground and smashed a fist into Bystrom's chin. His head snapped back but he didn't go down. Dain's strength was about gone but he smashed two more blows to Bystrom's chin. Bystrom's knees finally buckled and he went down.

"Had enough?" Dain whispered.

Bystrom was gasping for air. Dain would like to take credit for putting Bystrom down but he knew that crash on the sand had a lot to do with it.

Bystrom nodded. "Enough," he breathed.

Men swarmed out from the creek bank to surround the two fighters. All attention was focused on Dain. He had championed them all in stopping Bystrom.

"Everybody back to camp and hit the sack," Forsyth ordered.

The men scrambled out of the creek bed. Dain expected to get a private reprimand from the colonel. But Forsyth turned without another word and headed for the camp.

"I think he approved of what you did," Ron said quietly to Dain. "If we were in the regular army, he'd have plenty to say, but he could have said more than he did, anyway."

"I'd take that as approval," Dain said.

Dain picked up his shirt and put it on. He had several sore spots that would hurt for a day or two, he was sure. He looked at Bystrom slowly walking up out of the creek bed. He was the picture of dejection. Maybe he wouldn't forget what had happened to him tonight.

Forsyth looked over the men as they prepared to break camp the next morning. "I hope you'll save your fighting for the Indians from now on," he said and the matter was dropped.

They crossed the small divide to a stream that some called Beaver Creek, but Stillwell said it was Prairie Dog Creek. The Beaver was farther west. They followed this little creek bed to its beginning, then turned almost due south toward Fort Wallace.

The land was still as empty as a vacuum, and between the ravines leading into the little streams, virtually level. There weren't even any trees. A flat treeless plain was a land that Dain had never expected to see and there were miles of it here.

During the day they saw two herds of buffalo that barely lifted their heads as the men passed. There were antelope everywhere, it seemed, and virtually acres of prairie dog towns. The curious little creatures barked sharply at them as they passed, then dived down their burrows when the horses got too close. Ahead was a haze that Stillwell said marked the Smoky Hill Valley. There was a fascination about this empty land that gripped Dain.

Dain was disappointed that they hadn't gone on in the direction he thought the Indians had gone. There was no sign of Indians where they were now. No campsites, no trails, just open prairie.

They came from the north, down into the Smoky Hill Valley, to Fort Wallace. The fort was on the north slope of Pond Creek, a short stream that ran into the Smoky Hill River. Colonel Bankhead was the commanding officer.

"I thought we were chasing Indians," one man complained. "How long will we be here?"

"Until we get orders to move out," Lieutenant Beecher said. "That could be anytime."

The news didn't set well with most of the men but it was especially aggravating to Dain. He had joined the scouts in the hope of catching the Indians and finding Susan and Hiram. But here they were, awaiting orders to go after Indians. Dain thought they'd had those orders when they left Fort Harker.

During the next day, Dain wandered over the fort and got acquainted with a corporal who proudly led Dain over the grounds, describing the fort to him. Considering how isolated the fort was, he was surprised at its efficiency.

There were two barracks made of local stone that was soft enough to cut with a saw when first exposed to the air by peeling off the sod. That rock became as hard as concrete after a few days of exposure to the sun and wind. The walls of the barracks were two feet thick so they would give good protection from winter storms. Each barracks had forty double beds, giving shelter to eighty men. There were also some wooden barracks for temporary shelter until stone buildings could be constructed.

The kitchen and mess hall were also temporary wooden structures, partly roofed with tenting material. The mess hall had no floor. The parade ground ran north and south with the officers quarters at the north end and the guardhouse and magazine at the south end closest to the creek. The storehouses were to the southwest of the parade ground and they were built of stone, just a little larger than the stone barracks. The grain house, the corporal told Dain proudly, would hold fifteen thousand bushels.

The guardhouse and the hospital were both built of stone. The hospital was forty feet long with two wings, each forty-eight feet long. It looked as if they expected more business than most forts generated. There was a well at the foot of the slope but it was shallow and the water so brackish that most soldiers preferred to drink water from the creek. It wasn't far down the gentle slope from the barracks to the creek.

After two days of frustrating idleness at the fort, Gus Bystrom began to recover some of his old form. He didn't pester the other men any more but he began bragging about the Indian fights he had been in.

"To hear him spout off," Ron said, "you'd think he could go out alone and lick all the Indians on the plains."

While Dain found Bystrom's bragging irritating, he had no personal trouble with him so he ignored his boasting.

Then suddenly the order came to saddle up, check the provisions in their haversacks, ammunition and equipment. They were moving out in thirty minutes.

"Why the sudden rush?" Dain asked.

"Indians hit a freight train up at Sheridan," Stillwell called, running for his horse.

"Any fight?" Ron asked.

"At least two freighters were killed," Stillwell said. "The Indians may still be there. We're going to try to catch them."

That was the news Dain had been waiting for. He hoped this band of Indians was the one that had kidnapped Susan. With anticipation and excitement, Dain rushed to check his equipment. He wondered what lay ahead. The thrill of pending danger coursed through him. Would he find Susan before he returned to this fort? Or would he ever see this fort again?

Eleven

DAIN WAS AMONG THE FIRST ready to go. Gus Bystrom was the last. Lieutenant Beecher called the roll to see if all were there.

Two men were being left behind. One had been thrown from his horse the day before they arrived at the fort and had a fracture. Another was sick and they couldn't wait until he was ready to ride. So the company of scouts that had numbered fifty was now only forty-eight. Counting the three officers, the full strength of the company was fifty-one men.

"Be ready for a fight at any time," Forsyth ordered. "This raid on the freighters could be just a ploy to get soldiers to come from the fort. Forward by twos."

"Is that possible?" Ron asked Stillwell as the column moved out.

Jack Stillwell was riding just ahead of Dain and Ron. Pierre Trudeau, a real veteran in this group, was riding beside him.

"If there is a big batch of them, it could be," Stillwell said. "One of their tricks to get soldiers out of a fort is to taunt them with just a few warriors. The soldiers think they can whip those few and rush out of the fort. Then they run into an ambush. I reckon the colonel is wanting us to be ready in case of an ambush."

Dain looked around him at the empty prairie. He couldn't see where an ambush could be set. The prairie was comparatively level in all directions. They were riding northeast toward the end-of-track town of Sheridan. They were crossing the divide between the north and south forks of the Smoky Hill River so the land was fairly level. Unless the Indians could hide behind a blade of grass, there was no place for an ambush.

Off to the left was the beginning of a railroad grade. If they followed that grade they would come to Sheridan. But they were following the road cut by the freighters who loaded at Sheridan for destinations as far away as Santa Fe. The stagecoach also picked up its passengers at Sheridan instead of Atchison or Kansas City. The railroad would put the stage line and the freighters out of business if and when the line was completed to Denver. It had been a freight train bound for Santa Fe that had been attacked, apparently almost as soon as it had left the railroad.

"See that knob just ahead?" Stillwell said. "Sheridan is just on the other side of that."

"You been there?" Ron asked.

Stillwell nodded, a grin on his face. "It's a wild town. All the idle railroad workers are staying there, waiting for the line to get more money so they can go on building. Three out of every four businesses in town are saloons. And they are wild ones!"

"We should have stopped there instead of going to Fort Wallace," one man up ahead said.

"It's not army," Stillwell said, "although there is a small company of soldiers there to make sure that goods bound for Fort Wallace get sent there instead of somewhere else."

Dain marveled at how far away that hill Stillwell had pointed out proved to be. He guessed that hill could be seen for at least twenty miles.

There was a cut through the north side of the hill where the railroad grade would be. On the other side of the hill was the north fork of the Smoky Hill River, running to the southeast. Stillwell said that the town of Sheridan was spread out along the railroad tracks to the east of the river.

Dain was anticipating the town when Forsyth suddenly held up a hand for a halt. He looked past the riders ahead and saw a smashed wagon and three or four dead oxen. He knew they had arrived at the site of the freighters' fight with the Indians. From here they would likely take the trail of the raiders. At last, Dain would be on the trail of Indians and the possibility of finding his sister and nephew.

While the cut for the railroad track ran along the north side of the hill, the wagon road circled around the south side. It was much easier traveling for a wagon. Apparently the Indians had been waiting on the west side of that hill, out of sight of town, and had surprised the freighters.

Examination of the battle site was brief. Sharp Grover, the head scout, dismounted and walked quickly around the area. He examined one of the arrows he found sticking in a dead ox.

"Cheyenne," he said. "Same killers that raided along the Saline and Solomon. Not very many of them were here."

"How do you figure that?" Forsyth asked.

"Not enough tracks—and look at these wagons. They are wrecked but very little has been stolen from them. If there had been a big bunch of warriors, they would have taken everything they could carry and burned the rest. But a small bunch would have to hit and run before people from town came out and roasted them. This was a small raiding party."

"Where did they go?" Forsyth asked.

Grover made a quick round of the site. Then he pointed due north. "Unshod track going this way. Not more than ten or twelve. Looks like they took one wagon pulled by oxen."

"That means they can't go very fast," Forsyth said. "Let's go get them." He waved an arm to the north.

Excitement ran through the men. Dain felt it intensely.

Two riders came dashing around the hill. Apparently they had been afraid to come out until they saw the soldiers.

"How many killed?" Forsyth asked as the men reined up in front of him.

"Just two. The other whackers got back to town. It was a small train, only eight wagons."

"Did you see the Indians?"

The man nodded. "We saw them but we weren't in time to do much except protect the men who got away. I figure we were lucky they didn't hit the town."

"How many Indians were there?" Lieutenant Beecher asked.

"Looked like a lot to me," one man said.

Dain realized that these men were still scared. A frightened man would see dozens when there would really be only a few.

Forsyth motioned the column on and they rode to the north, leaving the men from Sheridan behind. They rode at a slow lope, a pace the horses could keep up for long distances. Dain felt the same urgency that apparently was driving Forsyth. They were close to the Indians. They might never have a better chance to bring them to bay.

Less than two miles from the battle site, they found the abandoned wagon with the eight oxen, all dead. One had been partially butchered and the best meat taken.

"Small bunch," Grover repeated. "They cut only enough meat for a dozen. A big bunch would have butchered all the oxen."

Forsyth pushed on, urging all the speed he dared from the horses without playing them out. But they didn't seem to be gaining on the Indians.

"Could have seen us," Stillwell said. "If they know we're following them, we won't catch them."

Dain didn't like to hear that. He instinctively trusted Stillwell's judgment. For a man of his age, Stillwell seemed to understand this frontier very well. But Dain wanted to catch the Indians, whip them and see if Susan and her son were there.

They were following a plain trail, one that Dain could have followed. But the sun was sinking fast. If they were going to catch the Indians before dark, it had to be soon.

Darkness, however, fell with no sighting of the Indians. Forsyth called a halt when Grover could no longer see the trail.

"Why don't we just keep on going?" Ron asked. "We might catch them in camp."

"And we likely wouldn't catch them at all," Stillwell said. "If they know we're following, they might turn off their course as soon as it is too dark for us to see their trail."

"Will they know we've stopped to camp?" Dain asked.

"Of course," Stillwell said. "They'll keep tabs on us. If we camp, they will likely camp somewhere up ahead. But they'll get an earlier start than we can. We have to wait until we can see the trail."

It was frustrating to Dain. He was so close to them yet they were as out of reach as if they'd been on the moon. He was as restless as a lion in a cage. After supper, he made his way around to the spot where Sharp Grover was relaxing.

"Do you think these are the same Indians that raided along the Saline?"

Grover nodded. "Very likely."

"If we catch them, will my family be with them?"

Grover hesitated. "I didn't mean these Indians were likely to be the same individuals who raided your place. But they are Cheyenne and it was Cheyennes who raided along the Saline and Solomon."

"You don't think I'll find them, do you?"

"Honestly, no," Grover said. "By now the raiders have probably turned their captives over to the women and children in the main camp."

"Where will that be?" Dain demanded.

"No telling," Grover said. "But these Indians are almost certainly heading that way. I'm guessing their raiding is over for a while. They'll take it easy, feast and have war dances. They'll do that where the whole tribe is together. That's where you'll find your family if you find them at all."

"Why wouldn't I find them?" Dain asked sharply.

Grover shrugged. "I hope you do. We're out to punish Indians and we'll rescue any captives we can. But the Indians don't like to give up captives."

"Do they kill them rather than give them up?" Dain asked, a cold chill running through him.

"They've been known to do that. But there is always the chance that we will find your sister and the baby alive and rescue them. We certainly will if we can."

As the camp settled down after supper, Dain heard Gus Bystrom reciting his stories about Indian fights. Not only was he bragging about how he had almost single-handedly whipped a party of warriors up in Nebraska but he was intimating that some of his companions on this expedition didn't have the nerve to fight real Indian warriors.

It irritated Dain but he ignored it. Let the rest of them put up with his stories.

After a hasty breakfast the next morning, they were in the saddle again as soon as they could see the trail. Sharp Grover was out ahead, leaning far over his horse's neck to read the sign.

The level prairie began to break up into gullies that deepened into canyons running north. Dain guessed there was a river up ahead.

"Beaver Creek coming up," Stillwell said. "The Republican is next."

"Think we'll find the Indians there?" Dain asked.

"Maybe," Stillwell said. "But I figure we'll find them only when they want us to find them."

Dain found little consolation in that, just as he'd found no comfort in what Grover had said about Indian customs concerning captives.

Less than an hour after sunrise, Forsyth called a halt in response to a signal from Grover out in front. Grover dismounted and examined the trail. Dain fretted at the delay. Every minute the Indians were getting farther away.

Grover came back to the column. "Trail's breaking up," he reported. "The Indians are scattering so we have a lot of trails."

"Which is the main one?" Forsyth asked.

"The one that will disappear entirely about a mile ahead," Grover said. "One or two break off the bunch every hundred yards or so. This bunch has scattered like thistle seed in a high wind. There's no way we can follow them all."

"Let's try to catch up with the main bunch before it breaks up," Forsyth said.

"We can try," Grover said. "But we won't make it. They're doing this just to throw us off and they've succeeded."

"What do we do then?"

"The Indians have surely agreed on a place to get together after they've lost us," Grover said. "I'll venture to say they'll meet somewhere on the Republican."

"Then we'll go to the Republican and see if we can find their trail there," Forsyth said.

Grover nodded. "Best thing to do now. We sure can't follow these trails they're leaving."

"What makes you so sure they'll meet at the river?" Beecher asked.

"It's obvious they started north without any thought of being followed so quickly," Grover said. "Taking the wagon and oxen were proof of that. Then when we got on their trail, they scattered but they'll get together again soon. They won't change their plans."

"We'll take care of them when we do catch them," Forsyth said.

Grover hedged. "Probably," he said. "But we're not going to catch them until they're ready to be caught. When they join up with the main war party, they might be willing to let us catch them."

"This isn't the main party?" one man asked.

"Only a splinter," Grover said. "They usually split up when they are raiding. That way they can hit a lot of places quickly and be gone before any organized force can be sent after them."

Dain didn't like what he was hearing. He wanted to catch the Indians as quickly as possible and rescue Susan and the boy before they were harmed. Grover was talking as if the Indians were in command of the situation. That didn't leave the scouts in a comfortable position. Dain, especially, felt totally frustrated.

Twelve

T HE SMALL BAND of Cheyenne warriors had left the scene of the short battle with the Mexican freighters as quickly as they could. They didn't expect any trouble from the people in Sheridan. Those people were not soldiers. The warriors had learned that it took people of a settlement a long time to get organized to make a serious assault against raiders.

They also knew that Fort Wallace was only a short ride southwest of Sheridan. There were soldiers there. The soldiers would come after them.

Black Sky hadn't killed either of the Mexicans who had died during the raid on the freight wagons. But he had counted second coup on one of them. The raid had been swift and deadly for the leading wagons. The rigs in the back of the caravan turned around quickly and headed back toward Sheridan while the warriors were taking possession of the first wagons.

Those escaping had only to go around the edge of the hill to be in sight of the town. If the Indians followed them, they would get in trouble. Those people who wouldn't organize themselves to follow the Indians would fight for their homes. Black Sky had learned that most of those white men were very accurate with their rifles. Only fools would follow those wagons into town. And there were no fools among the ten warriors who had conducted this raid.

Wild Fox tied his pony to the back of one wagon that was still intact and grabbed the whip to drive the oxen north. This was the last raid they would make before the tribes gathered to plan their big drive against the white settlers in Kansas and Nebraska.

The oxen moved so slow that the others grew impatient. Wild Fox could not get the lumbering beasts to move any faster. Black Sky was getting nervous. They should be putting distance between themselves and the site of that raid. The soldiers would come. They always did. Somehow through those magic wires they had, the soldiers would know what had happened. The soldiers would soon be on their way.

"Kill the white man's buffalo," Wild Fox shouted, stopping the wagon. "Too slow."

Black Sky agreed with Wild Fox. In a couple of minutes, the eight oxen were dead and Sparrow was peeling the hide off the fattest one and cutting huge slices off the hip. Black Sky joined the others in ripping through the load in the wagon. It was mostly cloth, something the squaws might like but not anything they could carry to them. They found a few small things in the front of the wagon. Black Sky got a watch. He had seen one once but didn't know how to use it. However, it was shiny and something he could wear to show what he had taken from the white men. The men they had killed had skin almost as dark as the Indians but they were working for the white men and that made them white men, too.

They didn't take time to burn the wagons. Not many white men could read sign as Indians could and often they went off in the wrong direction. A fire would point them in the right direction.

After they left the wagon and the dead animals that had pulled it, they made much better time. Black Sky no longer worried about the soldiers catching up with them. They could outride the pony soldiers anytime.

Black Sky and his nine companions were behind the rest of the warriors returning from the raids to the east. They had been told not to be late arriving at the gathering place where the water of the river began to flow. But the ten of them had yearned for one last raid and had moved down close to the iron trail where the iron horse ran. They knew they could find plenty of places to strike along that trail.

They had circled around the town beside the hill and waited for whatever came their way. It was the wagon train that had apparently gotten its loads from the big wagons that had come in on the iron trail. They had taken two scalps, counted some coups, and had collected some trinkets. Now they had to catch up with the rest of the camp and go to the big meeting with the other tribes.

Just before sundown, they stopped to rest the ponies and Wild Fox suggested that someone go back and see if the soldiers had found their trail. Black Sky volunteered. He turned his pony and rode back. He was surprised at how quickly he spotted the soldiers. He'd never known soldiers to come from a fort that fast.

Wheeling back, he soon caught up with his companions. He explained that the pony soldiers were not far behind.

"We will leave them no trail," he suggested and the others nodded.

They rode on and soon one man turned off to the west. A little farther another turned off to the northeast. Since their goal was to go to the river, the one the white men called the Republican, and turn west, they would leave their plainest trail in the other direction. Black Sky and his two good friends, Wild Fox and Sparrow, rode off together to the northeast, leaving the clearest trail the soldiers would see.

Well away from the route they had been traveling, they turned to the north and separated. At the Republican, Black Sky turned west and camped that night close to the river.

It was noon the next day when the ten warriors got together again on the Republican, confident they had left no trail for the soldiers to follow.

Black Sky was impatient now to get to their camp. That camp, led by their chief, Many Horses, should be up the river a ways. There were several Dog Soldiers in Many Horses' camp. Black Sky was a member of that society. The Dog Soldiers came from several camps and were considered the best fighters the Cheyennes had. There were several soldier societies among the Cheyennes but the Dog Soldiers was the biggest one. The next biggest soldier societies were the Kit Fox Society and the Crazy Dog Society. But both together would not number as many as the Dog Soldiers.

On a raid like the one they had just completed along the rivers to the east, the Dog Soldiers had split up according to their camps. Black Sky had gone with Many Horses. He was eager now to get back with the leader of the Dog Soldiers, Roman Nose. He was a great warrior and a special friend of Black Sky. But he belonged to a different group and Black Sky hadn't seen him since the raids began. He wasn't sure he had even been on the raids.

It was late afternoon when they spotted Many Horses' camp ahead. They gathered a short distance from the tepees. The two warriors who had taken the scalps of the Mexicans took the lead and they charged the camp like a raiding party. Many Horses' warriors leaped to their arms but then shouted a welcome as they recognized the newcomers. The charge told everyone that the men had been successful on their raid and the leaders, waving the scalps, brought proof of it.

Black Sky had been on several charges like that. Every successful battle was announced on their return by a charge on the camp by the triumphant warriors.

Many Horses was in the center of camp, waiting to welcome the warriors. "We have waited for you," he said. "But we must hurry. We are the last Cheyennes to go up the river to the big meeting. It is good that you got scalps and counted coups. But there are bigger battles ahead. The *Tsis tsis tas* will lead the battles against the white men."

Black Sky was sure that the *Tsis tsis tas*, the Cheyennes, would be in the forefront of every battle. There were more Cheyennes in this area and, in his opinion, they were the fiercest fighters.

Black Sky wondered how many of the *Suhtai* would be at the meeting. The two related Cheyenne tribes, the *Tsis tsis tas* and the *Suhtai*, didn't often fight together but Many Horses said they would this time.

Black Sky was eager to report the coups he had made but that would wait until they got to the main camp. That would be better. There would be many more people there to appreciate the coups that the warriors could report. Many Horses' camp was small.

Black Sky looked at the weapons around him. They were hardly what was needed to go against the soldiers following them. All the warriors had bows and arrows but only a few had rifles and most of those were old, not like the one he had. Roman Nose had managed to get many of the rifles that the Cheyennes and Sioux had captured when they enticed the arrogant army officer, Fetterman, into an ambush up on the Big Piney in the northern country. It was close to the fort that the white men called Phil Kearny.

Many of the eighty soldiers killed that day had seven-shot repeating Spencer rifles. Roman Nose got some and made sure all his men had one as far as they would go. Black Sky had gotten one of the first ones. With these, the Indians should be able to match the hated white soldiers. But he knew that the Indian riflemen were not as accurate with their weapons as the white soldiers were.

Many warriors refused to use a rifle. They were more effective with the bow and arrow. They would need both when they made their drive down the rivers to push the white man back. They had given the white men everything they had asked for. They had allowed them to make a trail through their country on their way to the big water where the sun set. They had signed treaties with the white men and the white men had broken them almost before the Indians had agreed to them.

Now they were settling on Indian hunting grounds, plowing up the grass and driving the buffalo farther and farther away. Lately they had begun to slaughter the buffalo. They didn't need the meat. They had plenty of winter supplies. They took the hide but they didn't use it for tents or warm clothing. They wasted everything. The Indians were going to starve and freeze if this kept up.

Black Sky had heard the chiefs talking about it. If the white men weren't driven back across the big river, the Indians would starve. Black Sky would never starve! He'd die fighting the white men before he'd let them kill off the buffalo.

Black Sky walked around camp as soon as he had cared for his pony. He was looking for Little Dove, Many Horses' daughter. He and Little Dove had made no agreement, but as far as Black Sky was concerned, it was settled. He knew that he had only to give Many Horses an acceptable gift and Little Dove would be his. But he didn't want Little Dove if she didn't want him.

Locating Many Horses' lodge, he found Little Dove in front. Instinctively, he knew she had been anticipating his visit. He motioned to her and she came eagerly. She was a small girl, a long black braid down her back, her smooth skin like the brown berries they found in the mountains when they went that far west. She was wearing the blue beaded moccasins that she wore only on special occasions. He couldn't miss the significance.

"I missed you, Little Dove," he said softly.

"I was afraid for you," she said. "There is always danger and you were following the iron trail. Many white men there."

"We took three wagons. I counted coup on a man Sparrow killed. White soldiers came after us but we gave them many trails to follow."

"Did they follow those trails?" she asked.

"I don't know. We haven't seen them. Would—would you like it if I gave Many Horses a gift for you?"

She smiled, then dropped her eyes, nodding her head.

"I'll find something," Black Sky said. "Maybe more horses?"

Again she nodded but said nothing. Black Sky had all the answer he wanted. Now he had to get some horses somewhere. He could give them to Many Horses and claim Little Dove as his wife.

Many Horses came from the lodge. "Black Sky," he said, "Wild Fox says that soldiers followed you from your last raid. He doesn't know if they are still following. Go back and see. We will leave here at light of day; you can catch up. If they are not coming, we will go slower. If they are following, we must hurry to keep ahead of them."

Black Sky nodded. "I will go. Where are the other Cheyenne camps?"

"Ahead near the start of the water. We are to meet them there. The *Suhtai* are to be there. There will be Sioux, Arapaho and Kiowa, too. We will be very strong when we go to war."

"Good," Black Sky exclaimed. "We can drive the white men back across the big river to the east. I will see if the soldiers are coming."

Black Sky ate his supper, then got a fresh horse and rode back down the river. If the soldiers were down there, they should be in camp now. Maybe he could run off some horses.

He rode nearly half the night. He was sure the soldiers wouldn't be too close even if they were still on the trail. Black Sky's group had hurried to catch up with Many Horses' camp. The soldiers would be trying to read trail so they wouldn't be coming so fast.

It was nearly midnight when Black Sky saw a small light ahead. Moving slowly, he saw that the glow was the embers of a dying fire. Could it be the soldiers? Dismounting, he crept forward. He was still some distance away when he saw a sentry cross between him and the glowing coals. Then he saw other sentries and the dim outline of men rolled up in blankets. The soldiers had not been thrown off the trail. Not only that, they were much closer than he had thought possible.

Going back to his horse, he mounted and hurried back up the river to Many Horses' camp. He had considered trying to steal some horses, but with sentries out, he knew he'd have had no chance of getting away with them.

Reaching camp at dawn, he found Many Horses just coming out of his lodge to wake the people. Black Sky reported that the soldiers were only half a day behind. Many Horses wanted to know if more soldiers were behind those.

"I don't know," Black Sky said. "These soldiers don't have blue clothes except for the three leaders. Perhaps these are scouts."

"There may be more soldiers behind them," Many Horses said.

In less than two minutes, he had the camp stirring and by sunup the camp was on the move up the river, moving fast now.

"Maybe we should stop and fight them now before more soldiers join them," Black Sky suggested to Many Horses.

The chief shook his head. "We must get together with our people. Then we will be strong enough to face them. The soldiers have many rifles."

Black Sky agreed with that. But he didn't like to run.

Many Horses saw the disappointment in Black Sky's face. "There are times when it is braver to run than fight," he said. "The soldiers may give up and go back if they can't catch us. They don't usually go too far from their main camp. If we are going to drive the white men across the big river, we must not waste time and maybe some braves in a fight we probably couldn't win."

Black Sky recognized the chief's wisdom but it didn't ease the urge within him to strike instead of running like frightened dogs.

By mid-morning, they passed a spot where a big party had turned into the trail. The tracks showed that this was a bigger group than their own. Black Sky wondered how big the camp would be when they all got together up where the waters started flowing.

In late afternoon, they caught up with the bigger group. Now they had enough men to wipe out the soldiers behind them. But again Black Sky's idea was rejected.

"There will be many *Tsis tsis tas* warriors when we get together, the most that ever fought together," Many Horses insisted. "We will drive out the soldiers as well as those who turn over the good grass."

Black Sky said no more. Many Horses had seen more summers than Black Sky had. He was wiser. It would take all the wisdom of their smartest chiefs to drive out the whites. He had seen how many of them there were on those raids along the eastern rivers.

There were several members of the Dog Soldier Society in the camp they had overtaken. But Roman Nose was up ahead in another camp, Black Sky was told. They would not fight until all the groups got together and plans were made for the war to drive out the white settlers.

"Did those soldiers following us have any Pawnee scouts with them?" one chief asked Black Sky.

Black Sky shook his head. "No Pawnees."

As a Cheyenne, Black Sky hated the Pawnees more than he did the

white invader in their land. The Pawnees were not only bitter ene-
mies of the Cheyennes but now they were working as scouts for the
soldiers. Their tracking skills made the white soldiers much more
dangerous to the Cheyennes.

They hurried up the river. According to the chiefs, this group was
the last to go to the meeting place. There would be hundreds,
maybe thousands, waiting for all the groups to come together to
plan the raids down the two rivers, the Republican and the Smoky
Hill. Black Sky didn't know many of the details but he did know that
they planned to make the raids before snow came.

They camped at the confluence of a small stream with the bigger
one. Several creeks ran into the Republican out here but there wasn't
much water in any of them this time of year. They had passed the
spot where the South Fork of the Republican joined the main river.
The creek where they were camped this night was the Arikaree
Creek.

Black Sky's two good friends, Wild Fox and Sparrow, were just his
age, nineteen, and as impatient to hit the enemy as he was. As darkness settled in, they approached Black Sky with a suggestion that
they ride back and steal some of the soldiers' horses and maybe
count some coups.

The idea fired up Black Sky's impatience. He knew it would be
against Many Horses' orders. But he remembered in almost every
battle they had fought, some of the warriors had slipped out ahead.
The Dog Soldiers had a reputation for doing that. They had the
advantage of surprise. The older chiefs always scolded them for their
impatience, but if they were successful, they got no punishment. It
would be the same now.

Black Sky wanted to put on his war paint but that would give away
their plan. If they were going off to a real battle, he'd ride his regular
horse and lead his war pony which was faster and used to fighting.
But that, too, would give away their plans. They simply slipped outside the camp, got their horses and quietly moved away before
mounting and riding down the river.

Black Sky knew they were going against long odds but he felt
confident they could sneak up on one of the guards, overpower him,
then run off some horses before the camp came awake. The prospects of that made Black Sky's head giddy. He had to get horses
somewhere; what better place than from the enemy who was trailing
them?

Black Sky was surprised when they came to the soldier camp so soon. He hadn't expected them to be making better time than the Indians were. The three dismounted and Black Sky and Wild Fox slipped up close to the camp. Sparrow stayed back and held the horses in case they had to make a run for it.

They moved in fairly close to the path the guard was walking. Black Sky thought he could sneak up on that guard and kill him without rousing the camp. But Wild Fox touched his arm.

"There are too many," he whispered. He held up both hands and closed his fingers five times.

Black Sky made a quick estimate of the sleeping forms of the scouts and he agreed with Wild Fox's count. There must be close to fifty. They'd have to strike fast, then ride swiftly to get away.

Wild Fox began inching backward. Black Sky had to check himself. They had to stop these white soldiers. He could get rid of the guard right now. But he had to have the cooperation of his friends. He crept back to the place where they had left Sparrow with the horses.

"We can do it," he whispered. "We'll kill one guard, then we'll dash through the gap he leaves, hit the horses and drive away as many as we can."

Wild Fox shook his head. "Too many. We'll be killed and for nothing."

"It's an honor to be killed in battle," Black Sky said.

"It's no honor if we're disobeying orders," Sparrow said.

Black Sky squelched his anger. "Others do this. We can, too."

"It will take a lot more than three of us," Wild Fox said.

Black Sky's anger boiled over. "Are you afraid? Cheyenne warriors are brave."

Wild Fox flinched. "Many Horses would call this foolish, not brave."

It was Black Sky's turn to recoil. Wild Fox was right. Many Horses would be furious if he knew what Black Sky was considering now. He couldn't afford to antagonize Little Dove's father.

Thinking of Little Dove, he realized that if he wanted her for his own, he'd better be a little more careful. Later, all the warriors would go against these soldiers. He'd count some coups then. Patience would get him what he wanted without risking his life.

Quietly they mounted their ponies and headed back. Black Sky was keenly disappointed. He had hoped to have something to brag about when they got to camp. Now they'd have to sneak in and hope no one saw them so they wouldn't have to explain where they'd been.

Black Sky guessed they were about halfway back to their camp when he caught the odor of burning buffalo chips. Someone had a fire somewhere and there shouldn't be anybody near here. The soldiers were downstream and Many Horses said they were the last Cheyenne village to be moving up the river.

Black Sky halted. The others stopped, too, sniffing the air. Black Sky tested the faint breeze. He pointed to a valley running into the stream from the north.

Without hesitation, Black Sky put his horse into the stream. Somebody was over in that valley and he intended to find out who it was. It might be enemy or friend but he had to know.

Wild Fox and Sparrow followed Black Sky's lead. They rode cautiously up the valley, water dripping off the horses' fetlocks. The valley wasn't deep but the slopes on either side were very steep and made the shadows in the bottom dark enough to hide anything that didn't move.

Finally Black Sky saw a faint glow ahead. He held up a hand and dismounted. Wild Fox went with him as he crawled up close enough to see who was near the fire.

Black Sky discovered a small camp. A chill ran through him as he spied a group of Pawnees. If ever there was fair game for Cheyenne warriors, these Pawnees were it.

"Their horses are up on the east slope," Black Sky whispered. "We can ride right through the camp and drive off the horses."

Wild Fox nodded. "There are only four of them. They're a long way from their hunting grounds down the river."

"Probably no buffalo there," Black Sky whispered. "Let's get our horses."

If he should get killed in this fight, Black Sky knew they'd sing of his bravery in camp. He thought of the words he'd heard in an old man's death chant. "Nothing lasts forever except the earth and sky." He'd chant the same words if he got a death wound.

They got their horses, then rode slowly as close to camp as they dared without risking detection. They would get no reprimand for fighting Pawnees, no matter where or what the odds were.

Black Sky untied the blanket he was carrying tonight and the others did, too. They had planned to use the blankets to scare the soldiers' horses into running. They'd use them now to frighten the Pawnees' horses.

With a sudden whoop, Black Sky dashed toward the horses, waving the blanket over his head. The startled ponies broke for the top of the hill. One Indian, who had apparently been standing guard, fired his rifle at the raiders.

Black Sky swerved toward the warrior. It wasn't likely that he had a repeating rifle, so that one shot would be all he had. Black Sky grabbed his hatchet from his belt and, dodging the knife slash the Pawnee made at him, struck down with his hatchet. The Indian dodged the fatal strike but the blow sent him reeling. Black Sky circled and reached down to touch the Indian. He couldn't tell how seriously he was hurt but he had counted coup on him.

Then he joined the other two chasing the horses. Two rifle shots came from the camp but neither hit anything. The Pawnees couldn't pursue them without ponies.

It took a while to get around the ponies and head them upstream. They needed to get these horses into camp before the camp began its move for the day. Black Sky was eager to get to Many Horses' lodge with the prizes before the lodge came down at daybreak.

It was just dawn when they reached the camp. The Pawnee horses had run themselves out and were as docile as kittens now. Black Sky drove them directly to Many Horses' lodge.

"Six horses!" Many Horses exclaimed. "Where did you get them?"

"Found a Pawnee camp. They had six horses, two of them for packs. They were hunting on our ground."

"Did you kill them?"

"One maybe," Black Sky said. "Counted coup on him. I brought you these horses for Little Dove."

"How did you know about the Pawnees?" Many Horses asked.

Black Sky had to tell the chief that they had gone after the soldiers and found there were fifty of them. They had found the Pawnees on the way home.

"You were ordered not to go after the soldiers," Many Horses said, but that was the extent of the reprimand. "I'm glad to know how many soldiers there are. Were there more soldiers behind them?"

"We saw no sign of any," Black Sky said.

"I'm afraid there are many soldiers following these. We must join with the others. Then we can face them, no matter how many there are. The Pawnees must have been looking for buffalo."

Black Sky thought of the way the white men were slaughtering the buffalo and wasting both the meat and hides. His anger rose. The Indians had to have the buffalo to survive. There could be no peace until the white men were driven across the big river and forced to stay there.

Black Sky brought his mind back to the horses he had brought in. "Will you accept these horses for Little Dove?" he asked.

Many Horses nodded. "Plenty horses. But we have many big battles just ahead. You might be killed. Little Dove must not be a widow. When the big fight is over, Little Dove shall be your wife."

Black Sky agreed. "I will count many coups in the fights ahead," he promised.

Thirteen

DAIN WAS GETTING increasingly frustrated; they weren't catching up to the Cheyennes. They had lost some time when the Indians scattered and had decided to go straight on to the Republican River. Dain hoped that Grover was right in assuming that the Indians would come together again on the Republican.

All the rest of the day they moved north, following no trail and seeing nothing to indicate they were following Indians. Dain was becoming more aggravated with each mile.

Night caught them in the broken hills and deep valleys that Grover said led to the Republican. They found a small stream running down one of the valleys and camped. Dain was disappointed they hadn't gone on in the dark. After all, they knew they were going as far as the river before they picked up the trail again.

"Got to give the horses a rest, too," Ron said.

Every delay took more out of Dain than extra travel without rest would have done. Before the scouts rolled into their bedrolls, Forsyth had a conference with Sharp Grover just a short distance from Dain's bedroll.

"Are you sure we'll find the trail on the Republican?" Forsyth asked.

"As sure as I can be about anything concerning Indians," Grover said. "I think their plan was to throw us off the trail, then, when we couldn't find it again, hope we'd go home."

"We're not going home until we find them," Forsyth said sharply.

"I figured as much," Grover said. "That's why I suggested we come up to the river. Indians like to travel along rivers."

"Is this the same bunch that raided along the Saline and Solomon?"

"Part of them, I'm sure," Grover said. "There were a lot more than a dozen on those raids, though."

"They'll all likely get together somewhere," Forsyth said.

"You can bet on it, Colonel. And when they do, there will be a pretty big bunch of them."

"We started out to fight Indians," Forsyth said, "and we're going to do just that, no matter what the odds."

Dain liked that determination. It was Dain's only hope of finding the two captives. If the soldiers couldn't find them, then he certainly couldn't do it alone. Also, in the back of his mind was the distinct possibility that Jed Wolfcry would be with the Indians when they found them. If he was, he'd get to him some way.

Sunrise found them in the saddle. They were at the Republican before the sun was an hour high. Stillwell called Forsyth's attention to a wickiup on the opposite bank. He doubted if it was occupied but they couldn't afford not to look. They were in Indian country and anything unusual needed to be checked out.

Stillwell and two men were sent across to look over the wickiup. They were back in ten minutes. "Nobody's been there for three weeks," Stillwell reported. "But there has been plenty of traffic past there recently, all headed upstream."

"That's where we're headed, too," Forsyth said. "I'm guessing some of those tracks were made by the Indians we trailed out of Sheridan."

"Probably," Stillwell said. "But they're not alone any more."

The company moved up the river bank on the south side. The main valley of the Republican was a fairly wide one but the river bed itself was more sand than water this late in the season. Dain could only imagine what this valley looked like during a spring flood.

"Sure ain't any place to hide here," Trudeau muttered. "I like to see places where I can dig in if we run across trouble."

"No place to hide means there isn't any place for the Indians to lay an ambush."

Trudeau nodded. "I reckon that's one good thing."

Dain agreed with Trudeau. This was a totally empty land they were riding through. But there were the tracks that proved there had been someone here recently. The Indians' passing had frightened off all the game and it was empty now, void of all life as far as Dain could see.

But there were tracks, more and more of them as they moved up the river. Dain was getting a little apprehensive. Where were all these Indians coming from? And where were they going? It appeared that Colonel Forsyth was determined to find out.

Then they found a place where a large group had turned into the trail. There were the telltale ruts dug in the trail by the ends of travoises.

"Some families joined the group here," Grover said.

Dain felt a shiver of excitement. If families were up ahead, then maybe Susan and Hiram were among them. Grover had said they'd probably be with the family groups if they were still alive. He wouldn't allow himself to think they weren't.

An hour later, Forsyth asked, "Are we gaining or losing ground, Grover?"

"Maybe gaining a little," the scout said. "But we'll have to do better if we want to catch them before they get the whole bunch together."

"Looks like the whole bunch is together now," Bystrom complained.

"You obviously have never seen the trail a whole tribe leaves when they move north or south," Stillwell said. "We can handle a bunch this size."

"Meaning we can't handle a big bunch if we run into them?" Bystrom asked.

"It wouldn't be healthy to try," Grover said.

"Don't talk nonsense," Forsyth shouted. "We're going to fight Indians, no matter how many there are. We haven't come this far just to turn tail and run."

No more was said about the number of Indians they were following but from time to time Grover reported more tracks turning into the trail. Dain knew they were following enough warriors to worry Grover and Stillwell.

"How far ahead do you figure the main camp of Indians is?" Dain asked.

Grover answered. "Doesn't make any difference. That camp will move if they're not ready for us to catch up with them."

They rode until sundown. When they camped, Forsyth doubled the guard around camp. Dain realized they could be attacked at any time. They must be close to the Indians ahead of them. And according to the tracks, there were literally hundreds of warriors up there.

As they were settling into camp, Dain caught sight of something white over on a hill nearly a mile away. It intrigued him. He couldn't think what would show up white against the fall grass. He called Ron's attention to it.

"What do you think it is?" Dain asked.

"I have no idea," Ron said. "Maybe we ought to check it out."

"May be a trap," Dain suggested.

"Could be," Ron agreed. "Let's ask Grover."

They found Sharp Grover and pointed to the two white spots over on the hill. Grover studied them carefully through his binoculars, which were not too powerful.

"Can't make them out from here. Let's go take a look."

"Think it might be a trap?"

Grover rubbed his chin. "Maybe. They get pretty cagey sometimes."

They resaddled their horses. Forsyth walked to the edge of camp with the three riders. "Make sure your rifles are loaded and ready," he said. "Take it cautiously and watch in every direction."

Dain knew he was thinking ambush, too. But this was something out of the ordinary and, in enemy country, they couldn't afford to ignore it.

Grover led the way, watching in every direction. Dain and Ron followed, also watching to the east and west as much as straight ahead. They didn't pay much attention to the white spots they were going to investigate until they were fairly close. There was no sign of an Indian anywhere in the vicinity. Dain remembered the warning he'd been given. "It's when you don't see an Indian that he's the most dangerous. When he lets you see him, he's not dangerous."

"It's two people!" Ron exclaimed softly. "They must be dead."

Dain saw then that it was two women who had been staked out on the hillside and left to die. His heart rammed up in his throat as he nudged his horse up the slope for a closer look.

Then it seemed to stop beating entirely. He recognized both women. One was a neighbor lady who lived a few miles up the Saline from Dain. The other was Susan.

Swinging off his horse, Dain ran forward. Before he reached his sister, he knew she was dead. Ron grabbed him and stopped him a few feet from the bodies.

"Know them?" Grover asked in a tone that said he already knew the answer.

"That's his sister, Susan," Ron said, pointing to the woman on the left.

Dain fought to get free of Ron's grasp, then suddenly felt himself turning sick. Wheeling back toward his horse, he gripped the saddle horn to keep from falling. He'd never get that picture out of his mind. The two women had been staked on the hillside with four stakes that stretched them out. He vaguely heard Ron ask Grover a question.

"Were they dead when they were put there?"

Grover's answer was little more than a whisper. "No. That's one way Indians get rid of captives."

"What—what about Susan's baby?" Ron asked. "They took him, too."

"They probably killed him the first hour," Grover said. "They can't stand a crying baby. And a white baby will cry when he knows something is wrong. There's not much chance he's alive."

"How long would you say they've been there?" Ron asked.

"A couple of days," Grover said tonelessly.

"Then the Indians we've been following weren't the ones that had these captives."

"No. It had to have been a band ahead of these. It really makes no difference. Any of the Indians would have done the same thing."

Dain was sick. Ron helped him back into the saddle and they rode slowly back to camp. Grover reported to Forsyth. The colonel and others came to express their sympathies to Dain but he barely heard them. He had only one thought—he'd been too late getting to Susan. She must have suffered terrible torture before she died. If he could only have been here a few days earlier!

"It wouldn't have made any difference," Ron said quietly. "They'd have killed their captives rather than let them be rescued."

"I've been on a fool's mission," Dain said, gradually getting control of himself. He had clung desperately to the hope that he could rescue Susan and Hiram. They had been his last link to people he had trusted all his life.

"It's over now," Ron said quietly. "You'll be all right."

Dain knew he still had one person he could fully trust. Ron had never given him any cause for doubting his friendship.

"How many Indians do you think are ahead of us, Grover?" Forsyth asked as darkness closed down.

"Too many," Grover said. "The trail looks like a highway."

Forsyth pinched his lips together. "We're going to keep after them. We came to fight Indians and we're going to fight Indians!"

Forsyth sent out a burial detail with shovels and a lantern and a four-man guard. Dain started to follow them but Ron stopped him.

"That's a tough job you don't need," he said. "Stay here and pull yourself together."

"I don't have much left to live for," Dain said emotionlessly.

"That's wrong," Ron said quickly. "You've got Valina waiting for you back in Alpha."

Thought of Valina was like the flashing light of a meteor in his mind but then it was gone. The vision of Susan staked out on that hillside filled the void. He wondered if he would ever get over that.

The burial detail came back to camp and Colonel Forsyth came over to Dain.

"You have my permission to go home, Dain," he said. "I know you came along to rescue your sister. Your part of the mission is over."

Dain started to agree, then a picture of Jed Wolfcry flashed across his mind. Susan's death was the result of Wolfcry's treachery. He was as much responsible as if he'd staked her out himself.

Dain's mission suddenly focused on Jed Wolfcry. He had to find him and make him pay for his treachery. He had already concluded that Wolfcry was surely with the Indians.

"I'm not going back," he said to Forsyth. "I'm going to make the ones who killed my family pay with their lives or I'll die in the attempt."

Fourteen

DAIN FOUND IT impossible to sleep that night. He could never clear his mind of the picture of Susan staked out on that hillside. Jed Wolfcry had to answer for that. Dain couldn't see just how he was going to get close to Wolfcry. But his only chance would be with Forsyth because he was the only one who was going to get near the Indians.

He wondered momentarily if he could be wrong about Wolfcry showing the raiders where Susan had hidden. Maybe Susan had been in the yard with Bert when they attacked. Then he remembered that the bureau had been pulled out from the wall. Bert and Susan had rehearsed what they would do if Indians struck. No matter what happened outside, Susan and the baby were to get into the hiding place and stay there until the raiders were gone. If Susan had been with Bert, Wolfcry wouldn't have pulled the bureau away from the wall. Wolfcry was as guilty of Susan's death as any murderer could be.

Forsyth had them on the move at sunup, hoping to catch the closest Indians before they joined the main camp. But each mile seemed to show more tracks in the trail. It was a real thoroughfare.

"Were all these tracks made at the same time?" Dain asked Grover.

Sharp Grover shook his head. "Some of these tracks were made a week ago. But somewhere up ahead all the Indians who made these tracks are going to get together."

"I'm guessing a thousand," Stillwell said to Grover. "How about you?"

"At least that many. Maybe a thousand warriors, not counting the families. We're bucking long odds any way you cut it."

"Maybe we ought to turn back while we still can," one man suggested.

Dain sensed the nervousness in the men. It hadn't been there a couple of days ago when they'd been trailing only a few Indians. When the first doubts arose in the scouts, Gus Bystrom laughed at them, making remarks about the yellow streaks down their backs. Yesterday when the trail became a highway, however, Bystrom had been quiet. Now one of the men that Bystrom had taunted spoke up.

"Are you still chomping at the bit to get at the Indians, Bystrom?"

Bystrom scowled, then drew himself up straight. "Ain't no Indian going to scare me out."

"How about a thousand of them?"

Bystrom looked around at those watching him. He shrugged disdainfully. "Ain't enough Indians in this territory to scare me."

Dain looked at Bystrom's cousin, Ken Calhoun, riding beside the big man. He was looking straight ahead, no expression on his face.

It was a beautiful morning. There was a slight haze drifting over the valley that hinted of a change in weather. The valley was wide here and the September sunshine was warm. It was a pleasant day for a ride. Dain thought that Susan would have enjoyed it. As he thought of Susan, Dain's day suddenly clouded over. He didn't see the sunshine any longer or hear the meadow larks in their fall concert.

"You'd better change your tune, Bystrom," one man said. "There are a lot of Indians ahead of us."

"I've fought Indians more times than you have," Bystrom bragged. "I know Indians. They won't fight. When they find out we're still coming after them, they'll break into little groups and hightail it out of the country."

Dain didn't believe that and he saw that others didn't, either. But, looking at Bystrom, he thought that he really did believe it. Anyway, considering the bragging he had done, he could hardly admit that he was afraid now.

They discovered that the trail turned along a small stream running into the Republican from the southwest. None of the tracks went on.

"Doesn't look to me like they're splitting up," one man said dryly.

Forsyth and Beecher searched their maps. One thought they were on a creek called Delaware Creek; the other thought it was called Arikaree Creek. It made no difference to Dain. The Indians had gone up this tributary and Forsyth was turning that way, too.

About noon, Dain thought he saw an Indian off to the southwest, watching their progress up the creek. He called Ron's attention to the spy. At almost the same time, Stillwell pointed to the northwest, where another head appeared.

"They've got us named and numbered by now," Stillwell said.

"Think they'll attack soon?" Dain asked.

"Not until they get a decided advantage," Stillwell said.

"Colonel," one man said, "I think we're riding into something we can't ride out of."

Forsyth turned to Grover. "How do you feel about it?"

"We've got our hands full," Grover said.

"Afraid?" Forsyth asked.

Grover shook his head. "Just uneasy. Anyway, we can't retreat now. If we started back, they'd come after us like coyotes after a crippled calf."

"We came to fight Indians," Forsyth repeated. "Let's do it."

Dain rode in silence, feeling the tension growing in the men. He watched Stillwell in particular. He was the youngest member of the scouts, about eighteen or nineteen, but he had an understanding of the situation beyond his years.

"How many warriors do you figure are up ahead?" Dain asked him.

"Hard to say. Probably two thirds of the Indians are women and children and men too old to fight. But from the looks of the trail we've been following, there still are a lot of warriors."

"All Cheyenne?"

"Probably," Stillwell said. "Tribes don't usually mix much. There'll likely be both Northern and Southern Cheyennes. Could be some Sioux, too. They share this territory."

There were no new tracks turning into the trail now. It was a wide trail and in places the grass was worn down to the roots. Dain saw an arrow at the edge of the trail and pointed to it. Stillwell dismounted and picked it up.

"This is an Arapaho arrow," he said, frowning. "If there are

Arapahos here, there may be Kiowas, too. We could be riding right into a gathering of the nations."

"Why would they be gathering?" Dain asked.

"I wish I knew," Stillwell said. "But you can be sure it's not to offer us a peace pipe."

"Maybe they'll break up now and go their own ways," one man suggested. "I never knew different tribes to work together."

"True enough," Stillwell said. "But I've never seen anything like this trail we're following, either. Anything can happen."

Dain saw a doll made of a wolf skin along the trail. A little farther, he saw a blackened pot that had apparently bounced off a travois.

"Looks like they might be getting in a hurry," one man said. "Maybe we are closer to them than we thought."

"They're in a hurry to get away from us," Bystrom said. "I told you they'd run."

Stillwell shook his head. A couple of items lost off their loads didn't mean the Indians were panicky. If anybody was going to panic, it should be the scouts.

Dain watched for Indians spying on them but he didn't see anything. He remembered the adage about the Indian you didn't see being the one to be afraid of.

The trail was still broad and worn down through the grass. There had been many travoises over this road, the ends of the poles plowing small furrows as they were pulled along. Dain was sure there were enough warriors ahead of them to wipe out a regiment of soldiers. And there were just fifty-one men riding into this trap.

The creek, reduced to little more than a trickle at this time of year, had cut a wide swath through the valley in its yearly flood. Most of that was dry sand now. Up ahead, some bluffs pressed down close to the creek where it ran between them.

There was plenty of room along the banks below the bluffs for passage of the scouts. Forsyth sent two men ahead to make sure there was no ambush just beyond those bluffs. It was all clear and they rode through the gap, breaking out into a broad valley with the stream running slowly through it, holding closer to the north side of the valley. The grass was very good here for September and Forsyth called a halt.

"We'll camp here even if it is early," he said. "We'll give our horses a rest and start out at first light in the morning. Tomorrow we will surely catch up with the Indians."

Dain dismounted with the others and proceeded to unsaddle his horse. Leading him down to the creek, he found he had to take him well out across the sandy creek bed to reach the little stream of water that was still running.

The stream was split here, going around an island in the middle of the creek bed. The island was about two hundred and fifty feet long, not more than fifty feet wide, and only about a foot above the water level. The water of the stream was only ten or fifteen feet wide on either side of the island and no more than a few inches deep. It was fully seventy yards from the bank of the stream to the island and it appeared to be about the same on the north side. There were a few alders and willows growing in the center of the island with a cotton-wood tree at the tip.

Dain guessed that this stream was a roaring flood during the spring when mountain snows melted and water levels rose. Likely most of the island would be under water then. Now there was hardly enough water to float a blade of grass.

Dain guessed the valley to be about two miles wide where they camped. The camp was on a gentle slope and it was over a mile to the south where the hills fenced in the valley. On the north side of the creek, the land rose a little faster for a short half mile and there the valley ended abruptly in a row of steep bluffs. The entire valley was covered with fine grass. There was sage grass on the island and along both banks of the creek. Farther back, the buffalo and grama grass took over and blanketed the valley all the way to the hills and bluffs. It was a pretty setting for their camp.

Although it was early, none of the men objected to the extra rest. They wouldn't find a better campsite, no matter how far they rode. The valley itself looked to be a mile and a half or two miles long, extending from the bluffs through which they had come to some low bluffs that crowded in on the creek to the southwest.

Supper was a light meal. The rations were virtually gone. The scouts had expected to replenish their rations with game shot along the way. There hadn't been any since they hit the Republican River. Now with so many Indians ahead of them, they knew there would be no game tomorrow. Or maybe the next day or the next. It wasn't a pleasant prospect.

They had already been on the road longer than expected when they left Fort Wallace. And they had come much farther than they had planned. They hadn't controlled where they would go. The

Indians had done that. They couldn't fight Indians until they found them. That had been their goal and had brought them all the way here to the northeastern section of Colorado Territory.

It was the most peaceful valley Dain had ever seen. But there was nothing peaceful inside Dain. He could see that none of the others were thinking about their peaceful setting, either.

There was tension in every face. There was no doubt in any of the scouts that they were about to meet a deadly foe that greatly outnumbered them. They just didn't know where or when it would happen. But the prospects tightened the nerves and made the skin crawl.

Fifteen

BLACK SKY was disappointed that Many Horses had postponed his wedding to Little Dove. But he understood. It made him realize how serious Many Horses considered these big raids coming up. If they pushed the white men all the way back to the big river, it would mean they would be fighting where the white men already had big camps. More warriors would be killed than had ever been killed in battle before. But this had to be done. The Indians would starve because the invaders were taking all the buffalo pasture and either killing the buffalo or driving them away. Black Sky clenched his fists. He would not go to a reservation created by the white men and die a slow death as some Indians were already doing. He'd die in battle!

With the prospects of battle and with all of Many Horses' camp together, the chief called for a war dance. In timber country, that would have meant a big fire. Here on the treeless plains, it was a much smaller fire of buffalo chips, but that wouldn't dampen the enthusiasm of the dancers.

At the start of the festivities, the warriors who had been out on the raids were called on to report their coups and show the scalps they had taken. Wild Fox had taken one scalp and counted one coup. Others reported their successes in battle.

Then it was Black Sky's turn. He looked over at the women. Little Dove was there with her hands clasped in front of her as she watched. He moved to the center of the ring. He had no scalps but he did have a first coup and two second coups. Cheyennes could count three coups on each enemy. The first warrior to touch the enemy counted first coup; that was the most important. The second one to touch him got second coup and the third one got third coup.

To verify the truthfulness of his report, Black Sky repeated the vow: "If I tell a lie, I hope that I may be shot far off." That meant he'd be killed far from home and his body could not be recovered; a sad thing for his family. No warrior wanted that to happen to him.

After all the warriors who had counted coups and taken scalps had reported, the dance began. Black Sky expected it to last most of the night. But a rider came into camp before the enthusiasm of the dance had reached its peak. The dance suddenly stopped as Many Horses hurried over to the far side of the circle to talk to the messenger.

Black Sky went over, too, but he didn't get there in time to hear the beginning of the message. He did hear the last.

"The chiefs say to hurry up the river where they are gathering. We will fight tomorrow or the next day."

The big battle would start soon, Black Sky realized. The first skirmish would annihilate the fifty soldiers that had been following them the last few days. Then would come the sweep down the Republican and Smoky Hill rivers to push the white settlers back beyond the big river.

The messenger rode off toward another camp to call them to the gathering. Many Horses told Black Sky to bring all the leading warriors to his lodge. Many Horses headed for his lodge on the highest ground in the camp circle.

In ten minutes, every warrior leader in camp had gathered at the lodge. Many Horses stood as straight as a tree and his bearing told everyone that he had something important to say.

"We go to the gathering up the river," he announced. "Soon, maybe tomorrow, we go to war. We must prepare for that. The leaders will not eat of the tongue or the hump of the buffalo before battle. That is bad medicine."

Black Sky realized that Many Horses had called the warrior leaders together not just to warn them of the coming fight but to make sure they didn't eat the forbidden meat. They would have bad luck if they did. Once the battle was over and they were victorious, they could feast on those delicacies.

Black Sky thought he had heard all the message that the rider had brought but now he found out he hadn't.

"The chiefs are worried," Many Horses said. "The spies they sent out today have not come back. They were to report exactly where the soldiers are tonight so we can prepare for them. We are to send scouts out to find them." His eyes fell on Black Sky. "Black Sky, you will go. Take two with you."

Black Sky was pleased with the assignment. It would be better than sitting here thinking about the coming battle.

"I will take Wild Fox and Sparrow," he announced.

The three ran toward their ponies. There was no need for talk. Black Sky did wonder what could have happened to the spies. They should have watched the soldiers until they were certain where they would camp, then reported to the chiefs. An ambush would surely be set once the chiefs knew when the soldiers would come.

They had ridden less than a mile when Wild Fox held up a hand. "Someone ahead. I hear horses."

They waited. Surely it would be the spies. But if not, they were prepared to fight. Four riders developed out of the dim light. Black Sky recognized them as Indians but he didn't recognize the riders until they got closer. Two were men he knew.

One shocked him when he got a good look at him. He was lighter-skinned than the others and Black Sky had never seen him before. Black Sky demanded to know why they were late getting back.

"We checked the soldiers very carefully," one warrior said.

Black Sky thought from the way he said it that something was wrong. "All you needed to do was see where they would camp," he said.

"Wolfcry had to get close enough to see every face," the spokesman said.

Black Sky searched the other faces. They were looking at the light-skinned warrior. Black Sky looked at him, too.

"Why?" he demanded.

The warrior called Wolfcry nudged his horse over closer to Black Sky. "I lived with the white men for a while," he said, anger twisting his face. "I learned to hate them. One man there beat me up. I swore I'd kill him. I had to find out if he is among those soldiers. He is."

"Then you can count coup on him when we fight them," Black Sky said. "Let's get back and report where the soldiers are. The chiefs want to know."

"They are closer than we thought they would be," the spokesman for the spies said. "They have been traveling fast."

Black Sky rode over next to the spokesman. "Are you late because you had to wait for Wolfcry to look over the soldiers?"

"Until nearly dark," the warrior grumbled. "We couldn't come back without him and he wouldn't listen to any of us. He came when he was ready."

Black Sky guessed that Wolfcry was not one to listen to orders. That could cause trouble in a battle.

Black Sky reported to Many Horses while the four spies went on to the camp from which they'd been sent. The camp was settling down. The war dance was over. They had to move early in the morning.

Many Horses assigned two warriors to go back to the place where the Arikaree Creek ran into the Republican to watch the soldiers to see if they turned up the little stream. If so, they were to hurry back to report to Many Horses, who would be moving on upstream.

The camp was up at dawn and moving by sunrise. Before noon, they were at the gathering place. There were many camps, including a half-dozen Cheyenne, several Sioux and one Arapaho and one Kiowa camp. All were in circles except the Kiowa camp and it was in a line. Black Sky had been told that Kiowas always camped in a row while Cheyennes camped in a circle if there was room.

Black Sky left Many Horses' camp and went to the Dog Soldiers'. They were off by themselves as was fitting for the best fighting warriors in the camps.

Black Sky could hardly wait to see Roman Nose. He was usually with his friend but they had been separated during the raids along the Saline and Solomon rivers many miles to the east.

Roman Nose was there and, at first, Black Sky didn't notice anything different about him. He was one of the tallest Indians Black Sky had ever seen. He was six feet three inches tall, even taller than most white men. He was not heavy for that height but he exuded strength and force simply standing there. Black Sky thrilled just to be associated with the greatest Dog Soldier of them all. He didn't have a handsome face, but in battle, he was the epitome of indestructible force.

"Who went with you on the raids?" Black Sky asked after they had greeted each other.

"I didn't go on the raids," Roman Nose said. "We have been

preparing for the battles that will push the white men off our hunting grounds. I will be needed there."

Black Sky understood that. As leader of the Dog Soldiers, Roman Nose was indispensable. Wherever he led, the warriors would follow. They had never lost a battle when Roman Nose was in the lead on his magnificent chestnut war pony.

Black Sky drew the task of carrying messages to all the other camps, including the *Suhtai* Cheyennes, the Sioux, the Arapahos and the Kiowas. The message was simple. The war chiefs of all the tribes were to meet immediately at the center of the Cheyenne camp to plan strategy. They now knew where the soldiers were and about when they would arrive here.

When the war chiefs met, Black Sky expected Roman Nose to lead the plans for the ambush of the soldiers. But the leader of the Crazy Dog Society was in charge.

The big Cheyenne camp was about a mile above the open valley of the Arikaree. The warriors would hide behind the bluffs that crowded in close to the creek at the head of that valley. When the soldiers came through the gap, they would pounce on them. It should be a quick battle, and with any luck, there would be very few Indian casualties.

The war societies would be in charge of the planning and the battles. Since the Dog Soldiers were the biggest society, they would have the choice spots in the ambush. Roman Nose would be in charge. That was as Black Sky thought it should be. What wasn't right was that Roman Nose wasn't taking charge of the meeting. In fact, he wasn't even in sight.

The Dog Soldiers would run the most risk in the ambush but they would also be in a position to count the most coups. Behind them would be the Crazy Dog Society, the Kit Fox Society, and all the lesser societies, plus the Sioux, Arapahos and Kiowas. The Sioux numbers were small compared to the Cheyennes so they had to take a back place.

Before the warriors left to locate their positions for the ambush, one of the old chiefs stood up and faced the warriors.

"We have been pushed off our good hunting grounds," he said. "We will run no more. We will kill the soldiers who are following us, then we'll ride down the two rivers and push the palefaces completely across the big river toward the rising sun."

Black Sky had no doubts about the outcome of the battle with the soldiers following them. There were at least twenty warriors for every soldier. The battle would be short if the ambush was a complete surprise. It was up to the leaders of the warriors to see that it was a surprise.

The chief had a final word for the warriors. "There must not be a soldier left alive. Let none get away to go back and tell what happened. We will strike swiftly along the rivers. We will leave no one alive and no building standing that will burn."

Black Sky shouted and raised his fist with the others. This kind of enthusiasm was what it would take to drive the white men off Indian land. If they did miss some houses in their sweep down the rivers, those people would lose no time running back to the east when they saw what had happened to their neighbors.

Black Sky knew it would be difficult in this ambush to keep some warriors from charging out ahead to count coup and strike a blow at the enemy. It was usually the young warriors who spoiled most ambushes. It would be surprising if a few eager braves didn't spoil this one.

Black Sky went in search of Roman Nose and found him by himself back in a draw that ran down toward the creek.

"Don't you know we're getting ready to strike the soldiers?" he asked.

"I know," Roman Nose said. "But I can't fight. My medicine is broken."

"That can't be!" Black Sky exclaimed in horror.

Roman Nose was invincible. Black Sky himself had seen him ride openly within twenty-five yards of a company of soldiers who fired repeatedly at him. Roman Nose, wearing his protective war bonnet, rode back and forth twice and was never touched by a bullet. From that moment, everyone knew that when Roman Nose was wearing his war bonnet, nothing could harm him. Now he was saying his medicine was broken.

"We have to have you as our leader," Black Sky said. "We are the Dog Soldiers, the best warriors in the tribe. We can't let them down."

"Someone else can lead the warriors."

"No one else can do it," Black Sky argued. "We are the best but we have to have you to lead us."

"I'll be killed if I fight," Roman Nose said. "You know the magic of my war bonnet. But there are certain things that will break that magic. One is eating anything that has been touched with iron. Yesterday, before you got here, I ate meat at a Sioux camp. Only after I ate did I learn that the woman used an iron fork to lift it out of the pot. My medicine is broken."

"You can break the curse."

"It takes a two-day ceremony," Roman Nose said. "I don't have time. The enemy is close."

Black Sky's heart sank. Roman Nose was right. There wasn't time to perform the necessary ceremony to take the curse off the war bonnet.

"We are planning to hide on this side of those bluffs that reach down close to the creek," Black Sky said. "We'll spring out and surprise them. None of us should get killed doing that. You'll be safe. I'll be close and make sure nothing happens to you."

"Even an ambush can go wrong," Roman Nose said. "It won't be that easy."

The two scouts sent out last night came riding in shortly after noon to say that the soldiers had turned up Arikaree Creek. The chiefs called the warriors to prepare for war.

Roman Nose agreed to lead the parade that the Dog Soldiers (*Hotamitaniu*) would make along with the other societies. Many of the warriors had put on some war paint, while others paraded without it. They would put it on before the battle began.

Black Sky took his usual place just behind Roman Nose. He was worried. Roman Nose wasn't wearing his war bonnet; he hadn't put any paint on himself or his horse. He wasn't ready to fight. Black Sky was sure he didn't intend to fight.

The parade was a ceremony they observed if there was time before a battle. Today they had time. The soldiers were still several hours away. There were strict rules to follow during a society parade. Every warrior wore a whistle around his neck made from the bone of a bird's wing. If he happened to drop something from his horse, he was not allowed to stop and pick it up. It was lost to him unless he blew his whistle and a companion rode up and hit his horse over the head, then led the horse back to the spot where he had dropped the item. The Dog Soldier could dismount then and pick it up. If nobody responded to his whistle, the item remained on the ground until someone picked it up or, at the end of the ceremony, the warrior went back and got it.

Black Sky made sure he had everything he was carrying securely fastened. He couldn't have his medicine broken by losing something.

After the parade, the societies rode down to the bluffs that crowded the creek and found places where they could spring out of cover in an instant, ready to do battle with the soldiers as they came through the gap between the bluffs.

Then they waited. They knew the soldiers were coming. Then a scout near the gap called back that the soldiers had just come through the gap at the lower end of the valley, nearly two miles away.

The warriors were excited. It was still early enough that the soldiers were sure to come beyond this point to camp. The moment they rode through this gap, they would be breathing their last.

A half hour later, the scout called back in a quieter tone. "They're stopping. I think they're going to camp out in the middle of the valley."

Consternation raced through the warriors. They had a perfect ambush set up. Black Sky doubted if they could control the young warriors through the night and spring the ambush tomorrow morning when the soldiers came through.

"We may have to go out there and kill them," one lead warrior suggested.

"We'll lose too many braves if we do that," another said. "Let's wait for them to come to us. They'll come this way in the morning."

Black Sky wondered which plan would prevail. He doubted if waiting would work. There were too many eager young warriors who would find waiting too hard.

Black Sky worried about his friend when the battle finally took place. Would Roman Nose fight? And if he did, would the magic of his war bonnet protect him?

Sixteen

THERE WAS A LIGHT HAZE screening the sun as it set. Dain thought that tomorrow it might rain. But right now it was a beautiful evening. Some of the scouts seemed to notice and enjoy the peaceful surroundings. Worry lined other faces; peace was the farthest thing from their thoughts.

Dain marveled at the emptiness of the land. They were many miles from civilization as he knew it. He doubted if white men had ever set foot before where the scouts were camping tonight. The emptiness surrounding them was complete. There were no animals, large or small, and only a few birds ventured to sing their lullabies. It was a false emptiness, Dain knew. The very emptiness was created by the recent presence of the Indians which had frightened all of Nature's creatures into hiding.

As darkness settled over the valley, Forsyth called for the attention of the scouts. "Make doubly sure your picket pins are secure," he ordered. "If we are as close to the Indians as I suspect, they could sneak back tonight and try to stampede the horses. If an alarm is sounded, I want every man on his feet instantly, one hand holding his horse's picket rope, his rifle in the other hand. Understood?"

Heads nodded. Dain looked at Sharp Grover standing close to Forsyth. Apparently one or both of them felt that an attack before morning was likely. Dain had heard that Indians seldom fought at night because they believed that they wouldn't go to the next world if they were killed in a night battle. So the likely time for an Indian attack would be dawn.

They had eaten most of their remaining rations for supper. The Indians had frightened off the game so all they had found to supplement their meal were some plums on bushes along the creek. At least, the season was right; the plums were ripe. But a diet of plums would be a poor substitute for a balanced meal.

Dain drew one of the first guards. Before going out to the edge of the camp to watch, he made doubly sure that his picket pin was driven well down into the sod. He couldn't afford to lose his horse.

Gus Bystrom had the guard post next to Dain. Dain expected Bystrom to do some bragging about the many Indian fights he'd been in. But the big man had nothing to say tonight.

It was a still night, only the faintest of breezes whispering through the grass. Dain noted that it was a southeast breeze. Southeast winds often brought rainy weather, Dain had learned in the short time he'd been on the plains. But tonight, there was a beautiful clear sky above and a quiet hush hovered over the prairie. It was as if Nature was waiting with baited breath for something to happen. Or maybe it was Dain's nerves that were waiting expectantly.

Dain was relieved at his guard post at the same time that Gus Bystrom was. Dain couldn't believe that he hadn't heard a word from Bystrom when they met in their beats on guard duty. There had been no bragging about the Indian fights Bystrom had been in and no ridiculing other scouts for being anxious about what they were getting into.

Dain wouldn't trust Bystrom as far as he could spit. He really didn't know anybody in the group except Ron well enough to trust. Without Ron to lean on, he'd be pretty miserable in this group.

Dain dropped into an almost dreamless sleep. He didn't think he'd been asleep more than a few minutes when a rifle exploded out on the guard line and the shout went up, "Indians!"

Dain leaped up as if he'd been lying on a coiled spring. Remembering what Forsyth had said, one hand gripped the rope holding his horse and the other grabbed his rifle.

It was still dark, Dain thought. Indians didn't attack at night. Then, as sleep was swept from his eyes, he saw that it was getting light in the east. Some might call this dawn.

Then he heard the whoop of the Indians. Every man raised his rifle ready to shoot while still holding tightly to the rope of his horse.

The Indians materialized out of the shadows, the dried hides they were shaking making a frightful racket. The Indians themselves were but shadows in the dim light. Dain fired once but he was sure he had missed. It was like firing at wisps of smoke.

In a minute they were gone. They had dashed toward the horses but had been met by rifle fire. So far as Dain could see, every man still held his horse. Dain heard the thud of hoofbeats fading away to the west.

Then it was quiet. Forsyth ordered every man to saddle his horse and stand at the ready. By the time this was done, the light was growing stronger. Roll call was made quickly. Every man was present but two horses had pulled their picket pins and had been driven off by the raiders. Two of the four pack mules had broken free and gone with the Indians, too.

The packs were quickly loaded on the backs of the two remaining mules. Some of their supplies, especially the extra food, had already been used so the loads were not excessive for either mule. The extra ammunition was on one mule and the medical supplies on the other. Every man had his full quota of ammunition in his belt.

They waited as the light grew stronger. It was deathly quiet again. One man ventured the opinion that this might have been an isolated raid by some young warriors who just wanted to steal some horses.

"Not likely," Grover said. "We know there are at least a thousand Indians ahead of us. This raid was likely intended to get the horses and leave us afoot. It didn't work."

"Will they try something else?"

"You can bet on it."

"We'd better use our horses to get out of here," Bystrom said. "There ain't no Indians back the way we came."

"We'll stay right here till we see what is going on," Forsyth said.

Dain was surprised to hear Bystrom sound retreat. "Doesn't look like Bystrom wants to show us how to fight Indians," he said to Ron.

"Talk is easy," Ron said. "Backing it up is sometimes a little harder."

As dawn spread its soft light over the valley, the landscape materialized out of the misty morning air like a vision in a dream. The valley was quiet, peaceful. Dain wondered if that raid had been an isolated incident.

The horses were nervous, as if they sensed a danger the men only imagined. The men stood by their horses, calming them, waiting. There was no sound except the champing of teeth on bridle bits. If there was any movement in the valley, it was hidden in the dim dawn light.

The sun got closer to the eastern horizon and the light grew stronger in the valley. Suddenly Dain caught his breath as hundreds of mounted Indians came pouring between the bluffs at the upper end of the valley a mile away and charged down toward them. There were enough to run over them without slowing their charge, he was sure.

"Mount up!" Forsyth yelled and every man swung into his saddle, gripping his rifle, ready to fight or run.

Suddenly the grass to the west seemed to explode with hundreds of Indians on foot. During the lull, warriors had apparently come out into the valley under cover of darkness. When it got light enough for them to be seen, they had dropped down in the grass and crawled forward. Stillwell had said that an Indian could hide in inch-tall grass like a snake. There were hundreds of Indians on foot running toward them now.

"To the east!" Bystrom bawled. "We can outrun them."

"Shut up!" Grover shouted. "That's exactly what they want us to do. You can bet there are hundreds of Indians down in that gap we came through yesterday just waiting for us."

"Where to then?" someone shouted.

"To the island!" Forsyth shouted. "Dismount and lead your horses. Stay on the right side of them."

Dain saw the wisdom of that but he hated to sacrifice the speed his horse had. But the riders would make too big a target for the Indians if they stayed in the saddle.

The men leaped off their horses, caught the bridle reins close to the bit and hid themselves from the Indians by staying on the right sides of their horses. They made excellent time running toward the island, the horses trotting rapidly beside them.

It seemed like confusion yet there was order in the rush toward the island. It wasn't far to the creek bank and they plunged out onto the sand, sending it flying as they raced for the island. Dain was aware that Ron was beside him and that the Indians were firing, although most of them were still out of range. The mounted Indians were passing those on foot now and were rapidly getting close enough that their bullets would begin taking their toll.

Dain whipped a look to the west over his horse's neck. Indians were still pouring through the gap between the bluffs. The upper valley was being pounded by hundreds of ponies carrying warriors to battle. The valley floor seemed to sprout thousands of warriors.

Their estimate had been low. There were even more warriors than anyone had believed possible.

The sand stretched about sixty yards to the edge of the water that trickled past the island. It dragged at Dain's feet and made running a torture. Even his horse was slowed.

Just as Dain and his horse lunged up out of the creek bed onto the island, tearing through the sage grass that grew on the island, the horse flinched and stumbled, then regained his feet. Dain knew he'd been hit by a bullet. The mounted Indians were well within range of the scouts now.

Once on the island, some of the scouts stepped free of their horses to fire at the charging Indians. Others stayed behind their horses and fired across their saddles, using the horses for protection.

The howls of the Indians were filled with fury. Since this was Dain's first battle with Indians, he assumed that this was their usual method of fighting. But Grover set things straight.

"They're madder than scalded lizards because we got to this island," he shouted at Forsyth. "They didn't expect this. If they'd sent some warriors to hold this island, we'd have been trapped and we'd all have been dead by now."

"They may have some trouble digging us out of here," Forsyth said. "Half of you keep firing. The other half start digging holes to hide in while you fight."

That made more sense to Dain then any order he'd heard since he started on this mission. He yelled at Ron above the din of rifles and Indian yells.

"You dig. I'll keep shooting."

Ron dropped to his knees and started clawing at the tough sage grass roots. Dain tossed the knife he had taken from Wolfcry to Ron. With that, Ron soon tore through the grass roots. The sand beneath the grass was loose and fairly easy to scoop out.

The dismounted warriors were getting closer to the island now. Dain fired carefully at one and saw him drop like a rock. Other scouts were firing, too, with good success. The warriors took the hint and dropped down in the grass. Dain had to watch for a target and when it appeared it was only for a second.

The mounted warriors made bigger targets but they were circling now, almost out of rifle range. They were screaming their rage. Their easy victory had gone sour and they were furious and frustrated.

Out on the sand in the middle of the creek bed, Dain saw one of the pack mules stretched out. Losing the mule was not so bad but that mule had been packing either ammunition or medical supplies. They couldn't afford to lose either. From the size of the pack, Dain guessed it was the medical supplies.

The horses had been tied to the shrubbery and the men were behind them digging their pits. The Indians who had crept up close to the creek bank in the sage grass were using the horses as their targets now. One by one the horses were going down, floundering in their death throes. The men had to watch for flaying hoofs.

The fury of the Indians' yells grew louder as they realized that the scouts were digging into the sand and would use those sandbanks as well as the dead horses as breastworks from which to carry on the battle.

A stream of mounted warriors came up from the east where they had apparently been waiting for the scouts to come dashing down the valley to escape the first onslaught of the warriors from the west. Choosing the island instead of dashing in retreat down the valley had kept the scouts out of that ambush.

With the warriors from the thwarted ambush joining in the big circle going around the island, it seemed to Dain that all the Indians in the world must be out there. The digging was proceeding at a furious pace as some scouts dug while others fired at any Indian who showed his head within rifle range.

The mounted Indians were riding in circles around the island, churning up the sand as they raced across the mostly dry creek bed. They were careful not to present a decent target, riding on the far side of their horses with only a leg presented to the rifles on the island. Their shots, fired under the necks of their running horses, were not especially effective. The Indians hiding in the grass along the banks were a different matter. Some were good shots and they forced the scouts to keep their heads down below the sand breastworks.

"Make every shot count," Forsyth yelled. "We may need all our ammunition."

Dain guessed that if they could kill an Indian with each bullet they had, they still wouldn't have enough bullets. He was aware that they weren't hitting many of the enemy with their shots.

One by one, the horses were being killed. Dain almost felt the bullets when his own horse was hit three times. Still the horse stood, quivering as if he had a chill. Then two more bullets brought him down. He kicked a few times, then lay still.

"My horse is down, too," Ron said. "They've made it impossible for us to leave. Now they'll kill us at their leisure."

"We can make them pay a price for the privilege," Dain said.

Dain looked around the crude rectangle the men had made with their pits around the island. All were digging their holes deeper, using the added protection of their fallen horses.

Dain saw the last horse stagger and fall. Now they were fifty stranded men, without a horse to ride. Someone out on the creek bank saw the same thing.

"There goes their last horse," a voice shouted.

Dain caught his breath. "There must be a white man out there."

"Hear that?" Grover called to Forsyth. "Must be one of Bent's boys with them."

"Likely," another man said. "No Indian could speak English that well."

Dain wasn't so sure of that. He knew that a couple of William Bent's boys lived with the Indians. But Dain was thinking of Jed Wolfcry.

He wondered if it had been Jed who had yelled. He'd like to believe that. It would mean that Wolfcry was with the Indians and Dain was this close to him. Just how he was going to confront Wolfcry was a problem but he'd take almost any chance to get to face him and make him pay for the loss of his family.

The mounted Indians began to drop out of the circle they had been riding around the island. They apparently had decided that the damage they were doing to the scouts wasn't worth the risk they were taking. The warriors on the creek bank could do better and their firing did get heavier.

"Dig, dig, dig!" came the call. Dain took his turn at digging while Ron watched for an Indian head to shoot at. Exposing even an arm was risky business. The Indians shot at anything that moved on the island. Dain had heard that Indians couldn't hit anything with a rifle but he'd discovered that there were some out there who could come dangerously close with every shot.

Looking around at those he could see from his pit, he saw blood on more than one man. At this rate, every scout would soon be killed or wounded. Then the Indians could charge in and kill all that were still alive.

Dain didn't have to use his knife in the sand. Once Ron had carved through the sage grass roots, the loose sand scooped out easily. He dug his tin plate out of his haversack and found that it worked almost like a shovel to heap the sand in front of the pit he and Ron would share. The pit was still too small and too shallow to afford protection for both of them.

Dain traded places with Ron again. As he watched for a target, Dain considered their situation. Fifty-one scouts, some already wounded, maybe some dead, against hordes of Indians, perhaps numbering in the thousands. Dain saw only one possible outcome. The scouts could only hope to sell their lives dearly.

To add to their troubles, word came filtering down from pit to pit that Dr. Mooers, the army surgeon and only medical man in the group, had been hit in the head and was delirious. Colonel Forsyth said there was no hope of his recovering.

There were wounded all around Dain and now there was no doctor. Then more bad news was passed—that all the medical supplies had been lost when the pack mule had been killed crossing the dry sand of the creek bed.

Not far from Dain's pit was the hole that Gus Bystrom had dug. He had dug sand like a badger and had the deepest pit on the island. Now he cowered in the bottom, not lifting his head or his rifle to fire at the enemy.

Dain discovered that he was not the only one who had noticed Bystrom's cowardice. A man on the other side of Bystrom yelled to a companion during a sudden lull in the firing.

"Look at our brave Indian fighter! He's showing us how to fight Indians."

Now others jeered at Bystrom. Dain expected him to speak up in his own defense or at least use his rifle. But he only scrounged lower in his pit, making sure no part of him showed for a target for some Indian sharpshooter.

Dain couldn't see any other man hiding in his pit. Bystrom was the only coward in the group. And he had been the one who had ridiculed the others for being nervous about the prospects of the coming fight.

The only feeling Dain had for Bystrom was anger and disgust. Bystrom had to be humiliated at the scorn turned on him but Dain felt no sympathy. It did mean the scouts had one less rifle to use against the warriors. The fury of the Indians was apparent. Their easy victory had become a bitter fight. The volleys they were slamming into the island spoke of their frustration and determination to correct their error in not occupying the island themselves.

"How long can we hold out?" one man called to anyone who would answer.

"We'll still be here when all the redskins are done for," another man shouted back.

A cheer came from several throats. Dain realized that not all the determination was on the Indian side.

Dain noted a spot where a rifle was consistently peppering shots into the embankment he and Ron were building. He centered on the spot and when the Indian lifted his head to fire, Dain fired first. The rifle went silent.

Dain and Ron changed places again. A few riders were still racing back and forth just out of effective rifle range. It was a temptation to fire at them but Forsyth had advised them to fire only at targets they had a good chance of hitting. Forsyth himself was down in his pit, wounded in the hip and with a broken leg. But he still kept command of the scouts.

The riders were encouraging the warriors along the river banks. But those warriors were becoming more cautious. The sharpshooters on the island were teaching their lessons well.

The Indian women and children had gathered on the bluff to the north of the battleground and were cheering their warriors on. In spite of this, the fighters along the riverbanks were showing more wariness than courage now and the firing on both sides was settling down to carefully chosen shots.

News filtered around the row of pits. Forsyth had three wounds, the last a glancing blow to the head, but he assured them it was not serious. Two scouts were dead; several wounded. Some of the wounded would be able to fight if the Indians rushed them.

"Think they will?" Dain asked.

"They'll give it everything they have," Stillwell said. "If they make a concentrated charge, we'll have our hands full."

Listening to what Stillwell didn't say, Dain realized they would have little chance if the Indians were willing to sacrifice enough men. They could simply overrun them with sheer numbers.

"Some of those Indians must have Spencer rifles," Grover said.

"They probably came from Fetterman's men," another man said.

"The Sioux killed more than eighty men there and took all their weapons. Likely the Cheyennes got some of those rifles."

Now that the snipers were becoming more cautious, mounted warriors were dashing toward the island, firing their rifles, then peeling off when the scouts fired back. Then a second group would charge, then a third. None were a serious threat to charge over the island.

"Each little band of warriors tries to show that it is braver than the others," Stillwell said. "They don't fight together well."

That was little consolation to Dain considering the situation. They had to whip all the Indians out there to survive. There was small chance of that.

The riders were called back then by the sharp tones of a bugle. Dain heard it and stuck his head up, then dropped down quickly after seeing the riders heading away. The snipers along the banks weren't pulling back.

"Got to be a white man out there," Ron said.

"Maybe not," Dain said. "The Indians probably captured a bugle when they massacred Fetterman's men at Fort Phil Kearny. Anybody could learn to blow a blast on a bugle. That wasn't any bugle call I ever heard."

"It seemed to have a message for the Indians," Ron said.

Dain stole another look over the embankment. The Indian horsemen were heading downstream toward the gap in the bluffs that they had come through yesterday afternoon. Dain guessed that well over half the mounted warriors out there were riding away.

"Are they leaving?" Bystrom asked, peeking out of his pit for the first time since he'd dug it. He was ignored.

"Looks like bad trouble, Colonel," Grover said. "They're not giving up so the only reason they're going down there is to organize a charge. There will be several hundred warriors, the elite of the fighters."

"What chance will we have, Grover?" Forsyth asked.

Grover shook his head. "We'll just do the best we can."

Seventeen

BLACK SKY had been on guard the first part of the night. So he had slept through the latter part of the night. Those who had been able to sleep the first part of the night were up early and preparing for battle. The war societies had decided that they would not wait for the soldiers to come into their ambush. They might discover it and avoid it. The warriors could slip up and surround the camp before daybreak and there would be no chance of failure.

The leader of the Crazy Dog Society suggested an ambush laid at the gap downstream from the soldiers' camp. With a dawn charge of Indians from the west, the soldiers might run east. The warriors hiding there could kill them as they came through the gap. Fifty Crazy Dog soldiers were assigned that duty and told to go at midnight, detouring far to the south of the soldiers.

Wild Fox nudged Black Sky awake well before dawn and he got up and began preparing for battle. Many of the warriors were already starting out on foot. They would crawl as close to the soldier camp as possible. Then the mounted warriors would charge out of the gap and surround the soldier camp or drive them toward the ambush. No soldier would escape. This would be the first step in driving the white men back across the big river to the east.

Before this day was over, the soldiers would be dead and the warriors would be riding down the Republican and Smoky Hill rivers. Both groups would sweep to the east, killing every settler, burning every building. When the soldiers came out from Fort Wallace, they would ambush them and, once they were gone, the warriors would race on without serious opposition until they met the soldiers from Fort Hays and Fort Harker. There were enough warriors to overpower those soldiers, too. Black Sky had doubts about that but the chiefs were certain. It made no difference. This was a matter of life and death for the Cheyennes and other tribes. They had to eliminate the white invaders or starve to death. The only alternative was to go to a reservation. Black Sky would rather die than do that.

He had his war paint partly on when he heard distant rifle fire. Instantly he knew what had happened. Some warriors had gotten overanxious. They had ridden out into the valley and charged the soldier camp, hoping to steal the horses and leave the soldiers afoot.

That ruined the surprise. Unless those rebel braves had succeeded in their raid, the rest of the warriors would have a tough battle on their hands. They had been depending on surprise to kill the soldiers and not risk any Cheyenne lives. That surprise was gone now.

Before Black Sky was ready for battle, the raiders returned. They had only two horses and two pack mules. The chiefs scolded them severely. Black Sky knew they'd get more punishment after the battle was over. He agreed they deserved it. Their impetuous action would probably cost the lives of many warriors.

Many of the warriors who had been up longer than Black Sky had their war paint on. Only a few warriors painted their horses so Black Sky didn't feel so naked with an unpainted horse. But he always put paint on the chest and front legs of his war pony, mainly because Roman Nose did that. He hoped someday to be as great a warrior as Roman Nose.

Black Sky raced for his war pony. Wild Fox and Sparrow had their horses close to his.

"Have the warriors without horses had time to reach the soldiers' camp?" Black Sky asked.

Wild Fox shook his head. "Not yet. But they are the warriors with good rifles and are good shots. They will be ready if the soldiers come this way."

"How about that new man who came to us?"

"Wolfcry? He was the first to volunteer. He saw that man he hates among the soldiers, you know, and he thinks he'll have a better chance of killing him if he is on foot. He can creep closer. He says he is good with a rifle."

The horses were ready then and they charged through the gap into the big valley. It was later than Black Sky had thought. It was light enough that he could see the black cluster of men and horses that were the soldiers.

There were warriors all around Black Sky. There was no organization to this charge. Each man was riding hard, hoping to get to the soldiers in time to count coup on some of them.

When Black Sky worked his way up to the place where he could clearly see the soldiers, he was surprised to see them leading their horses at a trot toward the creek. They must think they could defend themselves better in the creek bed. The banks really weren't high enough to be much protection.

Black Sky urged his horse to top speed. The soldiers were getting away although they couldn't get far on foot, leading their horses. But the warriors had no targets to shoot at, either, because the men were not in their saddles.

The soldiers hit the creek and kept right on going. Then Black Sky saw where they were headed, the island. If they had time to dig into the sand there, it might be very hard to get at them.

One of the war chiefs realized what they were doing and his scream of rage echoed over the valley. Black Sky realized that the warriors had made a bad mistake in not sending men down to occupy that island. If they'd been there with rifles, they could have stopped the retreat to the island and kept the soldiers out in the creek bed where they could have all been killed in a few minutes. It was too late now.

A wild war cry swept through the riders and Black Sky picked it up, adding all the volume he could. Those soldiers had to know they were hearing their own death cry.

The riders swept on, passing the men on foot. Those men were running now, shooting now and then. Black Sky swung his Spencer rifle around and aimed at the men running for the island. He fired but he didn't have any specific target. The men were all hidden by their trotting horses.

The two pack mules were lumbering along behind the horses. Bullets from the warriors killed one of the mules and he flopped into the sand halfway between the bank and the island.

Black Sky realized that even the warriors on foot weren't going to be able to help much because they couldn't get any closer than the bank of the creek and that was at least seventy yards from the island. If the soldiers kept down in the sand, the Indian sharpshooters wouldn't have much to shoot at. Their accuracy at that distance would be questionable, too.

Black Sky fired only a few shots at the soldiers before they reached the island. Then he joined the other warriors galloping around the island in a big circle, firing under his horse's neck at the soldiers. He was sure they scored some hits but the soldiers were firing, too, and their accuracy drove the warriors into a much wider circle, at long range for the soldiers' rifles.

Things had not gone at all as planned. They had expected the soldiers to stand and fight where they were or dash away to the east. In either case, the warriors would have finished the battle in a few minutes. Now they would have to find another way to kill those soldiers digging in on the island. The fifty Crazy Dog soldiers that had been waiting in ambush near the gap at the lower end of the valley rode up to join the warriors riding around the island fortress.

Black Sky soon realized that the Kit Fox and Crazy Dog soldiers had stopped riding around the island and were gathering, planning their own strategy. The different war societies seldom worked together and apparently they weren't going to do it today, either. Black Sky stopped to rest his pony.

The Kit Fox soldiers gathered on the slope south of the island and suddenly made a dash toward the island. If they could overrun it, they'd be the heroes and they would be the ones who would count the coups.

Before they reached the creek bank, the rifles on the island began mowing them down. The charge broke at the creek bank and the warriors swung to the east and west. Black Sky saw that it was going to take a lot more effort than that to overpower the soldiers.

The women and children had climbed to the top of the bluff on the north side of the river where they had a perfect view of the entire battlefield. They were screaming encouragement to their men but there were some wails mingled with the shouts as the Kit Fox soldiers were turned back, leaving some dead on the creek bank.

The warriors on foot had crawled up close to the creek bank and, hidden in the sage grass, were firing at any target they saw on the island. They had killed all the horses so the soldiers couldn't run away.

It was a stalemate. The Indians couldn't get at the men, digging into the sand behind their dead horses; the soldiers couldn't get away. The soldiers would die but it was going to cost the Indians some warriors to overpower them or some time to starve them out. They couldn't afford either.

Sparrow came by where Black Sky and Wild Fox had been resting their horses. It was becoming obvious that it was foolish to wear out their horses riding around that island when they couldn't get a decent shot at any of the soldiers.

"The chief wants the Dog Soldiers to charge them," Sparrow reported. "He said there are enough of us to run right over the island."

"We'll lose some warriors," Wild Fox said. "We must have Roman Nose to lead us."

Black Sky had been aware of Roman Nose's absence. At first, he hadn't missed him. But as they rode aimlessly around the island, he became aware that they had no leadership.

He knew why Roman Nose wasn't here. His medicine was bad. He was sure that if he fought before he got rid of the curse on his medicine, he'd be killed. But not many knew of that curse.

One of the lesser chiefs, Eagle Wing, came over to them. Eagle Wing knew that Black Sky was a close friend of Roman Nose.

"Where is Roman Nose?" the chief demanded.

"His medicine is bad," Black Sky said. "If he fights today, he will die."

"We need our greatest warrior," Eagle Wing said. "Come, we will talk to him. You lead the way."

Black Sky knew about where Roman Nose would be. His camp was close to the gap where they had laid the ambush yesterday. Black Sky doubted if Roman Nose had left his camp this morning.

Black Sky rode with Eagle Wing. Wild Fox and Sparrow followed. They left the battlefield behind where a thousand warriors surrounded the island. They found Roman Nose near his camp, walking around dejectedly.

Black Sky dismounted. "We've been looking for you," he said. "We need you to lead the Dog Soldiers."

"The battle is not going well?" Roman Nose asked.

"The soldiers are dug in on a little island in the river," Black Sky said. "We can't get at them. Chief Eagle Wing says we must charge them."

"You know why I can't fight today," Roman Nose said. To Eagle Wing, he continued, "At a Sioux camp, I ate meat and bread that had been taken up with an iron fork. I have not had time to go through the ceremony to remove the curse from my war bonnet."

"Don't wear your war bonnet," Eagle Wing said.

"That war bonnet is what keeps me alive," Roman Nose said

angrily. No one had ever challenged the magic of his war bonnet before.

"Your men are dying out there," Eagle Wing went on. "And here you stand, hiding behind a hill."

"They can fight without me," Roman Nose said.

"They will not fight without you," Eagle Wing said.

Black Sky knew that the chief was right. He also knew the fear that Roman Nose had because his medicine was broken. Eagle Wing had hit Roman Nose in a vulnerable spot. Roman Nose was a brave warrior. Nobody dared say that he was a coward.

"I will fight," he said.

Black Sky wasn't sure he liked this decision. He would have been afraid to ride into battle with the Dog Soldiers without Roman Nose leading. But with Roman Nose leading, he'd be afraid for his friend because his medicine had been broken.

"I will prepare," Roman Nose said. "I will tell the Dog Soldiers when I am ready to fight."

Eagle Wing turned back toward the valley. Wild Fox and Sparrow went with him but Black Sky stayed with Roman Nose.

"Will you wear your war bonnet?" Black Sky asked.

"I will not go into battle without it," Roman Nose said. "If its magic is good, no enemy bullet or arrow can touch me."

They went back to Roman Nose's lodge and he took down his magnificent war bonnet. Roman Nose had told Black Sky how he got this bonnet and why it held such magic power.

Several years before, Roman Nose had asked a powerful shaman, White Bull, for something to wear or carry into battle that would protect him. White Bull said he'd had a vision just a short time before of a great war bonnet that he was to make for someone soon. He was sure this was the time.

Everything about the bonnet was special. First, White Bull had made paint from stones, bones and clay pounded to a powder then mixed with charcoal from a tree set on fire by lightning. Some of this paint was put on the headband.

Right on the front of the war bonnet was a buffalo horn and directly behind the horn was the skin of a kingfisher tied to the hair at the base of the buffalo horn. On the right side was the skin of a hawk.

Two rows of eagle feathers trailed all the way to the ground; the feathers on the right side were painted red and those on the left were white. Partway down the row of eagle feathers was the skin of a barnswallow, tied to the white feathers. On the red feathers was a bat skin. The bat flies high and at night it can't be caught. The barnswallow flies low and anyone shooting at the person wearing the bonnet will shoot at the person but the real person will be the swallow flying low so he won't be hit. The kingfisher worn on top of the head was there for the purpose of closing any holes that might be made in the warrior—when the kingfisher dived into water, the water closed over it immediately.

When White Bull gave Roman Nose the war bonnet, he also gave him instructions on how to wear it and what must not be done so the good medicine it carried would not be broken.

"After you put this on your head," he warned, "you must never shake hands with anyone. If you do, you will certainly be killed. Also, you must not eat any food that has been taken from a dish with a metal implement. That, also, will break the bonnet's magic."

The bonnet further required the wearer to prepare his horse for battle correctly. A scalp lock must be tied to the horse's jaw or bridle, and zigzag lines must be drawn down the front of the horse's legs to represent lightning.

Roman Nose had complete faith in the war bonnet. More than once he had ridden back and forth in front of his warriors, sometimes within twenty-five yards of the enemy who fired repeatedly at him and never touched him. Black Sky had seen that demonstration twice. He believed in the magic of the war bonnet as much as Roman Nose did. That was the reason he always rode just behind and to the right of Roman Nose when they rode into battle. The magic of the war bonnet also protected him, Black Sky believed.

Black Sky helped Roman Nose paint the zigzag lines on the front of his chestnut war pony and down each front leg. Then he painted the same zigzag lines on his own horse and he painted the black and red lines down his face the same as Roman Nose did.

Black Sky put on his war bonnet which was simply a circle of raven feathers standing upright on a chaplet around his head. It had no tail. All the Dog Soldiers had bonnets like this.

Roman Nose and Black Sky rode through the gap and out into the valley. It was midmorning and the rifles were rattling down around the island. Black Sky couldn't see that anything had changed since he rode out to find Roman Nose. He was sure it wouldn't change until the Dog Soldiers made their charge. That should end the battle quickly. By tonight they should be camped down the rivers on their way to drive out the settlers.

Staying well to the south of the island, they stopped even with the battle. Roman Nose waved his hand and one of the Dog Soldiers blew a blast on a bugle that a Sioux had given him. The Dog Soldiers began leaving the fight and coming up the slope toward Roman Nose. Roman Nose looked over the battlefield. Then he turned and rode off toward the bluffs down the valley that closed in on the creek.

He hadn't said a word but no word was needed. Every Dog Soldier rode silently behind Roman Nose until they had passed through the gap and out of sight of the island where the soldiers were pinned down by the snipers.

"We will run right over them," Roman Nose said. "Kill all you can as you go over them. Then we'll come back and finish the job. Get ready."

Black Sky took his rifle and held it to the sky, then to the ground. Then he held it to the north, east, south and west. He was imploring the help of the god of the sky and the god of the earth and of the spirits of the four points of the compass. Finally he raised the rifle to the sun.

Each warrior ran his long rope twice around the belly of his horse and over his knees. That was to help keep the rider on his horse, even if he was wounded. No warrior wanted to fall in battle where the enemy could get to him. If he was wounded, he would turn toward his own people and depend on the rope to hold him on his horse till he got there.

Roman Nose assigned Medicine Man to lead the right side of the charge while he led the left side. Trotting their horses through the gap, they spread out in a long line. Black Sky was at his usual place, just to the right and behind Roman Nose. The line stretched out almost sixty abreast. After they all got through the gap, Black Sky looked back and saw that there were about five ranks of warriors. There had to be five or six times as many warriors as there were soldiers. And the warriors had Roman Nose to lead them. The soldiers couldn't possibly have a leader as great as that.

Each warrior wore his war bonnet of black raven feathers and held his position in line as Roman Nose expected. Their line was long enough to sweep completely across the island as they rode over it. No soldier would escape.

Black Sky had never been prouder than he was as they trotted up the valley. They were absolutely invincible. He knew they made a magnificent picture riding up the valley before they made their charge. Already he could hear the wild cheering of the women and children on the hill north of the island, waiting to see the hated white men annihilated.

The only thing that nagged at Black Sky was Roman Nose's certainty that his good medicine had been broken. It just couldn't be. There had never been such a wonderful specimen of a warrior. Roman Nose was almost a head taller than any man behind him, broad of shoulder, the picture of the invincible warrior.

Roman Nose halted the warriors, then rode slowly along the entire line, cautioning the impatient ones to wait until ordered to charge. Black Sky knew that the delay must be wearing on the nerves of the soldiers and likely Roman Nose was using this to make the battle easier.

Roman Nose came back to his spot in front of Black Sky. Rising as high as he could considering the ropes lashed over his knees, he lifted his rifle at arm's length above his head, saluting the women and children on the hill. Then, twirling the rifle around as if it was a small stick, he gave his war whoop which, coming from that deep chest, echoed over the entire valley. Every man behind him echoed the war whoop.

Excitement almost choked Black Sky as he screamed, then kicked his pony into a dead run as the line swept forward like one continuous wave. The battle was on.

Eighteen

DAIN HAD NEVER SEEN anything like it. He didn't know a great deal about Plains Indians but he'd heard that they fought individually, never as a unit. They never made a massive charge as white soldiers did. Yet if he'd ever seen a disciplined organized movement, it was the one coming up the valley now.

This wasn't a charge yet. But there was no doubt in Dain's mind that it was going to develop into one. He used his small binoculars. Most of the scouts had a pair among their personal things.

Those Indians had come through the gap, then halted as the big Indian at the head held up a hand. Without any orders, the warriors behind him had formed a long line. Then more Indians had formed another line behind the first one. A third and fourth line had developed. Dain couldn't see if there were more lines behind that. A swift count showed between fifty and sixty in that first line. If they came straight at the island, they would overrun every foot of it and many of the Indians would be out in the sandy bed of the creek on either side.

Dain had no doubts about the Indians' intentions. This sweep would completely annihilate the scouts. It could hardly end any other way provided the Indians held to the discipline they were showing now.

The lines began moving forward at a slow trot. Every man in the pits was turned toward the advancing Indians now. Forsyth's orders were to load every rifle and revolver to the limit. Each scout would have seven shots in his rifle and six in his revolver.

"Don't shoot until I give the order," Forsyth said. He was propped up in his pit. With a wound in his hip and the other leg broken, he wasn't able to move much. But nobody questioned his orders.

Keeping as low as possible and still watch the proceedings, Dain swallowed the cold lump in his throat. He felt he was witnessing his last scene on this earth. A cold calm settled over him.

He concentrated his binoculars on the big Indian in front. He was magnificent. He had to admire that warrior.

"Who is that big Indian?" he asked of no one in particular.

"Roman Nose," Stillwell said from the next pit.

"He must be the big chief of the whole tribe," Dain said in awe.

"He's not a chief," Stillwell said. "He's the leader of the Dog Soldiers, their best fighters." He breathed softly. "I never saw Indians following orders like that," he almost whispered.

Dain still watched Roman Nose. He had a huge war bonnet that flowed from his head down over the back of his horse. There was a rope around the belly of his horse pulled tight over his knees. He had a rifle lying across the horse's mane, cradled in the elbow of his left arm. He was totally naked except for a bright red sash tied around his middle and moccasins on his feet. His face was streaked with black and red lines, giving him the look of a monster from a nightmare. Even the front legs of his horse had black zigzag streaks down the length of them.

Still out of rifle range of the scouts, Roman Nose reined up his horse, then rode slowly down the length of the line. Final orders, Dain guessed. He was surprised at how calm he was now that he was facing death head-on. Roman Nose came back to his original place at the front of the line, then turned to the bluff north of the island where the women and children were waving and screaming encouragement to the warriors.

Lifting his rifle high in his right hand, he saluted the women and they responded with renewed cheers and screams. Then, turning to face the scouts on the island, Roman Nose lifted his rifle high in his right hand and shook it at the scouts.

Then throwing back his head, he uttered a wild war cry. Dain had never heard anything even remotely like that. Behind their leader, the warriors each added his own war cry until the valley echoed with the sound like the crash of thunder after a lightning strike.

Roman Nose's hand and rifle came forward, pointing directly toward the island. His horse bolted ahead. Every warrior followed. The lines kept straight. It was a charge that would have done credit to the best-trained cavalry unit in the U.S. Army. The scouts seemed to be hypnotized by a sight they could scarcely believe. Perhaps it was the inspiration of the Indian leader. Dain doubted if there ever had been or ever would be another like Roman Nose.

Every rifle was cocked and waiting orders from Forsyth. Even the rifles of the men unable to fight now had been taken over by the uninjured scouts; those rifles were loaded and laid beside the scouts ready to use when their own guns were empty.

The charge came forward, sixty warriors abreast and five or six ranks deep. Dain stretched a little higher for a better look and so did some around him.

Grover suddenly screamed. "Get down! Everybody, get down!"

Dain hadn't realized he was half standing in his pit watching the charge. He dropped like a rock and so did the others. They were none too soon. The snipers along the creek bank opened up with a withering barrage, apparently intended to keep the scouts down so they couldn't fire at the charging Indians. Dain guessed that even the warriors along the creek had been captivated by the magnificence of Roman Nose's Dog Soldiers. Grover's yell had brought them to their senses, too.

Dain crouched in his pit, rifle in hand, finger on the trigger. He didn't dare poke his head up to see where the Indians were. To jump up now and shoot at the Indians would mean almost certain death. The snipers would have to stop soon or they'd risk hitting their own warriors.

As Dain expected, the snipers suddenly stopped shooting. The charge must be close. Forsyth reared up in his pit as far as his wounds would permit.

"Now!" he screamed.

Dain came up along with every man around him. The charging Indians were only twenty yards from the foot of the island. Dain picked the warrior directly in front of him. He had never shot at a man before with the intent to kill. But now, knowing what these warriors would do to him if they got the chance, there was no hesitation.

He didn't even pause to see if he had hit his first target. He picked another warrior and fired again. His firing seemed right in unison with the other scouts'.

The first volley had knocked over many warriors and some horses. The second volley hit more horses than men but it left big gaps in the ranks of the charging warriors. Those warriors closed ranks, filling the gaps the first two volleys had made.

The third volley made more holes in those front ranks but still the charge came on. Medicine Man was still on his horse on the right. Roman Nose was riding unscathed on the left. There was little doubt in Dain's mind that the Indians were going to ride right over the island and every scout would be killed by bullet or lance. There were more lances than rifles among the warriors.

The fourth volley from the scouts came as the Indians were almost on the island. Medicine Man went down over to the north. But still Roman Nose came on, untouched. Dain realized that as long as he was leading, those warriors would keep coming, even if it meant certain death for them.

Moving his sights a couple of inches, he got the big man in his view. As he pulled the trigger, he realized that those around him had picked the same target.

Roman Nose and his great chestnut war pony went down together, right at the edge of the island. The horse's head was actually on the land. It couldn't have been more than a few feet from the rifle pits at the end of the island.

Dain jerked his eyes away from the fallen leader and sent another shot into the Indians who were on the edge of the island now. But suddenly the wave split, half the Indians racing along the south side of the island, the other half along the north side. Dain knew without consciously thinking about it that it was the fall of Roman Nose that had broken the spirit and the charge. Without their great leader, the Indians could not carry on.

Dain's last shot in his rifle was made broadside at the Indians racing past the island. He dropped the rifle and grabbed his revolver. He emptied it before the last Indian was out of range.

A triumphant shout went up from the men as they stood up, firing their revolvers after the fleeing Indians. Then suddenly Grover screamed at them.

"Get down! Get down!"

Again Dain dropped flat on his stomach. Momentarily he had forgotten himself in the exhilaration of surviving the charge. The surprised and raging Indians along the banks of the creek sent a blistering barrage over the island. They kept up the bombardment for two minutes. No one raised a head.

"If we hadn't killed Roman Nose, we'd all be dead now," Stillwell said in the lull that followed the bombardment from the snipers.

"I thought we were goners," Ron said.

"I don't think we were all in it," Stillwell said. He slid over the edge of his pit and down to Bystrom's pit. He took the rifle from Bystrom's hand. He examined it, then dropped it back on top of Bystrom.

"Just what I thought," he said disgustedly. "Not one bullet has been fired!"

"He ought to be thrown off the island," Ron said. "He's taking up space we could use."

Bystrom cowered in the bottom of his pit and didn't say a word. Dain was disgusted, but in a way he felt sorry for him. His bragging had apparently been an effort to cover up his cowardice. He had obviously expected the Indians to run from the menace of the scouts. When they didn't, his bravado had vanished.

Word filtered down through the pits that Lieutenant Beecher had been killed during the charge. Dr. Mooers was dying. So Colonel Forsyth, three times wounded, was the only officer left to command the unit of scouts.

Dain took a look down the creek. He was surprised at the number of dead warriors and horses scattered over the sand and in the shallow water. That testified to the marksmanship of the scouts under fire. Most were veterans of the recent war and had been tested before.

The wailing from the hill to the north also spoke of the effectiveness of the scouts' defense. Dain had thought the cheering of the thousand or so women and children on the hill had been loud. But it hadn't disturbed him like this wailing as they mourned for their dead.

Colonel Forsyth propped himself up on an elbow. "Can they do any better than that, Grover?" he asked.

"I don't think so, Colonel," Grover said. "I've never seen anything like that in all my days. Their leaders are dead. I doubt if they'll have grit enough to charge us again."

Dain hoped Grover was right. He knew it wouldn't take nearly as strong a charge to overpower them as the one that Roman Nose had mounted. The scouts had not come through unscathed. Besides the death of Lieutenant Beecher, there were several more wounded and probably some dead.

After the charge, the shooting settled down to sniper fire from the grass along the creek banks. Forsyth's orders were to keep down and not fire back at a sniper unless they could see what they were shooting at. They might need their ammunition more later on.

There was one sniper who was more accurate than the others. Dain noticed that the bullets coming from that one spot on the bank were always uncomfortably close. Ron had noticed that, too.

"Do you suppose that is the white man we think is over there?" Dain asked.

"Could be," Ron agreed. "If he's an Indian, he's had more experience with a rifle than most."

Dain couldn't help thinking of Jed Wolfcry. He'd had experience with a rifle. And Dain was certain he was with these Indians.

Dain and Ron used the lull in the fighting to deepen their pit until they could be reasonably comfortable and well out of sight of the snipers.

While they were doing that, Dain noticed that some mounted warriors were heading down the valley. He wondered if they were going to make another charge.

"What do you think they're up to?" Dain asked Stillwell in the next pit.

"Maybe another charge," Stillwell said. "Those were the Dog Soldiers under Roman Nose that we turned back this morning. I don't think they'll try it again. But there are other warrior societies. Each one usually fights alone, not together. We can be thankful for that."

Suddenly Dain thought of Valina. He hadn't thought of her all morning. He'd been too busy trying to stay alive. Even though they had won this skirmish, their chances of getting off the island were as slim as a shadow. He'd likely never see Valina again. That thought made him want to leap up and kill every Indian that stood between him and his Kansas home. But reason told him he didn't dare lift his head above his sand pit.

About two in the afternoon, the riders they had seen leaving came back in a weak imitation of Roman Nose's charge. There was no precision or organization nor were there the number of warriors.

They charged toward the island, each man strictly on his own. The scouts waited until the snipers stopped firing, then rose up and poured two volleys into the Indians. That was enough for them. They wheeled and raced away.

Bystrom stayed deep in his pit through this charge, too. The Indians had barely gotten out of rifle range when the scouts began ridiculing Bystrom for being such a coward, reminding him of his "brave" deeds. Dain knew he must be suffering the worst kind of humiliation but it didn't jar him into getting up and fighting.

About sundown, another charge came, this time from the west. Grover identified this group as Sioux. While they were a fairly large group, they apparently were already half convinced of the futility of trying to run over the entrenched scouts. Their charge was little more than a token as they veered to either side before they had much more than come within rifle range of the island.

Dain realized that they would probably not see any more serious charges. But that didn't mean they had any chance of getting out alive. They were without food; all their horses were dead, so they had no way of getting out of the country even if the Indians were gone. They would die here; the Indians would see to that.

Dain's dismal thoughts were interrupted when Ron said he was wounded in the leg. Since that last charge had not come close, Dain hadn't thought of anybody getting hurt. Apparently a spent bullet had hit him. The wound wasn't serious, he thought, but it would hamper his movements and would likely make it hard for him to hold a steady aim with his rifle.

Forsyth called for a report. Word was passed in from pit to pit. Four were dead, including Lieutenant Beecher. Ten were seriously wounded. That included Dr. Mooers, who hadn't spoken an intelligible word since he'd been hit in the early fighting. There were men who had lesser wounds, men who could fight if needed. That left twenty-eight able-bodied men. Dain was sure many of those were slightly wounded, like Ron, who wouldn't report his injury.

The wounded needed medicine but the medical supplies had been lost when the pack mule was killed crossing to the island. The doctor was dying. As Dain saw it, there was little hope for tomorrow.

Nineteen

THIS WAS A DAY Black Sky had never expected to see. He was as thrilled as he'd ever been when Roman Nose brought his warriors through the gap and lined them up for the charge against the soldiers on the island. With so many warriors moving together, those few soldiers could not possibly survive their charge.

Black Sky had taken his usual place just behind and to the right of Roman Nose. Roman Nose's good medicine had always protected Black Sky, too. He hoped for the same today.

When Roman Nose looked at the sky and voiced his war cry, Black Sky did the same. His cry was drowned in the cry of more than three hundred other warriors. It was as much a victory cry as a war cry. There was no way those few soldiers could stop this many determined warriors. And they were determined. The way they followed Roman Nose's instructions proved it.

Black Sky was appalled at the way the warriors were falling when the soldiers opened fire. He had never seen a slaughter like it. Still he concentrated on staying with Roman Nose. Together, they would ride over the hated soldiers and they would count coups on every one.

Black Sky felt almost as if a bullet had hit him when he saw Roman Nose's horse go down. That chestnut horse had carried the same medicine as Roman Nose and had never been hit even when Roman Nose had defied the soldiers by riding close to them.

But now the chestnut war pony was down. Black Sky took his eye off the enemy to see what Roman Nose would do without a horse. But as he galloped past the horse onto the edge of the island, he saw that Roman Nose had been hit, too. In fact, it looked as if he were already dead.

With an effort, Black Sky jerked his eyes away from Roman Nose and he saw that the other warriors were peeling off and going around the island. He suddenly felt totally alone.

Jerking the reins of his horse, he swung to the left, back into the water and out onto the dry sand of the creek bed. Every second he expected to feel a bullet cut him down. He knew why the others had swung away from the island. If Roman Nose's medicine had gone bad, then it would be bad for all the Dog Soldiers. They had depended on Roman Nose and his good medicine.

Black Sky hadn't realized how completely he himself had put his faith in Roman Nose's medicine. He suddenly felt as vulnerable as a baby where he had felt totally protected just a minute ago.

Riding hard, he made it past the island and out onto the grass of the riverbank. After seeing Roman Nose go down, he'd had the terrifying feeling that he would never ride away from that scene.

Some of the warriors began riding around the island beyond the range of the soldiers' guns and shooting at the island in frustration. Black Sky joined them for one full circle of the island, then gave up. He had never felt so low. He almost wanted to go up on the hill and join the women in the wailing for the dead. He was sure none of them could feel any worse about losing a husband or a son than he did over losing his good friend, Roman Nose.

He had screamed his fury, frustration and sorrow as he rode around the island but now he turned his horse away, feeling as if he were dead inside. He had followed Roman Nose into every battle in which he had fought. What would he do now?

One thing he could do. He could make those soldiers pay for killing his best friend. There was no way those soldiers could get away. They had no horses. The minute any of them tried to get away, they'd catch them and they'd make them pay for killing the Cheyennes' greatest warrior.

But the fury slowly died in him, replaced by deep sorrow. From a distance, he turned and surveyed the island and the scene of that fateful charge. He couldn't believe the number of horses and warriors that were strung over the battlefield. It was the worst loss he'd ever seen in any battle.

Black Sky's attention centered on only one fallen warrior. Roman Nose was lying just a couple of feet from his horse. Both had apparently been killed instantly. The rope wrapped around the belly of the horse and Roman Nose's knees had held him until the horse hit the ground.

Black Sky felt one strong urge. He had to get Roman Nose's body away from there before the white soldiers got to it. They might scalp him. Black Sky believed that a warrior who was scalped and mutilated would not be allowed to go to the camp of the dead where all good warriors went when they were killed.

Roman Nose had been the greatest warrior the Cheyennes had. Every effort had to be made to give him a decent send-off to the camp of the dead. And since Black Sky had been his special friend, it was up to him to see that they got the body and gave it a decent burial.

Black Sky considered making a dash to the island to recover the body. But he knew that would end in disaster. Since Roman Nose's magic was gone, no warrior would be safe from the soldiers' bullets. He'd be dead before he ever reached Roman Nose.

He saw the Crazy Dogs gathering. They were going to try to overrun the soldiers. Their only hope would be that Roman Nose's charge had hurt the soldiers so much that they couldn't put up much resistance. Black Sky didn't think it would be that way.

He wasn't surprised when the charge split up before the warriors got within twenty yards of the island. More dead warriors were lying over the field now. They did bring back their wounded. All the wounded from the Dog Soldiers' charge had been brought back with great risk to the rescuers. But the dead were left where they fell. Tonight, under cover of darkness, they would try to recover them.

The snipers along the creek banks kept up a sporadic fire, enough to keep every soldier confined to his pit. Occasionally a soldier would peek out. If a warrior saw him, he fired. One warrior, Wolfcry, never missed a chance to fire at any part of a soldier that was exposed. Black Sky marveled at his hatred for the soldiers. Black Sky hated them with a fury but Wolfcry's hatred was even deeper.

There was one man among those soldiers that Wolfcry had vowed to kill. Black Sky didn't know the whole story behind Wolfcry's hatred. Now that man was on the island and Wolfcry was determined to get him. He wasn't going to be satisfied to wait until the warriors killed all the soldiers. He wanted to personally kill this one man.

Black Sky pondered the battle they had fought. Why hadn't more than three hundred warriors been able to overrun fifty soldiers? It had to be the curse on Roman Nose's war bonnet. The good medicine of that bonnet had carried Roman Nose safely through every battle before. But the medicine had been broken when he ate food touched by an iron implement. Roman Nose had said he'd die if he went into battle today. And when he died, it meant that the medicine for all the Dog Soldiers had gone bad, too. They had no heart to continue once their leader was gone.

There were many Sioux warriors here. Some of them, along with Arapaho and Kiowa warriors, joined the Cheyenne warriors as snipers along the creek banks. But like the Cheyenne warrior societies, when they made a massive attack, they worked alone.

The Sioux chief was certain his warriors could finish the job that the Cheyennes had started and he gathered his warriors for a charge just before sundown. Black Sky watched, expecting it to fail as the others had. He wasn't surprised when it did.

As darkness fell, the snipers pulled back when they could no longer see what was happening on the island. Only one man stayed at his post, firing occasionally. That was the half-white Indian, Wolfcry. He apparently hated to give up, even for one night.

The chiefs and the leaders of the warrior societies met together a half mile from the island while the women went back to their camps beyond the bluffs upstream from the island. Black Sky stayed with the chiefs. He wanted to know the plan to recover the bodies of the warriors killed today.

The chiefs, however, had other things foremost on their minds. They gave orders for warriors to make separate camps all around the island, back far enough to be safe from the soldiers' rifles but close enough together that no soldier could slip between them and go for help.

Black Sky faded back before he could be assigned to one of those small camps. He had his work laid out for him tonight. He couldn't recover Roman Nose's body if he was stuck in a camp to watch for messengers trying to sneak away from the island.

Black Sky found Wild Fox and Sparrow and pulled them aside. "We have to get Roman Nose and give him a proper burial," he said.

They both agreed. "We'll have to be careful," Sparrow said. "He's right on the edge of the island."

"We'd better do it right away," Wild Fox said. "The soldiers might get to him if we don't."

Black Sky led the way down to the creek bank. Clouds were heavy and the night was as dark as the inside of a cave. That was just what Black Sky wanted. Their eyes, accustomed to the dark, still could not make out the island. But Black Sky knew from the creek bank just where the island was and he knew where Roman Nose had fallen. He was sure he could find him.

"We'll have to move quietly," he whispered.

The night was still but they could hear nothing as they stepped out on the sand. Before they got halfway across the sand, a wind sprang up and it began to rain. That was good, Black Sky thought. The spirits were with them. They wanted Roman Nose to be recovered. The wind and the rain would cover any sound they might make.

When they were close to the spot where Black Sky thought they'd find Roman Nose's body, he heard some shuffling ahead. It must be the men on the island shifting around. In the dark, they wouldn't be confined to their pits if they didn't mind the rain. Or maybe there were other warriors nearby trying to recover the other bodies that had fallen close to the island.

Black Sky came to the body of a horse. He couldn't be sure it was Roman Nose's horse. But he guessed it was. The wind and rain covered any sound they were making. He moved beyond the horse and found the body of a warrior. A hand run down the back located the long row of feathers and he knew he had found the body of Roman Nose. He also knew that the soldiers had not been here ahead of him. They would have taken that war bonnet if they'd found it.

Carefully, the three dragged the body through the shallow stream and across the sandy creek bed. Roman Nose had been a big man. He'd be hard to carry. Once they reached the creek bank, they lifted the body and took it out on the grass some distance.

"I'll get my horse and we'll take him to camp," Black Sky said. He hurried off to get his horse where he'd left him when he started this mission.

In fifteen minutes he was back and the three warriors lifted the body over the back of the pony.

"Where will we bury him?" Wild Fox asked.

"That will be up to his wife," Black Sky said. "She will be in the main camp. We'll take him there."

Leading his horse, Black Sky set off up the valley and through the gap between the bluffs. He knew the location of the camp where Roman Nose's widow would be. There was a fire in front of the lodge where she waited. She was expecting someone to bring her husband's body to her.

There was loud weeping and mourning from the widow and all the relatives of Roman Nose. Black Sky joined in. When the wailing had subsided, he asked the widow about the burial.

"He must be buried like the great warrior he was," she said. "On a scaffold beside a river. There is a medicine man here. We will take my husband inside the lodge and the medicine man will come."

Black Sky helped carry the body into the lodge where the ceremony would take place. They laid the body straight with arms at the side, the position in which he would be buried.

The medicine man arrived in a short time, apparently knowing that he would be called on for this ceremony. It was a short and simple ceremony to assure that the one who had died would find his way to the camp of the dead where he'd have all the pleasures of life, many of which he hadn't had in this life.

The medicine man lighted his sacred pipe and when it was going well, he offered the first smokes to the powerful god in the sky by pointing the pipe stem up. Then he pointed it downward, offering the smokes to the equally powerful god in the earth. Then he offered the smokes to the spirits, pointing the pipe stem first to the east, then to the south, then to the west, and finally to the north.

In his chant, the medicine man asked the spirits to guide Roman Nose as he followed the footprints that would lead him to the Milky Way and there he would locate the camp of the dead where he would find his friends who had already died. His life there would always be pleasant.

With the ceremony over, Roman Nose's widow, with the help of relatives, dressed him in his best clothes. Then they laid him on a blanket and robe, body extended, arms by his side. They folded the robes and blankets over the body until it was completely encased in them. The entire bundle was then lashed tightly with ropes.

While the widow and relatives mourned some more, Black Sky slipped away to find Little Dove. Many Horses was camped right beside this camp and he found her quickly.

"I just wanted to make sure you knew I was all right," he said.

She nodded. "I knew. I saw the battle. I saw the great warrior,

Roman Nose, go down. I saw you turn aside and escape. I was never so frightened in my life."

"We brought Roman Nose to his lodge. The ceremonies are over. We will take him wherever his widow says and bury him."

"How long will the battle here go on?" Little Dove asked.

"I don't know. It will start again at dawn. After tomorrow, we'll know. I hope we can finish it tomorrow. We have so much to do after we get rid of these soldiers."

"I'm afraid for you, Black Sky," she said softly.

"I will come back to you," Black Sky promised. "I must go now. We will bury Roman Nose as a great warrior should be buried."

Black Sky hurried back to the lodge of Roman Nose. A travois had been brought to take the body to the burial place. Roman Nose's widow helped the women relatives of Roman Nose take down the lodge. The lodge poles would be used to build the scaffold for his body.

The body was placed on the travois. Another travois carried the personal things that would be placed on the scaffold with Roman Nose. Those things included his rifle, his bow and arrows, axes and knives, his pipe and tobacco. He would need them in the camp of the dead. The lodge poles were also put on the travois. They brought along his favorite horse, second only to his chestnut war pony.

Black Sky thought the widow might have him buried somewhere close by on the Arikaree Creek but she wanted to go over to the south fork of the Republican River. It would be quite a trek. But to Black Sky, no amount of inconvenience would be too great to give Roman Nose the best possible send-off to the camp of the dead.

Most of the relatives went along with the funeral caravan. The women had slashed their legs so that blood ran down. Black Sky knew they wouldn't wash that blood off until they stopped mourning Roman Nose's death.

Black Sky had no idea what time it was when they stopped on the south fork of the Republican River. He helped erect the platform from the lodge poles they had brought from Roman Nose's lodge.

The platform was high because the lodge poles were long. It was a struggle to get the body up on the platform but it was done and all the special possessions of the great warrior were put on the platform with him so he'd have them in his next life.

Then the final act of the burial was performed. Roman Nose's

favorite horse was led under the platform and there he was shot.
Roman Nose would have that horse to ride in the next life.

Then began the long trek back to the Arikaree. They hurried because there was a job there to finish. They got to the battle site just before dawn. Black Sky, Sparrow and Wild Fox joined the Dog Soldiers. There was none of the enthusiasm for the battle that had driven them yesterday but there was grim determination. Those soldiers had to die! They had killed the greatest warrior any of them had ever known.

Black Sky inquired if any of the soldiers had tried to escape during the night. No one had seen any sign of them. Black Sky knew that there was a possibility that many of the soldiers had slipped away. As night guards, some warriors were not the best, he knew.

As dawn began to lighten the sky, several warriors, who apparently expected the soldiers to be gone, started boldly toward the island. Black Sky could understand their thinking even if he didn't share their convictions. Indians trapped like that would have slipped away under cover of darkness. And last night with the wind and rain, it should have been easy to slip away.

A rifle shot told him that his hunch was right. The soldiers were still right there waiting to resume the battle.

The Dog Soldiers strung out in a line and rode rapidly around the island, staying just beyond the rifle range of the trapped men. But while they were comparatively safe doing this, they were also too far away to do any damage to the soldiers.

The Indian snipers crawled up through the grass to the bank of the creek, led by Wolfcry, and began their bombardment. There was little response from the island but anytime a warrior showed himself, he drew a shot. This could go on for days. The soldiers would eventually starve but much time would be lost. Most of the warriors would lose interest and go away. Black Sky might do that himself.

No charge was made against the island this morning. Black Sky headed over where he saw the Cheyenne chiefs gathering. He asked one about the raids to the east along the Republican and Smoky Hill rivers. The chief shook his head sadly. There would be no raids now.

"Sioux, Arapaho—they are tired of this fight already," the chief said. "We have lost many of our best warriors. We can't go on the warpath now."

Black Sky recognized the truth in those words. Yesterday over a thousand warriors had failed to whip fifty soldiers. Too many war-

riors were dead; too many disheartened. The bond that had drawn
the tribes together for this great campaign down the rivers was broken. Black Sky had never felt so depressed. His best friend was dead.
The war against the white invaders was lost before it had ever really
begun.

They would kill these fifty soldiers who had put up such a fight,
even if they had to hold them here until they starved to death. But
the invaders had so many soldiers. The white soldiers would triumph
in the end. Black Sky wanted to cry. How was it possible for those
high hopes of yesterday morning to lie shattered in the dust today?

With only a few riders circling the island now and then and the
snipers keeping the soldiers down in their pits, Black Sky headed up
the valley toward the camps. Many of the women were on the hill
overlooking the battleground but even their encouragement
couldn't inspire the warriors to try overrunning the soldiers again.

There were warriors who wanted to stay and kill the soldiers.
Black Sky would let them do it. His heart was no longer in the
battle.

He'd go find Little Dove. She'd be in her father's camp. Many
Horses would let Black Sky marry Little Dove now. There were no
big battles ahead of them that anyone could see.

He'd take Little Dove down along the Washita River. There were
still buffalo there. He'd make her happy in what little time was left
for them. Soon the white man would kill all the buffalo. Then the
Indian would starve or go to be penned up on a reservation. Either
would be death, the way Black Sky saw it. With a heavy heart, he
rode toward Little Dove.

Twenty

A S DARKNESS SETTLED DOWN over the island after the first day of battle, Dain stood up, stretching aching muscles. The Indian snipers had stopped firing shortly after dusk. Grover had said it was almost certain they had gone back to camp for the night except for the guards they would put out to make sure nobody left the island. Indians didn't fight at night unless forced to.

Ron tried to get up but his leg wouldn't allow it. Dain wanted to report Ron's wound to Colonel Forsyth but Ron objected.

"What good would that do? He has enough to worry about without another wounded man. I can fight when I need to. I just can't retreat very fast."

Dain recognized his attempt at humor. Retreat was one word that had no meaning in their position. They would live or die right where they were. And the chances of living were slim indeed.

"Reckon they'll be back in the morning," one man said.

"You can lay odds on that," Grover said. "We'd better be ready for them at dawn. If they don't muster up enough courage to run over us then, they probably won't try it any more."

"Get your weapons loaded and everything ready for battle in the morning," Forsyth said. "Then try to get some sleep."

He assigned guard duty to those who were still without wounds. Four guards would be sufficient. They didn't expect any Indians to try to sneak onto the island but a guard on each side and one on each end would be enough to spot any intruder.

"At the first light of dawn, come back to your pits," Forsyth added.

Dain would take his turn at guard after midnight. Now he was supposed to sleep. He doubted if anybody would sleep any tonight. Those with wounds couldn't and the rest would be worrying about what the dawn would bring.

Dain had things on his mind but they weren't all about the battle tomorrow morning. Jed Wolfcry was surely out there somewhere with the Indians. But there was absolutely no way that he could see of coming to grips with Wolfcry. Even if Dain survived the battle, Wolfcry would be gone with the Indians.

He had signed up for this campaign to find and rescue his sister and nephew. That had failed. His other objective was to catch up with Jed Wolfcry. Now he was probably close to Wolfcry but if he'd been on the moon, he wouldn't have been any more inaccessible. So he was going to fail in that, too. To make his trip a complete failure, he in all probability would not survive this battle. A thousand Indian warriors would almost guarantee that.

There hadn't been time to eat anything since last evening. Dain felt lank but they had used almost the last of their rations yesterday. Breaking that charge of Roman Nose this morning was the high point of the day and Dain felt they could repulse any attack the Indians might launch. But there was no way to whip starvation with rifles.

The only food available on this island was the horses. The thought of eating their horses would have been revolting a day or two ago. But now hunger overrode the reluctance to eat horse meat.

Dain was already out of his pit with his knife ready to peel away the hide from the hip of his horse when Grover called to the men.

"Cut steaks off your horses. Spread the meat out on the bushes and maybe the sun will dry it so it will keep longer. Or bury it in the sand. The cool sand should keep it from spoiling for a while."

Grover was facing the reality that they could be here on this island for a long time. There wasn't anyone here who didn't realize that now.

Dain cut off three chunks of meat. One he laid aside to eat tonight. One he spread out on a bush close to his pit in the sand. The other he buried a short distance from his pit where the sand down deep was cooled by the water below it. He did the same for Ron. The weather would have a lot to do with how long that meat stayed good. Right now the weather was cool and cloudy, quite different from the hot humid afternoon they had spent crouching in their sand pits. When this meat spoiled, they'd be faced with a choice.

Either make a dash for freedom and almost certainly be killed or stay here and slowly starve to death.

From upstream to the southwest came the steady beat of a drum and the wailing chant of voices. Dain turned to Stillwell in the next pit.

"What does that mean?"

"It's the death chant," Stillwell said. "They're mourning the death of their braves. That's mostly women chanting."

"Maybe they've had enough," Ron said hopefully.

"I doubt it," Stillwell said. "They know we can't get away. They'll be back to try to finish us off."

Dain listened to the chant of the Indians but there was a closer sound that disturbed him more. It was the moaning of the wounded. They needed a doctor and medicine. There was no hope of getting a doctor. Dr. Mooers would never regain consciousness. But the medical supplies they had brought should be out there where the pack mule had gone down in the creek bed.

Dain knew that the colonel would not approve of a foray to try to get the medicine. But it was beginning to rain now and the wind had come up. That would cover any sound made by someone crawling out to the mule to retrieve the medical supplies.

Dain whispered his plans to Ron. Ron was against it. There certainly would be Indians watching to see that no one left the island. Dain assured him that he'd be very careful. He'd take his revolver with him.

Knowing that Ron would not tell anyone what he was doing, Dain slipped out of his pit and moved down to the edge of the island. It was as dark as the inside of a barrel and the rain was coming down hard now. Dain felt that he could just walk out there and no one would see or hear him. But there might be warriors close and any foolish move could mean his death.

Cautiously he moved in a crouch out to the spot where he thought the mule had fallen. He had to search awhile for the mule before he found it. But the pack that the mule had been carrying was gone. Apparently the Indians had already been out here since darkness fell and taken the pack. Likely they had taken it away from the scouts who would use it to ease the suffering of the wounded.

Dain turned back toward the island, moving less cautiously now that he was heading back. The rain had slackened some and he could hear other sounds than the wind and the rain.

He was halfway back to the island when he heard a rustle close by. He guessed it was an Indian, probably looking for dead warriors who had fallen during the battle. Stillwell said that the Indians would come tonight and get their dead. They never left their dead on a battlefield if they could help it. Dain was amazed at how much Stillwell, not yet twenty, knew about Indians.

Dain dropped flat on the sand, revolver in hand. The night wasn't quite as black as he had thought it was. Against the clouds, he could barely make out a figure moving slowly over the sand. Dain hoped he wouldn't see him.

The Indian apparently was looking for bodies and he must have thought he saw one when he came close to Dain. He started to move forward, then stopped short. Dain guessed he had seen the clothes and knew it was a white man. The Indian brought around his knife and reached for Dain's head. Dain realized the Indian thought he was dead and was going to scalp him.

Bunching his muscles, Dain suddenly leaped away and brought up his gun. The Indian was no more than three feet away when he fired. The warrior staggered back and sprawled on the sand. Dain didn't wait to see if he had killed him. If there was one Indian out here, there might be more.

Making no effort to be quiet, he dashed for the island. A couple of rifle shots came from the creek bank but they were aimed by sound, not sight, and they didn't come close. They did let Dain know there were other Indians out there. He made it back to the island and into his pit.

"Glad you're back," Ron said. "Did you get hurt?"

"Not a scratch," Dain said. "I can't say as much for the Indian who tried to scalp me."

"How about the medicine?"

"The Indians beat me to that. The pack was gone."

"We almost shot you," Ron said. "When we heard that shot, we all grabbed our rifles. I yelled that you were out there so nobody fired."

"What did you find?" Forsyth called from his pit.

"The Indians already had taken the pack," Dain said.

"Thanks for trying to get the medicine for us," Forsyth said. "But nobody is to leave this island again without permission. If the Indians don't kill you, we might."

Dain realized he had been foolish but his only motive had been to get medicine for the wounded. He had failed in that, too.

Under Forsyth's orders, the men began digging trenches between pits so that they would be connected. That made communication much better. When they had finished with the trenches, they made one big pit near the center of the island. They called that their hospital and moved all their seriously wounded into it. It was about all they could do for them since they had neither doctor nor medicine.

The rain had virtually stopped when the men finished digging. They could hear soft rustling sounds out in the creek bed. Grover said that was likely the Indians gathering their dead.

One man, not far from Dain, dug down in his pit to fresh water. With the trenches connecting the pits, it made the water available to every man. They were in fairly good shape now as long as the horse meat stayed good.

In the short view, things were much better. They had meat to eat and plenty of water and Dain doubted if the Indians would launch another attack like the one under Roman Nose. But the long-range outlook was no better. The Indians had them trapped here and they'd keep them here until they starved to death.

When there were no more sounds out in the creek bed, Forsyth spoke up again, calling for all the men's attention. It was lighter now, with light from stars filtering through the breaking clouds.

"We must get help from Fort Wallace. Even if the Indians should go away, we can never get back to Wallace with our wounded. I'm sure the Indians have guards out to keep us from getting through but we must try. Are there any volunteers to try to get through to Fort Wallace?"

"How far is it?" one man asked.

"Grover and I calculate that we are about a hundred and ten miles from Fort Wallace. The first couple of miles will be the tough ones because the Indians will be watching for you."

It was hard to see raised hands in the dark but Dain saw a few close to him. His own hand was up. He knew the risk but he thought it would be better than staying here and dying of starvation.

"I want you to understand the danger," Forsyth said. "The Indians know we have to send for help. They'll try to catch any scout who slips off the island. You know their habits. They torture before they kill. You'll be faced with that if you're caught. Think that over, then let's see who really wants to make the try."

Again Dain saw several hands. His was still one of them. Forsyth looked over the volunteers and picked Jack Stillwell. Dain hated to see him go. He had been a real source of information about the Indians. But he didn't question Forsyth's decision to send Stillwell. Knowing Indians as he did, Stillwell would probably have a better chance than most of getting through.

Forsyth then picked one of the older scouts, Pierre Trudeau, to go with Stillwell. Dain didn't doubt that Trudeau was about as well qualified as Stillwell.

"Take water, meat, your revolver and ammunition," Forsyth said. "Leave your rifle here. It would be bunglesome to carry and harder to hide than a revolver. You may have to hide during the day."

Forsyth then wrote a note to Colonel Bankhead, commander of Fort Wallace, explaining the plight of the scouts and asking for immediate aid, reinforcements, ambulances for the wounded, horses for the able-bodied scouts.

Forsyth handed the note to Stillwell. "Take care. God be with you."

The two scouts took the precaution of wearing moccasins and walking backward so their tracks in the sand would look as if Indians had made them, moving toward the island. In the morning, if the Indians saw tracks of scouts leaving the island, they'd make a thorough search and find the scouts wherever they were hiding.

Dain watched the two slip away. He wondered if he'd ever see his friend Stillwell again. He tried to ease the discomfort of Ron's painful wound.

"Did you notice that Sharp Grover didn't volunteer to go for help?" Ron asked. "He is certainly the best-qualified man we have."

Dain hadn't noticed. "Maybe he thought he'd be needed here," he said. "And he is a little old to be playing hide and seek games."

For four hours, Dain watched, wondering if they would return or if they'd been caught or if they had actually gotten through. He was sure that, if they couldn't get through and hadn't been caught, they would come back.

Dawn came and the two scouts had not returned. Dain's turn as guard on the perimeter of the pits on the island ended when Forsyth called the guards back to their pits to prepare for the expected battle at first strong light.

Dain strained his eyes through the growing light. Suddenly he saw them, fully twenty riders materializing out of the morning haze. They were riding boldly toward the island.

"They must think we slipped away during the night," Grover said.

"Don't anybody fire until I say the word," Forsyth said. "If we can wipe out this bunch, it may be enough to make them quit."

Dain doubted that. As the light grew stronger, he saw hundreds of mounted Indians behind the twenty and he knew the scouts were in for more trouble. Apparently none of the Indians had given up.

Twenty-one

THE INDIANS reined up just out of rifle range. Then two rode a few yards farther, leaning over their horses' necks.

"Looking for tracks," Grover said.

"What if they find the tracks of Stillwell and Trudeau?" one man asked.

"They won't," Grover said. "Those two went down the river bed, not out there. Besides, they wore moccasins. Even the Indians couldn't tell whether an Indian or a white man was in those moccasins."

"They must think we're gone," McCall said. "How do they think we could get away?"

"They don't know how many of us are wounded," Forsyth said.

"If they get a little closer, they'll find out that we're still here and we're ready to fight," Grover said.

It struck Dain that if they thought all the scouts were gone, they must not have caught Stillwell and Trudeau. Or maybe they caught them and thought that all the scouts were slipping away and they caught only two.

The Indians were masters at setting ambushes; now the tables would be turned when these Indians got within rifle range.

The Indian advance stalled as the two trackers searched for signs. One of the scouts got overanxious and fired his rifle. The bullet fell short of its mark.

The Indians dropped flat on their horses' backs, then kicked them into a wild run around the island, keeping well out of effective rifle range.

Forsyth screamed in rage. Dain wheeled to see who was guilty.

There were several scouts in that area. The only thing he saw that was surprising was Gus Bystrom crouching in his pit like the others, his rifle at the ready. Dain supposed that, since there had been no fighting this morning, Bystrom had screwed up enough courage to at least look over the top of his embankment.

That was all changed now. The Indians riding wildly around the island were firing their rifles ineffectually at the scouts. Bystrom returned to the bottom of his pit.

Forsyth demanded to know who had fired the shot but no one answered. Looking at the men around Bystrom's pit, Dain could see in their faces that they knew. Apparently it had been Bystrom. Dain supposed he was so frightened at even being in this situation that he couldn't control himself when he saw the Indians and had fired his rifle, probably not voluntarily. Bystrom was the biggest liability the scouts had.

It was just a short time until Dain saw the grass waving out beyond the creek bank. The snipers were back. Apparently they had moved into the taller grass well above the island, then worked their way down the creek bank to their places opposite the island. That way the scouts couldn't see them coming.

Dain watched for a sign that there would be another charge this morning. It soon became clear that they had no intention of coming any closer to the scouts than that wide circle they were riding. The warriors intended only to keep them in the pits until they starved to death.

The women and children were back on the hill north of the island and their wailing and chanting drifted over the valley. They would mourn their losses for several days, Grover said. There was some rather weak cheering when the warriors moved a little closer to the island but that faded when the war ponies were pulled back out to the wide circle they had worn around the island. To Dain, that meant it wasn't likely for any more charges to be made.

Dain didn't understand the chants but he knew from what Grover said that the songs were for the dead. They had a depressing effect on Dain. There were dead here on the island to mourn, too. If those still living got careless, they could all be dead soon and there would be nobody to mourn them.

It was obvious to all the scouts now that their only hope of getting out of this alive was a rescue party. Even if the Indians left, only those who were not wounded would be able to walk back to civilization. And the Indians showed no sign of leaving. Likely they'd wait until the scouts got so weak they couldn't fight. Then they'd rush in, count coups and take scalps.

The Indians presented no targets for the scouts. They sent an occasional shot over the island to remind the scouts that they were safe only as long as they stayed down in their pits.

By noon when the scouts ate their raw horse meat, they found it already getting a bit strong. If they could just gather enough wood to have a fire and cook the meat, it would be better. But they couldn't stir out of their pits. The sun turned hot in the afternoon. That was spoiling the meat faster than they had expected. Starvation was coming closer and closer.

Darkness came and the snipers withdrew. Again Colonel Forsyth asked for volunteers to take a message to Colonel Bankhead at Fort Wallace.

"You don't think Stillwell and Trudeau got through?" someone asked.

"We can't assume that they did," Forsyth said. "We have to keep trying. It's our only hope."

Dain considered the request. He faced starvation if he stayed here. He had hoped to get to face Jed Wolfcry but that hope was dwindling. Even if Wolfcry was here with the Indians, Dain wouldn't be able to get to him. His great expectations when he signed up for this campaign were all coming to nothing.

If he could get through with a message and bring help, it would save all the scouts. He was thinking of Ron in particular. Ron's wound would never allow him to walk out of here even if the Indians did go away. He had to have help. Dain's hand went up as a volunteer.

This time Dain was chosen along with a scout named George to try to get past the Indian guards. Forsyth gave Dain a written message similar to the one he had sent out the night before. Dain didn't know the last name of the scout who was going with him. He knew there were three men in the company named George. In a place like this, names weren't that important.

Slinging their boots around their necks by the strings, they left the island, walking backward in their sock feet. The imprints in the sand should look like moccasin tracks if the Indians discovered them in the morning.

They headed down the creek bed. If they came close to Indian patrols, there was a much better chance of hiding along the creek bank or in the sage grass on the banks.

As the island faded into the darkness, Dain had the hollow feeling he'd experienced as a boy when he left home for a day or two. That island, as much as he wanted to get away from it, represented the safety of home in this hostile atmosphere.

It seemed like a long time, although Dain knew it hadn't been more than a few minutes and they hadn't gone far, when the sound of someone talking came to his ears. Dain couldn't understand the guttural tones but he knew it was Indians talking.

Dain touched George, who stood frozen in his tracks, and motioned toward the grass on the bank. As quietly as possible they crawled into the grass. The sound of voices still came to them. Dain inched forward to see if it was a camp that they could go around or if it was a patrol that they would have to dodge.

George went deeper into the grass away from the creek while Dain moved stealthily along the bank toward the voices. The voices stopped and Dain remained motionless. Had he made some noise that they had heard? Or was this just a normal pause in their conversation?

The voices started again and it seemed to Dain that they were closer now. He moved forward cautiously. He almost bumped into an old buffalo carcass that was lying on the bank of the creek. Apparently it had not been a victim of an Indian hunt. The tattered hide was still on it. The coyotes had cleaned out the cavity some time ago but the hide was still clinging to the ribs.

Moving carefully around the carcass, he crept close to the voices. So far, he heard the voices but detected no movement. Now the voices stopped but there was a rustling of footsteps. The Indians were moving.

In horror, Dain realized they were coming up the riverbank right toward him. If they found him, he'd be the target of all the torture that Forsyth had described before Stillwell and Trudeau went out last night.

Dain backed up an inch, still on his hands and knees. His foot bumped into a stiff leg of the buffalo carcass. An idea exploded in his mind. Backing as quickly and quietly as possible, he moved around the back legs of the carcass until he was even with the body cavity.

Pushing the ribs apart, he managed to squeeze inside the cavity and lay still. Outside, he could hear some activity. Apparently he had made some noise spreading the dried ribs enough to crawl inside the old carcass. The Indians must have heard it.

Dain remained motionless and almost stopped breathing as Indians moved around the carcass looking for the source of the sounds they had heard. Dain waited for them to think to look inside the carcass. Even though it must have been weeks since the coyotes cleaned out this carcass, the stench was almost stifling. Dain wondered how long he could stay here. The Indians apparently had come to the conclusion that they had heard a coyote or some other animal. Coyotes were plentiful in the hills on either side of the valley, attracted by the smell of the decaying flesh of the dead horses.

A bit of the tattered hide of the buffalo hung inside the cavity where Dain was lying and it touched Dain's nose. It tickled and he felt a sneeze coming. A sneeze would be the final disaster for him. Carefully, he lifted a hand and rubbed it across his nose to stop the sneeze, then moved the dangling piece of hide away where it didn't touch him.

He listened intently to see if his movements inside the carcass had attracted the attention of the Indians. But they were moving away, going back the way they had come. Dain remained quiet, listening. He heard the scrape of moccasins on sand. The Indians must be crossing the stream.

When there was no longer any sound outside, Dain crawled carefully out of the carcass and crept back toward the spot where he had left George. George had just returned from the spot back a ways from the bank where he'd hidden.

"They went across the creek," Dain whispered. "Maybe we can get through now."

They moved along the creek bank, pausing every few seconds to listen. Just when Dain thought they had surely passed beyond the range of the Indian patrols, he again heard guttural voices.

They stopped, sinking down in the grass. The voices slowly faded, this time going away from the stream.

Again they moved forward. Then Dain saw a twinkle of light ahead. They crept closer and saw a half-dozen Indians squatting around a small fire. They'd have to detour around that campfire. But when they swung to the south to get around the fire, they saw another. A little farther on was another.

Dain tried to move between the fires but he discovered Indian pickets there. Twice more they tried to find spaces between the little campfires that apparently surrounded the island but both times they found pickets moving slowly across the open spaces. Dain considered himself lucky that they were not discovered by the guards.

George had a watch and he held it up where the starlight gleamed faintly on the dial. It was only an hour till dawn. As much as Dain hated to admit defeat, he knew he had to this time. If they were caught out here when daylight came, they'd be tortured to death. They couldn't get past the Indian guards. Their only hope to survive sunrise was to get back on the island.

They barely avoided a patrol on the way back. Dain guessed it was the same group of Indians they had hidden from when they left the island. It was a real disappointment to have to report to Colonel Forsyth that he and George hadn't been able to sneak through the Indian guards. Some thought the Indians had started to go away but Dain convinced them they were still out there.

Dawn brought a resumption of sniper fire across the island. It wasn't dangerous to the scouts if they kept down in their pits but it pinned them to the island. There were no more threats of a charge. Dain realized that many of the wounded who could have fought two days ago couldn't do it now. A charge now would likely succeed.

Shortly after noon, five Indians appeared out on the plain south of the island. One was waving a white flag on the end of a rifle barrel.

"Going to talk to him, Colonel?" McCall asked.

Forsyth hesitated. "What do you say, Grover?"

Grover shook his head. "They've got nothing to gain by a truce. They just want a look at the shape we're in to see if they can take us."

The five Indians were riding slowly toward the island. Colonel Forsyth watched them as he considered Grover's advice. Then he nodded. "Fire three shots into the dirt in front of them," he said. "Let them know there'll be no truce."

The rifles roared and dust spurted up ahead of the Indians. They stopped, then wheeled and rode back, screaming defiance. It brought on another circling ride by the warriors who fired wildly at the island defenders.

"We called their bluff," Grover said. "We couldn't have told them any plainer that we're still able to whip them."

The snipers along the creek bank poured in a heavy fire but no Indian showed himself within range of the scouts' rifles.

Later in the afternoon, a single Indian shouted from the grass back a ways from the creek bank. "I dare you, Talmage, to come out and meet me!"

Ron jerked up on an elbow. "Is that redskin yelling at you, Dain?"

Dain nodded, excitement rushing through him. "I'm the only Talmage in this outfit. That has to be Jed Wolfcry. He's the only one who could know I'm here."

"Do you know that Indian?" Grover asked Dain.

Dain nodded. "He's the one who revealed my sister's hiding place to the raiders. He's only half Cheyenne. Been living with the whites. But he's a redskin to his very soul."

"Likely figured you'd be coming after your sister," Grover said. "Probably sneaked up on us while we were coming up the valley and saw you."

"I'm going to accommodate him," Dain said.

"Not now," Forsyth said quickly. "You'd be killed before you reached the creek bed. Those snipers are just waiting for someone to show his head."

Dain understood. Now that he knew for sure that Wolfcry was out there, he still couldn't get to him. Wolfcry probably figured on that. But somehow he'd find a way to get out there and kill him.

"We can't spare a single fighter," Forsyth said, apparently seeing the determination on Dain's face.

Dain nodded. He knew the colonel was right. He would be letting the others down as well as himself if he foolishly stepped out to meet Wolfcry and got cut down by the snipers.

Dain had seen something on this campaign that he had never seen before. There was a bond among these men. They cared about each other and, more important, they trusted each other. These men were proving themselves to Dain every day.

"You may get your chance," Ron said to Dain. "The boys will back you if the opportunity comes up."

Within an hour, the women who had been chanting their mournful songs on the hill to the north began to leave. When they stopped their mourning and silence fell over the valley, Dain turned to look.

"What does that mean, Grover?" he asked.

"It means that the women have ended their period of public mourning. It may also mean that they are pulling out."

"Leaving the area?" Forsyth asked hopefully.

"Probably," Grover said. "Many of the warriors may go with them."

"Can we go home then?" Bystrom asked eagerly, sitting up in his pit.

"No!" Forsyth snapped, putting a lot of anger into the word. "The Indians will keep us pinned down here till we die!"

Dain realized how angry Forsyth must be at Bystrom. But his anger was no greater than that of many of the scouts. Brave men usually hated a coward.

Jed Wolfcry hurled another challenge. "I'm still waiting for you, Talmage."

Dain knew that somehow he would get out there to meet that challenge.

Twenty-two

SHORTLY AFTER Wolfcry had shouted his second challenge at Dain, a fat Indian appeared out to the south, just out of the range of the Spencer rifles. He had been there off and on since yesterday afternoon.

Just his presence out there could be tolerated. But he had a loud voice and this afternoon he shouted every obscene English word he knew and accompanied each word with an equally obscene gesture.

"I wish we could shut him up," McCall said.

"He's out of range of our rifles and he knows it," Forsyth said. "At least, the snipers seem to be letting up. Maybe the fat man thinks he can irritate us from a distance just as well."

"Colonel," McCall said, "we have a few Springfield rifles in our outfit. I think those breechloaders might reach him."

Dain was watching the fat Indian just as the others were. He had stripped off every stitch of clothes and was screaming all kinds of insults.

"I'm glad he's that far away, at least," Ron said.

Forsyth raised himself as far as he could on his elbows. "McCall, bring those men with the Springfields over here. Tell them to be careful coming over. There may be a few snipers left."

McCall shouted for the men with the big rifles to come. Three crawled over from different pits. Men made way for them in the pits facing the south.

"Think you can come close enough to that savage to scare him?" Forsyth asked.

"It's worth a try," one said.

Dain knew from his military experience that those Springfield breechloaders had a range over a hundred yards beyond that of the Spencer repeating rifles. Their accuracy at that range was questionable but they might scare that fat Indian back into his clothes.

"Raise your sights to the limit," McCall said, sounding more like the general of the Pennsylvania regiment he had been during the war than just a scout in this group. "Aim well over the sight. You should startle the old fool, anyway."

The sights were adjusted and the men prepared to fire. McCall called for them to aim and fire. The three rifles fired as one.

Out on the plain, the fat Indian leaped into the air with a startled scream, then fell and rolled. Even from that distance, it was obvious that he was dead. The Indians who had been clustered around him kicked their ponies into a dead run and scattered in every direction except toward the island.

"Good shot, men," Forsyth praised. "I don't know when I've ever seen anything that pleased me as much as that."

The Indians began racing around the island again, firing wildly at the scouts. They were likely as angry over being outmaneuvered as they were at losing the fat brave. The scouts on the island stayed low in their pits and waited for the circling Indians to tire of their futile rage.

At sundown, Wolfcry's challenge came to Dain again. "Unless you're a coward, you'll come out and meet me."

Dain fought the urge to jump up and start running toward Wolfcry. He knew exactly where he was right now, standing behind his horse about fifty yards beyond the creek bank. He might never have that advantage again. But he remembered the caution of Ron and Forsyth. There were Indians just waiting to get a shot at any scout who got careless.

Darkness settled over the valley. The scouts began moving around to get their supper. The horse meat was spoiling fast now. But it was all they had.

The snipers were gone for the night. Someone slipped out of his pit and gathered some dry wood among the bushes. It wasn't big sticks but it did make a quick fire. In a short time, some men began cooking their meat over the fire while others brought more sticks. They hadn't felt it was safe to go far from their pits before, even at night, so they hadn't had any wood. This was the first hot food they'd had since the night before the Indian attack. Still, the men had to sprinkle gunpowder on the meat to kill the bad taste.

Dain had just finished eating his half-rotten meat when a yell came out of the darkness across the creek.

"Are you too big a coward to come over and face the man who staked out your sister and killed your nephew?"

Dain was startled. He supposed that Wolfcry had faded back to the Indian camps along with the snipers. But obviously, he was over there right now and he was really waiting for Dain to come over.

This was exactly what Dain had been hoping for. His blood was boiling. He had his chance now to meet Wolfcry and get his revenge or die trying.

"Could be a trap," Ron said.

"Maybe," Dain admitted. "But it's the only chance I'll probably ever have to get my hands on that killer."

"I don't like the idea of losing a good friend," Ron said. "I don't trust Wolfcry as far as I can throw a buffalo by the tail."

"Neither do I," Dain said. "But this is my chance and nobody's going to talk me out of taking it."

Dain began making preparations for crossing over the stream bed. He'd take his revolver but not his rifle. And he'd carry the big knife he had taken from Wolfcry back at his homestead.

Wolfcry yelled again. Dain didn't answer but he worked faster getting ready to go.

"Do you think there are any Indians over there with that English-speaking brave?" Ron asked Grover.

"Not likely," Grover said. "Indians don't like to fight at night. Unless this fellow has some good personal friends, he isn't likely to have anyone with him."

"I doubt if he ever had a good friend in his life," Dain said. "I'm going over to see."

"Hold on," Ron said, pulling himself up on his elbows, wincing at the pain the move cost him. "When you cross that creek bed, you should have somebody to cover for you."

"I'll make out," Dain said. He looked over the men in the flickering light of the dying fire, then lowered his voice. "I don't really trust anybody here but you. And you're in no shape to move anywhere."

"You're right about that. But if you find Wolfcry over there and get into a fight, which is what you're going over for, you're almost sure to stir up plenty of noise. There'll be Indian patrols all around this island. If they hear a scuffle, they're going to come running. You could have more on your hands than you can handle, even if you whip Wolfcry. You need someone over here with a good rifle who will cover your return to the island."

Dain couldn't argue with Ron about that. Wolfcry might not have any companion with him but Dain knew there would be plenty of Indian patrols around. There had been last night, anyway, when he and George had tried to get through to Fort Wallace. A scuffle would bring the nearest patrol on the run. He would need help to get back to the island.

Actually, the whole situation was preposterous. But Wolfcry had set the table with his challenge and Dain was going to the feast. He'd be taking a big chance and giving the advantage to Wolfcry but he'd risk all that to get his chance at him.

Ken Calhoun, who had crawled over after eating his supper, moved a little closer. "I'll cover you," he said.

Dain couldn't believe what he'd heard. Ken Calhoun was Gus Bystrom's cousin, about the last man on this island, with the exception of Bystrom himself, that he'd trust. Calhoun was a little man but he had done his part in the fighting even if his cousin hadn't.

"I want to see that loudmouth over there shut up," Calhoun said. "Think it over. If you want me, I'll be right over there." He indicated a spot on the other side of the embers that had been the fire. He crawled away.

"I wouldn't trust him as far as I could see a black cat at midnight," Dain said to Ron.

"I don't see any reason not to," Ron said. "I'll admit I wouldn't trust Bystrom. But Calhoun is different. He'll do what he says he will."

Dain contemplated the situation. How could he trust a cousin of Gus Bystrom? But it really made no difference in his decision. He was going to go after Wolfcry, with or without someone standing by if he needed help.

Dain made sure he had everything ready to go after Wolfcry. Ron was watching him closely. As much to please Ron as to protect himself, he went around to Calhoun. Calhoun picked up his rifle, checked it to make sure it was fully loaded, then moved silently down to the edge of the island.

"I'll stay right here and watch," Calhoun said. "If you get into any trouble, I'll let them know we're watching from over here."

Dain nodded and stepped off the island into the shallow water that hugged the island. He moved silently through the narrow stream of water, then across the broad span of dry sand to the riverbank.

Dain had two doubts in his mind. He wasn't sure that Wolfcry would be alone. He might have a warrior or two with him. And he doubted if Ken Calhoun would stay on the edge of the island to cover Dain's return with his rifle. He'd more than likely go back to his pit as soon as Dain was out of sight.

It was light enough to see across the creek bed by starlight but it would be almost impossible to distinguish anything at that distance.

Dain crouched on the sand at the edge of the creek bank, listening intently. If Wolfcry was at the edge of the bank, he was being very quiet. But a bird of prey or a carnivore could sit patiently without a sound for long minutes waiting for prey to come close enough for an attack. Dain remembered, as a boy, how his cat would sit close to the hole of a ground squirrel for half an hour without moving, waiting for the squirrel to poke his head out of the hole. He had visions of Jed Wolfcry crouching up on the creek bank just like that, waiting for Dain to crawl up out of the creek bed. Then he'd pounce.

Dain moved up the bank about twenty feet. There he stopped and listened intently again. If Wolfcry had been waiting for him back there, he'd have to move up the bank to keep even with him. And any rustle he made in the grass should be loud enough for Dain to hear.

His ears almost ached with the silence of the prairie. There was no sound to indicate that Wolfcry was up there somewhere waiting for him. He knew that he'd make some noise when he climbed up into the grass along the bank. It was only a few inches above the level of the stream bed but the grass would have to part to let him through. He imagined that would sound like a passing whirlwind to anyone listening for that soft rustle of grass.

Wolfcry might still be where he'd been at sundown when he yelled at Dain from behind his horse. That was fully fifty yards back from the river bank. Dain doubted if he was that far away. If he expected Dain to take the bait, he was surely up close watching for him. If he didn't expect Dain, he might already have gone back to the camp of the Indians.

As Dain crawled into the grass, the hair on the back of his neck felt as though it was standing on end. Wolfcry could be only inches away in the grass, waiting to pounce on him with a knife or maybe a revolver.

Pausing, he listened, holding his breath. Still he heard nothing. Maybe Wolfcry had given up and left. But he remembered that Wolf-cry had yelled at him after darkness had enveloped the valley. He'd been here then; he likely was here now.

To bolster his resolve, Dain recalled how much he wanted to get his hands on Wolfcry. Wolfcry had been responsible for Hiram's death and Susan's death and torture she had endured before she was finally staked out on that hillside. Dain had a huge score to settle with the half-breed. Whatever he did to him, it couldn't pay for all Wolfcry had done. Dain thought that hanging him by the heels and swinging him through a slow fire would be too good for him.

Dain crawled forward, knowing that he was making some noise. There was no way he could avoid it. If Wolfcry was out here, the half-breed would hear him. All the advantage of surprise was with Wolfcry.

He was nearing the edge of the taller grass that grew close to the river bed. He stopped, again listening for some movement. He had never been so tense. Ahead lay the shorter grama and buffalo grass. Neither was tall enough to hide anything bigger than a snake. So if Wolfcry was hiding, waiting for him, it would have to be in this taller grass.

Dain began to relax a bit. The shorter grass wasn't far ahead. He crawled forward more quickly, thinking he wasn't going to find Wolfcry.

Then suddenly the grass just ahead of him exploded. Just when he'd decided he wouldn't find Wolfcry, he had found him. And he wasn't prepared.

Twenty-three

DAIN BARELY HAD TIME to throw himself sideways as he saw Wolfcry lunging at him, knife flashing. Wolfcry was throwing himself full length at Dain and Dain got a fuzzy look at his hate-twisted, hideously painted face. He was as eager for this battle as Dain was.

Dain was strictly at a disadvantage. Even though he'd been expecting Wolfcry to jump him somewhere, he was still surprised at the suddenness and the ferociousness of the attack.

Jerking his knife out of its sheath, he lunged to his knees to meet Wolfcry's next assault. But Wolfcry was still trying to jerk his knife out of the sod where it had plunged when he missed Dain. He'd had the knife aimed at Dain's heart.

Lunging at Wolfcry, Dain started to bring his knife around toward the half-breed. But Wolfcry had his knife free now and was wheeling toward Dain. Dain hit Wolfcry's arm, sending the knife spinning away into the grass.

Dain got little consolation from that, however, because in the jolt of the collision, he had lost his grip on his own knife. He knew about where his knife had fallen but he had no chance to grab it as Wolfcry lunged at him.

Wolfcry wasn't as tall as Dain but he was as heavy and his weight was mostly muscle. Dain got a good look at his face in the starlight and he saw that he had war paint on his face and chest like any Cheyenne warrior going into battle. The zigzag lines from his temples down to his jaw made him look hideous but it didn't camouflage his features. Unlike the warriors Dain had been seeing riding around the island, Wolfcry wore long pants. The warriors usually had little or nothing on but a sash tied around their waists and maybe a breechcloth. A little of Wolfcry's civilization among the whites had apparently rubbed off. He preferred the trousers of the white man.

Dain also saw that he preferred the revolver and gun belt he had worn back in Alpha in preference to bows and arrows. Dain remembered that he had handled that revolver quite well the few times he had seen him with it in his hand.

Dain expected Wolfcry to try to get his knife again or use his revolver. He did neither. He lunged at Dain as if to tear him apart with his bare hands. That suited Dain. He was just as furious as Wolfcry and just as determined to destroy his enemy. In fact, Dain would get more satisfaction from literally tearing Wolfcry limb from limb than he would in using a gun or a knife on him.

Rushing to meet Wolfcry's charge, Dain had no illusions about this fight. Wolfcry was a very strong man and he was depending on his strength to overpower Dain.

With arms reaching for each other, they came together with a grunt that would have done credit to a pair of buffalo bulls, then they bounced apart. Dain's reach was just a little longer. He realized he had to use that to his advantage. If he let Wolfcry get him in a bear hug, it might be more than he could break.

As Wolfcry was reaching for Dain, Dain drove a fist into the half-breed's stomach. It brought an extra grunt from him and slowed his charge but didn't stop it.

Seeing that Wolfcry was going to close with him, Dain leaped to one side, grabbing one arm. Wolfcry was spun around. Dain smashed a fist into the painted face that snapped Wolfcry's head back. This wasn't going the way Wolfcry had planned. He was a mauler. If he could get his arms around Dain, he'd wrestle him to the ground and there he'd gouge out his eyes and beat him to death.

As he ducked away, Dain caught an arm across the side of his head. It hit him like a club and sent him reeling. Wolfcry gave a sharp cry of exultation and lunged for Dain again.

Backpedaling rapidly, Dain shook his head to clear his thinking. He managed to keep out of Wolfcry's reach. Then suddenly he braced himself and threw a fist at the half-breed. Wolfcry wasn't prepared for an attack and the blow smashed into the side of his face. Now it was his turn to reel backward.

Dain was still trying to sweep the fog out of his head and didn't try to follow up his advantage. He circled Wolfcry cautiously and Wolfcry was doing the same.

They sparred carefully like two wrestlers trying to find an opening. Then Wolfcry lunged at Dain and Dain dodged away, slapping at Wolfcry's arm. His fingers caught on something around his wrist.

Dain tried to get his fingers free but they were caught so he gave his hand a hard jerk. It came free but whatever was fastened to Wolfcry's wrist came with it.

Dain saw at a glance that it was a leather wrist band. Suddenly he realized that this was the same leather wrist band he'd found in his wagon when he was at Minneapolis buying lumber. It really had been Wolfcry who had ransacked Dain's wagon that night in camp, looking for this wrist band.

Dain's mind was whirling. Was this wrist band a medicine band that belonged to Wolfcry? He had gone to great lengths to recover it when he had lost it before.

Dain tossed the wrist band to one side as he prepared to meet Wolfcry again. Wolfcry jumped forward but not at Dain. He was going for the wrist band that Dain had tossed to one side.

Realizing the importance of this wrist band to Wolfcry, Dain lunged to intercept him. He didn't know much about Indians and their medicine pieces but he did know that if he could keep Wolfcry from recovering his medicine band, it might work to his advantage.

He hit Wolfcry just as his fingers were reaching for the leather band. He knocked the half-breed away from the band and he lit on top of him. Wolfcry fought like a demon to get free and Dain could see that he wasn't trying now to hurt him. He was struggling to get to that wrist band. Dain struggled just as hard to keep him from reaching it.

It was strength against strength and Dain wasn't sure he could win the battle. He got one hand free and he swung that fist as hard as he could and hit Wolfcry on the side of the head. Wolfcry's grip on Dain loosened for a moment and Dain jerked free.

Wolfcry rolled free and went for the wrist band again. Dain leaped into his path. Wolfcry stopped, an animal scream coming from his throat. Dain thought of a lion's scream he'd heard once.

Dain suddenly saw the glint of starlight on steel. Wolfcry was clawing for the gun in his holster. Dain threw himself backward and jerked his own gun free.

Wolfcry's bullet ripped through the space Dain had occupied only a fraction of a second before. Dain used his army training to steady his nerves a split second before squeezing the trigger. His bullet propelled Wolfcry backward three feet and he hit the ground hard.

Dain started to get to his feet but he felt something hard and cold under him. His fingers closed on the knife he had lost in the collision with Wolfcry earlier in the fight.

Grabbing the knife, Dain lunged to his feet, the knife in one hand, his gun in the other. Wolfcry was on the ground but he was bringing up his gun for another shot. Dain leaped forward, his boot crashing against Wolfcry's arm, sending the gun spinning away in the darkness.

Dain dropped like a rock on top of Wolfcry. He might have another knife on his person and Dain had no intention of letting him use it.

The moment he hit Wolfcry, he realized that the half-breed was badly wounded. There wasn't much fight left in him. He pressed down on Wolfcry and he suddenly went limp.

Dain watched him carefully. He wasn't going to be lulled into relaxing and allow Wolfcry to suddenly turn the tables on him. Whipping the knife around, he touched the blade to Wolfcry's throat and held it there. Wolfcry didn't even flinch. Dain pressed slightly on the knife.

"I'm going to cut your throat for what you did to my family," he hissed. "You're going to die for that."

Still Wolfcry didn't move. "Go ahead," he whispered finally. "You took my medicine. I can't win."

Dain realized that he was referring to that leather wrist band that he had torn off Wolfcry's wrist. According to Wolfcry's belief, apparently he considered himself invincible while he wore that medicine band. But once it was gone, his good medicine was also gone.

Dain wondered what kind of nerves the man had to lie so still for so long. Maybe he was dead. But just then Wolfcry opened his eyes and stared straight up at Dain. Dain had never seen such hatred reflected in anybody's eyes.

"You still won't win," Wolfcry gasped, his voice little more than a whisper. "Scurry will get Valina, whether you get back or not."

Wolfcry's threat sent a chill racing down Dain's spine. He started to press the knife against Wolfcry's throat, then suddenly realized that Wolfcry had stopped breathing. He had used his last gasp to threaten Dain.

Dain heard running feet on the prairie up the slope from him. The Indian guards had heard the shots Dain and Wolfcry had exchanged and were coming to investigate. From the sounds of the running feet, there must be several warriors approaching. Dain knew he had to get to the island before they got to him.

Leaving Wolfcry, he ran in a low crouch toward the river. It wasn't very light but it was light enough he might be seen if he ran upright.

He wasn't far from the river but he could hear the footsteps gaining on him. He hit the creek bank and dropped down into the sand, then he ran as hard as he could. He was sure he would be outlined against that sand.

He hadn't gone ten yards when the first shot from the Indians echoed over the creek. That was followed immediately by two more shots. None hit him but he did hear the snap of one bullet that was close to his ear as it passed.

Then, in what seemed like a miracle, Calhoun opened up with his rifle from the edge of the island. Dain could see the blossoms of the explosions as Calhoun fired. He was down right on the edge of the island. He was in as much danger of being hit by the Indians as Dain was. In fact, the shots from Calhoun would pinpoint his location better than the running figure of Dain crossing the river bed.

Dain hadn't expected Calhoun to stay at his post. And he certainly hadn't expected him to expose himself as he was doing in order to make his shots more effective.

The effectiveness of those shots became evident when one of the Indians behind Dain yelled in pain and surprise. Calhoun had hit his target. He was probably aiming at the gun flashes just as the Indians could aim at his.

Dain wasn't shooting; he was just making the best time he could toward the island. Suddenly the shooting behind Dain stopped but Calhoun kept his shots going until he had fired all seven shots in his rifle. By that time, Dain was at the creek bank and he lunged up out of the shallow water onto the dry land of the island.

"You all right?" Calhoun asked.

"Fine, thanks to you," Dain said. "Let's get to our pits."

Dain was sure he would never have made it across that sandy stream bed if Calhoun hadn't used his rifle to stop the Indians. It was a feeling he had never experienced before. He had not trusted Calhoun but had taken him mainly because Ron had said he should.

Calhoun had done all a man could do to help. From now on, he'd trust the little man in whatever he said he'd do.

They scurried back to the pits beyond the decaying horses. Before going to his own pit over by Ron Fulton, Dain swallowed hard and thanked Ken Calhoun again for what he'd done. That was something he'd had very little experience in doing.

Another shot or two came from the riverbank. A couple of scouts answered those shots and the Indian rifles fell silent. They wouldn't fight at night unless they had to and they didn't have to now.

Dain reported to Ron what had happened and how Calhoun had stopped the Indians chasing him.

"I told you he could be trusted," Ron said. "You can trust more people than you think."

Dain didn't feel like arguing with him. Right now he was thinking how great it was to find he could trust someone he had doubted. Then the mood was destroyed as he remembered what Wolfcry had said just before he died. He told Ron. A scowl replaced the frown of pain that had become a permanent part of Ron since he'd been wounded.

"I don't like that," Ron said. "I wouldn't put anything past Scurry. No telling just what Wolfcry meant."

"I've got to get home as soon as I can," Dain said.

"Nobody is going anywhere until we figure a way to get rid of these Indians," Ron said.

Dain was trying vainly to think of an argument against Ron's logic when Forsyth called for two more volunteers to try again to get past the Indians. From those who held up their hands, Forsyth picked A. J. Pliley and John Donovan. Like those on previous nights, they walked backward in their sock feet so the Indians the next morning would not realize that someone had left the island.

Those on the island doubted that Stillwell and Trudeau, who had gone out the first night, had made it. They were much more confident that these two would make it. There were far fewer Indians around now than there had been at the end of the first day's fighting. But there were still those one hundred and ten miles to cover to reach Fort Wallace. Then it would be several more days before help could reach them here on the island. Could they hold out that long? Dain doubted it and he knew others shared his doubts.

Twenty-four

DAWN BROUGHT a short flurry of shots from the snipers who had crept up to the riverbank before daylight. The ablebodied scouts answered the shots. It was important now that they make the Indians realize the scouts were still ready to fight.

If they didn't respond to those shots from the snipers, the Indians would conclude that injuries and starvation had weakened the scouts and they might make a charge in the hope of finishing them off. Dain knew that such a charge, if it had any size and determination, could easily crush the resistance of the weakened scouts.

The Indians soon scooted back from the creek bank and returned to their camps or to their horses, which they rode around in plain sight of the scouts but out of range of their rifles. They had obviously come this morning just to see if there was any fight left in the scouts. Convinced that there was, they had pulled back to wait for starvation to do what the warriors couldn't.

By afternoon, most of the mounted Indians had disappeared. Grover concluded that many of them were leaving. Indians were not known for laying siege for any length of time. And they didn't stick together well. If an Indian decided that some project wasn't worth the effort, he would go away. Grover was sure that many of the Indians had left this battle scene.

By late afternoon, there were only a few Indians on the hills around the island. They were the ones who were waiting for the scouts to starve.

"All Cheyennes," Grover said, taking the binoculars from his eyes. "I have seen Sioux out there and also some Arapaho and Kiowa. But only Cheyennes now. I'm sure the others have left."

Dain knew that if those few Indians stayed long enough they would get the victory. The horse meat was getting "extremely tender," as one scout put it. Dain had to cook his meat until it was brown and even then he sprinkled gunpowder on it to take away some of the rotten taste. He was thankful the Indians had pulled back enough they could gather wood for cooking the meat.

They went through another night with hunger pains gnawing at them. But these were overshadowed by the moans of the wounded. Dain didn't see how they could hold out much longer but he knew they had no choice.

There was no barrage of bullets to greet them that morning. The men stood up and walked gingerly around the island. One man even found a few plums on a bush and brought them back to share them. There was only a taste for each man. Dain thought that taste only revived the hunger pains that time had begun to dull.

As the afternoon wore on, the only Indians in sight were a few on horses on the tops of hills overlooking the valley. They were there just to remind the scouts that they were not forgotten.

Toward evening, Forsyth called for the attention of the scouts. "The Indians are thinning out," he said. "I think we can slip past them and escape."

"How about the wounded?" one man asked.

"There's no need for everyone to die just because a few of us can't walk out. I am recommending that the able-bodied men try to slip past the few Indians left here and walk back to Fort Wallace."

"And leave the wounded here?"

"We're going to die, anyway," Forsyth said, "unless help comes. The rest of you do have a choice."

"That's not an order, is it, Colonel?" McCall asked.

"No," Forsyth said. "It's just an option."

Dain's first thought was that maybe he had a chance to get back home and settle things with Scurry. Wolfcry's last words haunted him. What would Scurry do? Had Wolfcry just been trying to stab Dain with his last breath?

Then he thought about his best friend, Ron. If Dain escaped the island, he'd have to leave Ron here to die with the other wounded. He wouldn't do that.

"Here's what I say," McCall said. "We fought together; we'll die together if need be. How about the rest of you?"

Dain held his hand high along with the rest of the men. It was unanimous.

"Thank you, men," Forsyth said. "Let's pray that our messengers got through and that help gets here in time."

Nothing more was said about trying to leave the island. Starvation was their only real enemy now. Their one hope lay with the messengers. If the Indians had caught them or if they had gotten lost, then the fate of those on the island was sealed. Even if they got through with their message, it would take a long time to get help back here.

As evening fell, a coyote, attracted by the smell of the rotting flesh of the horses, crept across to the island. One scout saw him coming and waited until he reached the island, then shot him. He was quickly skinned and all the meat boiled in their cooking pots until there was some thin soup for every man. Each man did get a small piece of meat, too, and all declared it was better than any beefsteak they'd ever had.

The next couple of days, those men who were strong enough crossed the stream bed and picked the few plums they could find along the creek bank. The plums were ripe. Dain was one of the strong ones and he picked every plum he could find and picked up what had fallen on the ground.

The plums were boiled and the strong juice and the plums themselves were divided; the wounded were given a bigger portion first. Some said it was the most delicious food they'd ever had.

Dain knew this could not go on. They had picked all the plums in the vicinity. And with some Indians still around, there was certainly no game nearby. The horse meat had become impossible to eat. Dain thought that even a scavenging animal might turn it down now.

By the ninth day of the siege, Dain was feeling too weak to do much. There were still a few Indians watching like vultures waiting for a sick animal to die. They knew they didn't have to risk their lives to get these scalps.

Dain was contemplating whether he had energy enough to go up one of the valleys leading back from the creek. There might be plum thickets there. There could also be Indians, he knew, but he was willing to risk that to get something to eat, even if it was only plums.

Then one man rose up and pointed to the south. "Indians!" he yelled.

All eyes turned to the south. Weak hands picked up heavy rifles.

Dain doubted that he could hold a steady aim. Then one man staggered a few feet toward the south edge of the island. "It's an ambulance!" he shrieked.

Dain strained his eyes. The man was right. Then men on foot appeared beside and behind the ambulance. The few Indians who were still on the hills suddenly remembered other places they needed to be. Dain guessed there weren't enough Indians here to risk a battle with more soldiers. The siege was over.

It took the ambulance and the infantry accompanying it a long quarter hour to reach the island. There was a doctor and he immediately tended to the wounded the best he could. Then they moved the entire camp up on the slope away from the rotting carcasses of the horses. Dain thought it would take a week to get that stench out of his nostrils.

All surgery that could be postponed would be delayed until they reached the hospital at Fort Wallace. But Louis Farley's leg had gangrene and there was no time to waste. His leg was amputated on the spot. Louis Farley had received his wound on the first day of the battle while he was fighting alongside his son, Hudson. In nine days, gangrene had set in and the poison had spread over his whole body. He died before morning and was buried with the others who had been killed on the island.

They were still camped on the slope the next day when Colonel Bankhead and his men arrived from down the river. Jack Stillwell was with them. He and Trudeau had gotten through but they had been told that the only way they could get an ambulance to the island was to go straight north to the Republican then up the river to the Arikaree. Pliley and Donovan had found Colonel Carpenter and his all-black infantry west of Fort Wallace and they had come straight across country to the island, guided by Donovan. They were almost a day ahead of Colonel Bankhead's cavalry.

They rested for another day and regained much of their strength on the food the rescuing soldiers had brought along. Dain looked back over the battlefield and found it almost impossible to picture the battle here in this peaceful valley. The dead horses and the pits dug in the sand on the island were the sharp reminders. Otherwise, this was a totally empty land just beyond the fringes of the army camp. Dain wondered if it would always be an empty land.

On the third day after their rescue, they started back toward Fort Wallace the way Colonel Carpenter had come. At the south fork of the Republican River, they found thirteen scaffolds with dead Indians on them. Dain guessed that the one with the dead horse under the scaffold might be Roman Nose.

They took three more days to get to Fort Wallace, going slowly so as not to hurt the wounded any more than necessary. The ambulances were not too comfortable since there was no trail to follow.

Dain had been impatient all the way to the fort, wanting to get back to Alpha to make sure that Valina was all right. But he wouldn't leave Ron. At Fort Wallace, the surgeon decided that he would have to operate on Ron or he might be a cripple all his life.

Ken Calhoun came around to talk to Dain. He was going home to Minneapolis. He asked Dain if he wanted to go with him.

Dain did but he wouldn't leave Ron. "I have to stay to see how Ron comes through his operation. If all goes right, I'll head home tomorrow."

"Do you have any message I can take to anyone? I'll be going right by Alpha."

Dain nodded. "There is a girl there, a hatmaker. Her name is Valina. Tell her I'm all right and I'll be there within a day or two of the time you go through."

Calhoun grinned. "I'll bet you won't be late, either."

"I don't plan on it," Dain said, "unless Ron runs into problems with his operation. Is Bystrom going with you?"

Calhoun shook his head. "He'll go as far as the cars with me. He may take them on to Kansas City but he won't go back to Minneapolis. Would you? The story of the way he fought is going to follow him to Minneapolis. I think it's the wise thing to do."

Dain watched Calhoun get his horse and start out. He had borrowed a horse to ride to Sheridan. Dain felt better, sending word to Valina. It was odd, he thought, but he had no doubts whatsoever that Ken Calhoun would deliver his message. He trusted him completely. It was a warm comfortable feeling.

Dain saw Bystrom catch up with Calhoun as they started toward Sheridan, the end of track. Dain wished he was going, too, but he took some consolation in the fact that he didn't have to ride all the way to Ellsworth with Bystrom.

The doctor set Ron's leg, which Dain hadn't realized was broken, having to cut into the flesh and clean out the infection. It was a painful hour for Ron but the doctor said there was no doubt he'd be as good as ever once the flesh and bone healed.

Dain checked with Ron early the next morning. He was resting easy and the doctor said he was doing fine.

"Get on back to Valina," Ron said. "Don't waste any more time. No telling what Scurry might think to do. Tell Eve I'm all right."

Dain nodded. "I couldn't leave till I had checked on you. I'll be watching for you to ride into Alpha one day soon. I'll tell Eve you're doing fine."

Dain found a freighter going to Sheridan to bring another load of supplies to Fort Wallace and he caught a ride with him to the cars.

At Sheridan, he bought a ticket to Ellsworth. That was the closest station to Alpha. He'd buy a horse there. The army hadn't paid him for his service but they had given him some scrip he could use to buy a horse, replacing the one he had lost at the island.

Riding in the caboose of a freight train, he made the trip to Ellsworth, just a short distance from Fort Harker. He stopped at the fort only long enough to get the rifle and revolver he'd left there at the beginning of the campaign. The army had no appeal for him now. He just wanted to get to Alpha as quickly as he could.

He headed for the livery barn. Most barns had horses for sale or rent. He was surprised that the livery stable owner had heard about the battle out on the northeastern Colorado plains. "Yesterday evening a man came through who'd fought in that battle. But we'd heard about it as soon as the men got back to Fort Wallace. This telegraph is a wonderful thing."

"Reckon so," Dain said. "Has the word got out to the homesteads yet?"

The man shrugged. "Not likely. The only way it gets out to them is for somebody to go and tell them. The telegraph goes along the railroad and that's all."

Dain knew that the only news Alpha would have of the battle would be from people like Calhoun who had been there. He asked about a horse and found three that the livery man had for sale. One caught Dain's eye and he bought it with a saddle and bridle, using the scrip they had given him at Fort Wallace. The livery man could turn it into cash at Fort Harker.

Dain was ready to go. It was getting late in the day and he knew he couldn't get to Alpha tonight unless he rode most of the night. He was well out on the prairie with no sign of people in any direction when he decided to camp. If he'd had the horse he lost at the island, he could have let him go and he'd have gone home. This horse wouldn't know where to go.

Dain was up before sunrise the next morning and back in the saddle. Impatience prodded him. And the nearer he got to Alpha, the more he worried about what he'd find. He couldn't forget Wolf-cry's last words.

His place on the Saline was almost on his way to Alpha so he reined the horse a little to the left to ride past his homestead. The Indians hadn't left much but he hadn't really examined the damage at the time.

The sod house was still there. The raiders hadn't found any way to burn that or the sod barn. There were just the ashes of the shed he had been building for his cows for the winter. He wouldn't have any cows to worry about this winter so he wouldn't need the shed.

Then suddenly he reined up. There was a saddled horse standing by the burned ruins of the wooden shed. He didn't see any man but there had to be one close by. That horse hadn't gotten there by itself.

Was it Scurry watching for him? His fingers tightened on the butt of his gun as he nudged his horse cautiously forward.

Twenty-five

AS DAIN DREW NEARER the horse standing ground-hitched by the burned heap that had been his shed, the more convinced he was that this must be a trap set by Scurry. If it was anyone else, he would have shown himself before this.

Then suddenly a man stepped out of the sod barn beside the ashes of the wooden shed. Dain's fingers tightened on his gun, then relaxed. That little man was not Scurry. Ken Calhoun was not nearly as big as Scurry.

Relief swept over Dain but that was replaced quickly by apprehension. Why was Calhoun waiting for him? Something must be terribly wrong.

Dain urged his horse on to the sod barn. "What are you doing here, Ken?" he asked.

"Waiting for you," Calhoun said. "I stopped in Alpha and delivered your message to the young lady. How did you get so lucky? Valina is beautiful."

Dain nodded. "I know. But you didn't come back here to tell me that. What's wrong?"

"About what you figured," Calhoun said. "I found your girl and told her you'd be here in a day or two and that you'd killed Jed Wolfcry. Half the town was there. Guess they don't see many strangers. This fellow with long greasy hair about went wild when I said that."

"Scurry," Dain said.

"I don't know why this greasy-haired fellow was so upset because you killed Wolfcry. He swore he'd kill you and I think he meant it."

"I'm sure he did," Dain said. "Wolfcry worked for Scurry in his store. They seemed to think alike."

"I was afraid you'd walk into an ambush when you got to town so I asked Valina how I could warn you. She said you'd likely come by your place here. She told me how to get here and I've been waiting. Thought you might not get here till tomorrow. You surprised me."

"I appreciate the warning," Dain said. "I'll be watching for Scurry."

"Scurry's blowup sort of set the town on edge," Calhoun said. "I gathered that Scurry isn't the most popular man around. I heard people saying he ought to be lynched."

"I'd go along with that," Dain said. He reined toward the trail into town. "You've done me a big favor. I could very well have ridden into an ambush."

"I wasn't going to see a man who had fought with me on that island get bushwhacked by some four-flusher like Scurry." Calhoun swung into his saddle. "I'll just ride along with you. I haven't told you everything yet. Scurry was as wild as a sore-footed bear and he made some crazy threats. He said you'd never see Valina again."

A chill stabbed Dain. He tried to push it aside. "That would be reasonable if he intends to kill me on sight," he said.

"I hope that's all he meant," Calhoun said.

Dain caught his meaning. He remembered Wolfcry's last words. He wouldn't put anything past Scurry. If he couldn't have something himself, he might destroy it for everybody else. He could kill Valina if he knew he couldn't have her himself.

"When were you in town?" Dain asked.

"Just this morning. I didn't ride as fast as you must have. I camped just outside town last night. Went in this morning and looked up the hatmaker and told her what you said. Half the town was there. That's when Scurry went berserk. I decided I had to warn you. I was dozing in the barn when I heard you coming."

Dain thought back to the island when he had almost balked at putting any trust in Ken Calhoun. Now he not only completely trusted him but he could call him a friend. Only a good friend would ride back here to warn him about Scurry when he probably wanted to get on to Minneapolis to see his family.

They came within sight of the town and Dain reined up. "You'd better swing around town and go on home, Ken. You've done enough for me already."

"You may need me," Calhoun said.

"This isn't your fight," Dain said. "You thought it would be bad for me to get ambushed after coming through the battle at the island. It would be worse if you got killed for less reason than I'd have."

"I'd be glad to help if I can."

"I appreciate that," Dain said. "But Scurry is just one man and he is my problem, not yours. You've got your own family waiting for you in Minneapolis."

Calhoun hesitated as if weighing his desire to get home against his need to help Dain. Then he finally lifted a hand.

"Be careful, Dain," he said. "Good luck."

Calhoun reined off to the right to bypass the town while Dain rode on. There was no place out on the open prairie where Scurry could surprise him. He wouldn't have to watch for an ambush until he hit town.

As he approached the end of the one main street, he saw a man step out from the building at the end and move into the middle of the road. Dain rode up to him and stopped. He recognized Herbert Gunderson, a farmer who lived not far from Ron Fulton's place. In fact, Ron had borrowed a horse from him after the Indians stole his.

"We've got problems here, Dain," Gunderson said.

Dain looked at the rifle the man was carrying and the gun belted around his waist. He looked as though he was expecting an Indian raid.

"Scurry?" Dain guessed.

Gunderson nodded. "You must have talked to the little man who was here this morning."

"Calhoun was with me in the fight with the Indians," Dain said. "What about Scurry?"

"He's gone crazy. Ain't no other explanation. He is dead set on killing you. Swore he'd do it and he meant it. He seemed to fly to pieces when he found out you'd killed Jed Wolfcry. Now he says he'll kill Valina if he can't kill you."

"Where is Valina now?"

"At the millinery shop," Gunderson said, frowning. "We're partly to blame. When Scurry was spouting off like that, we should have corralled him. But we didn't and he slipped away from his store and he's in the millinery shop now. He's got Valina and her aunt prisoner there."

Dain caught his breath. If Scurry was as wild as Gunderson said, he might kill Valina. Dain would tear him limb from limb if he did.

"We have the town surrounded so Scurry can't get away," Gunderson added.

"How are you going to get him out of the millinery shop without risking the lives of Valina and her aunt?" Dain asked.

Gunderson shook his head. "We don't know. But we're making sure Scurry can't slip out of town."

Dain nodded. That was good but it wasn't doing anything for the safety of Valina and Martha.

Dain dismounted and left his horse. He also left his rifle. He wasn't going to need it. If he got into a fight with Scurry, it would be at close range and his revolver would be all he could use. His problem was how to get close to Scurry without risking Valina's life.

He found two other men about half a block from the millinery shop, which was at the north end of the street. They were hiding carefully behind a corner of a building.

"What are you planning to do?" he asked.

"We're afraid to do anything while Scurry is holding those women," one said. "He might kill them. You never saw a man fly into a rage like Scurry did. He's crazy."

"Isn't there any way to root him out of there?"

"We can't think of any. We might rush the place and we'd do it if it wasn't for Valina and Martha. But I think he might shoot them if we crowded him."

Dain studied the situation, fighting down the fear that squeezed up in his throat, threatening to choke him. It was hard to concentrate, knowing that any plan he came up with might end in Valina's death.

The building next to the one the men were hiding behind was Scurry's store. It was less than a block from the millinery shop and on the opposite side of the street.

An idea began to take shape in Dain's mind. It would be dangerous. But any idea he tried to implement now would be dangerous. He would try to put most of the risk on himself, not Valina and Martha.

The big drawback as he saw it was that he'd have to put complete trust in the men around him. He didn't know any of them well.

Dain's plan was based on Scurry's obsession with things he owned. What he owned was his and his alone.

"Can you gather some dependable men?" he asked. "I have an idea."

One man turned and left and was back in three minutes with five men. "This enough?" he asked.

Dain nodded. Then he outlined his plan. "We all know how Scurry loves everything he owns. He has a lot wrapped up in his store. We have to divert his attention from the hostages in the hat shop. Let's set a fire at one corner of his store where he can see it from the hat shop, then while he's watching that, I'll break in the side door of the hat shop. Think that will work?"

"I'll bet he'll rave about his store being burned," one man said. "He might even come out to fight the fire."

"If he does, we'll cut him down before he ever gets to the store," another said. "What do you want each of us to do?"

"One of you get some cloth, soak it in coal oil, and take it to the corner of the store where it can be seen from the millinery shop. Put it against the wall of the store and set a match to it. That will be risky. You'll be exposed to Scurry's gun while you are starting the fire."

"I'll do it," one man volunteered. "I'd love to see his store burn."

"What about the rest of us?" another asked.

"I'll need you to use your rifles. Give me time to get around to the side of the shop before you start the fire. There's no window there, just a door. Then when the fire gets going and you know Scurry's watching it, fire your rifles at the shop but make sure you shoot high so nobody gets hit. That's when I'll break in that side door. Once inside, I can tell where everybody is. I'll try to take care of Scurry. If I fail, then you'll have to come up with some other scheme." Dain was sure that if he failed, the war would be over. Scurry wanted Dain dead. Maybe if he got that, he'd let the women go.

Dain saw the determination in the men's faces. It was a great feeling to trust these men. He didn't know them but he trusted them to do what they were agreeing to do.

Dain quickly made his way around the building, keeping out of sight of the millinery shop. Once beyond the shop, he crossed the street quickly. If Scurry was watching the main part of town, which Dain was sure he would be, he wouldn't see him around here.

Coming up to the side door of the millinery shop, he paused.

He'd like to check that door to see if it was locked but he couldn't do that. The success of his plan depended on several men doing their job and it especially hinged on how well Dain could surprise Scurry.

Peeking around the corner, he saw a man dash out to the corner of the store in plain sight of the millinery shop and drop a bundle against the wall and touch a match to it. Scurry evidently was too surprised at the move to react to it. The man was gone in a matter of five seconds from the time he appeared.

The cloth, soaked in coal oil, exploded in a blaze that licked up the corner of the store. For a minute, Dain thought the cloth was going to burn up before the wood caught but then the flame began creeping up the corner of the store building.

That was the moment when Scurry began screaming. Dain waited another minute as the blaze began to grow at the corner of the store and Scurry's screams got louder. Practically everything he owned was in that building. If anything would coax Scurry out of the millinery shop, that would be it.

Scurry continued to scream and swear but he made no move to come outside. Dain moved over to the side door of the shop. He touched the doorknob. Scurry wouldn't notice a sound now. The door was locked.

Out front, Dain heard someone yell for Scurry to come out and save his store. Scurry only screamed and cursed louder. Dain knew that at last he had found something more valuable to Scurry than his possessions. That was his hide. He wasn't going out even to save his store.

Dain wished he knew where Valina and Martha were in the shop. He'd have to strike fast when he broke through the door and he didn't want to give Scurry time to hurt either of the women.

Taking a run at the door, he hit it close to the latch. The lock held. Dain knew his surprise was gone. Scurry would have heard that thump.

Just as he backed off to hit the door again, a half-dozen rifles opened up down the street, hitting the millinery shop about roof level. Scurry's screaming stopped abruptly. Evidently he hadn't expected anyone to shoot at him while he held the women hostages.

Dain made another crashing dive at the door. This time the lock gave way and he sprawled across the floor of the shop. Dain had his gun in his hand but he was in no position to use it as he slid across the floor.

Scurry had his attention on the front when the door burst open. He wheeled and fired but his shot went high. Dain rolled, bringing up his gun and firing as he rolled. His bullet hit Scurry in the shoulder and his gun fell from his hand and skidded across the floor.

Dain rolled to his feet, his gun aimed at Scurry. But the fight seemed suddenly to have gone out of him. Without his gun, he was out of it.

Dain looked for Valina and Martha and found them on the far side of the room, bound to chairs. Apparently Scurry hadn't wanted any interference in his fight with the people of the town and he hadn't trusted them not to get into the fight themselves.

Holding Scurry under the threat of his gun, Dain moved over to the chair where Valina was and, with one hand, untied the knot holding her hands. She quickly untied the ropes on her feet, then turned to release her aunt.

"Are you all right?" Dain asked Valina, not taking his eyes off Scurry.

"He didn't hurt us," she said, "but he tied us up when we wouldn't promise not to interfere with his fight. When he realized how mad the town was, he planned to use us for safe passage."

"Then he does know that the jig is up for him here," Dain said.

Valina ran over and picked up Scurry's gun and pointed it at him. For a second, Dain thought she might shoot him.

"You have to watch him," she said. "He's more than an Indian lover. He was raised by Indians."

"Indians?" Dain exclaimed. "How did that happen?"

"His mother died when he was young. He told me a few days ago when he didn't think you'd come back. He wanted me to know all about him, he said. His father married again—an Indian woman. They lived with the Indians. Jed Wolfcry was Addison's half brother. The boys thought they could make more money and live better in the white man's world."

Dain doubted that Scurry's confession of his past enhanced his chances with Valina, but in his own ego, Scurry probably was sure that Valina would be his as soon as she was certain that Dain would not come back.

"Outside, Scurry," Dain ordered, motioning toward the front door.

Reluctantly, Scurry obeyed, his spirit obviously broken. Dain was just a step behind him. Valina and Martha were only another step behind Dain. A cheer erupted from the men watching as they saw them come out. Two of the men grabbed buckets and dipped them into the water barrels that stood on the street and doused the fire they had started at the corner of Scurry's store.

Men came running from all parts of town and gathered around Scurry.

"Did you try to kill Dain by dropping him in a well?" one demanded.

"Did you help Wolfcry plan the raids along the Saline?" another yelled.

"You're worse than the Indians because you plotted against your own kind."

More accusations rained down on Scurry and Scurry didn't lift his head. Then one man yelled, "Lynching's too good for him but it's the best we can do."

Scurry's head came up with a jerk. But it had gone too far. They caught Scurry by the arms and began dragging him down the street. He dug in his heels but he couldn't stop them. He took turns cursing them and begging for mercy. They went out of sight around the corner of the last building on the street.

Dain hadn't lifted a finger to stop them. Now that the townspeople knew how Scurry had double-crossed them, they should decide what would be a just punishment.

When they were out of sight, Valina turned to look Dain over. "You didn't get any wounds, did you?"

He shook his head. "We almost starved to death but the worst of it was not being with you."

He opened his arms and she stepped into them as if it was the most natural thing in the world to do.

"Do you trust her now?" Martha asked through pursed lips.

"I'll trust her in anything she wants to do," Dain said.

"You'll have to prove it to me," Valina said. "And that may take a long while."

"How about a lifetime?" he asked and she nodded.

ABOUT THE AUTHOR

Wayne C. Lee is a former president of the Western Writers of America and the Nebraska Writers Guild. His first novel, *Prairie Vengeance*, was published in 1954, and since then he has written over fifty novels, including *Ghost of a Gunfighter* (1979) and *Hawks of Autumn* (1986). He was born in Lamar, Nebraska, and recently moved twenty miles to Imperial, Nebraska.